Lord Satyr

Lords of the Masquerade
Book Two

Jade Lee

Text by Jade Lee
Cover by Wicked Smart Designs

Dragonblade Publishing, Inc. is an imprint of Kathryn Le Veque Novels, Inc.
P.O. Box 7968
La Verne CA 91750
ceo@dragonbladepublishing.com

Produced in the United States of America

First Edition January 2021
Print Edition

The characters and events portrayed in this book are fictitious. Any similarity to real persons, living or dead, is purely coincidental and not intended by the author.

ARE YOU SIGNED UP FOR DRAGONBLADE'S BLOG?

You'll get the latest news and information on exclusive giveaways, exclusive excerpts, coming releases, sales, free books, cover reveals and more.

Check out our complete list of authors, too!

No spam, no junk. That's a promise!

Sign Up Here

www.dragonbladepublishing.com

Dearest Reader;

Thank you for your support of a small press. At Dragonblade Publishing, we strive to bring you the highest quality Historical Romance from the some of the best authors in the business. Without your support, there is no 'us', so we sincerely hope you adore these stories and find some new favorite authors along the way.

Happy Reading!

CEO, Dragonblade Publishing

Additional Dragonblade books by Author Jade Lee

Lords of the Masquerade Series

Lord Lucifer (Book 1)

Lord Satyr (Book 2)

The Lyon's Den Connected World

Into the Lyon's Den

CHAPTER ONE

"DO TELL ME what terrible thing your valet did," Isabelle, Lady Meunier commanded as she poured Jackson, Lord Sayres his tea.

Her tone was casual, but her eyes were sharp, and Jackson felt his gut tighten in reaction. This would be a dicey conversation, so he took his time answering. "My valet is exceptional, as you well know." An exceptional spy, to be exact, and Jackson no longer wished the man in his home.

"And yet, you released him," Isabelle pressed.

"I did." He toyed with the finger sandwich set before him. Though he was hungry, he tried to appear reluctant to eat. He'd learned that Isabelle noted every show of appetite—for anything—and inevitably found a way to use it to her advantage. "I passed him to Lord Denbigh who was in need." He smiled. "And as we were in need of information regarding Lord Denbigh's Irish relations, I thought it an excellent opportunity."

"There was no need to deprive yourself of a valet for such a thing. I could have provided another candidate."

"There wasn't time," he lied. In truth, he and his valet had been long searching for a way to get them both out from under Isabelle's thumb. Andrews' opportunity had come first. "Denbigh took his entire household to Ireland the next day. I had to put Andrews in place immediately."

Isabelle stroked her favorite ring, a large garnet that flipped up to allow poison to drip free. It was an implied threat. As far as he was aware, she'd never poisoned anyone. But she had ruined them financially, socially, and even once had a priest excommunicate an enemy. The lady was vicious when she felt betrayed, and so he stepped carefully.

"He has promised regular letters on Ireland," he said. "We may learn several interesting things soon."

"You understand that Andrews was my servant. You cannot dismiss my people without my consent."

"He is still serving you. Indeed, that is his intent. But you need no longer pay the cost of his salary. Lord Denbigh will pay him very well." Sayres had made sure of it.

"And yet, the problem remains. Andrews was *my servant* to deploy as I wish."

Jackson said nothing. It would do no good to remind my lady that England allowed no slaves inside the country's borders and that Andrews was free to seek employment wherever he wished. Isabelle felt ownership no matter the laws of the land and was displeased with this turn of events.

Or she should have been displeased. Instead, she continued to toy with her ring while her smile grew to an alarming grin. She never smiled like that except when she won.

Damnation, what had he missed?

Isabelle rang a small bell set at her elbow. The tinkling sound was pleasant to the ear, and yet it rang like a gong in Jackson's head. He was about to learn of his defeat. He knew it to his bones, and yet he kept his expression calm despite the way his heart sank.

A footman stepped into the parlor room. Except he was no footman. It was Andrews dressed as the lowest bootblack in Lady Isabelle's household. Bloody hell, what was the man doing here? He'd escaped!

"Andrews?" he said slowly. "You look remarkably solid for a man who is in Ireland."

The man hung his head, his gaze fixed upon the floor. "Lord Denbigh found another valet more to his liking. One my lady suggested."

How the hell had she managed it? How had she learned of Sayres maneuvering and switched in her own servant in the short twenty-four hours before Denbigh left? Good lord, the extent of Isabelle's tentacles never ceased to amaze him.

"Just as well," Sayres lied. "I found I've missed your service." He gestured behind him to the door. "You can wait outside. We'll ride together back to my flat."

He didn't really think it would work. Isabelle was not one to let an escape attempt go unpunished, but it was worth a try. As expected, Andrews did not budge.

"I'm afraid I've found service with my lady more to my liking." The words were spoken like a dirge. It was an obvious lie, but why? "I have happy news," continued the man in a tone that implied the exact opposite. "My wife shall present me with a child soon. She was most happy to learn that the babe will be born in England."

So that was what happened. Isabelle had learned that Andrews had wed. Sayres had told him to keep it secret, but somehow the news had travelled, and once known, Isabelle had leveraged the wife and the child. The method didn't matter. Far from escaping her control, Andrews now was deeper under Isabelle's paw. He would be punished for a time as a bootblack, but eventually, he would be sent somewhere else useful in Isabelle's vast information network. And he would go, fully chastened, in the knowledge that his own wife and child were in danger if he disobeyed.

That's what came of falling in love. The man was now trapped with no hope of escape.

"I give you my felicitations," he said, his own tone matching Andrews'. "I hope the child brings you every joy." Because he would have little joy in his life from Isabelle for a long, unhappy time.

Andrews lifted his gaze. "Working for you was a great privilege. I am sorry to see it end." There was truth in his words and misery in his gaze.

"But end it must," said Isabelle. "You may return to your duties," she said by way of dismissal. And once the door closed behind Andrews, Isabelle allowed her expression to become truly triumphant. "Now let us discuss your new valet. Here is how I wish you to use him—"

"No." His word was hard and loud. It was a risk to speak so strongly against her, but he had grown tired of her manipulations. Andrews was a lost cause now, and so Jackson gave her that win, but he had no wish to engage in yet another dance of control with yet another servant. "I have no need of a new valet."

"You have engaged another one? But you said, you have missed Andrews' service. I assure you, the man already at your flat is superior in every respect."

Meaning his loyalties were firmly lodged with my lady.

"I have no need of a new valet," he repeated. Then he leaned forward, choosing to speak plainly. "Isabelle, have done. I value our working relationship and have no wish for it to end, but I cannot have you paying my servants." It allowed her to spy on his every action and he could no longer tolerate such supervision, even from the woman who had taught him everything he knew about business.

"It is a *gift*, and one you did not refuse when you first came to London."

It was a gift that made him into her cicisbeo, and he'd left her bed years ago. He'd fallen into her clutches at nineteen as a randy boy excited to learn the bedroom arts from a woman of such renown. That was ten years ago, and even then he hadn't the stomach for some of her favorite entertainments. So he'd left her bed and become valuable in other ways.

Over the last nine years he'd been her investment analyst—

nothing more, nothing less. As a wealthy widow, she had money to spend, but as a woman, she couldn't access the kind of information she needed to make good decisions. Not easily. So she trained him to ferret out ventures, to investigate the men in charge, and determined their weaknesses.

In return, she paid his tailor bill and his valet. Nine years ago, he thought of it as his uniform. If she wanted him to discover certain information, she would have to outfit him such that he could move through society to learn whatever she wanted to know.

It worked beautifully for a time. What little money he had, he invested alongside hers. The returns had grown and now he had a sizeable amount to use as he saw fit. Isabelle wanted him to put it all in her canals. They were in need of repairs, and her own funds were spent elsewhere. But he wanted less entanglement with her, not more. More important, he wanted control, and Isabelle would never give him that.

"Isabelle," he said gently. "Surely you understand that I want to find a venture of my own."

"But you can have much more profit if you invest with me. I could make you an excellent deal."

"You will give me a controlling interest?" he pressed, already knowing the answer.

"You haven't enough money for that."

He arched a brow at her—neither confirming nor denying the statement—and she raised her eyebrows as if intrigued.

"If you have that much blunt, then we can find other investments," she said. "I have heard something exciting is brewing with Mr. Hollow near the docks. Something real this time."

He doubted it. Mr. Hollow enjoyed flights of fancy, pretending to opportunities that never materialized. "There are plenty of men who would jump at the chance to partner with you."

"But none with your insight. None who will climb into the water and work alongside the men to be sure it is done correctly. You know as a woman, I cannot do such a thing." She leaned forward, giving him a full view of her cleavage. "I trust you."

Isabelle trusted no one. He looked out the window because her assets—all of them—no longer appealed. "I will find my own venture, Isabelle, something I control." He set his tea down untouched. "Now do you wish to discuss Mr. Hollow's latest scheme? Or should I take myself off?"

She looked at him hard, her expression growing increasingly foul. "Let me speak plainly," she began.

Finally.

"I want your money for my canals. You want my support when you launch your sisters. Imagine how horrible it would be for them to come to London and find every eligible bachelor turned against them."

His brows narrowed. "You would do that to my family? To me?" he pressed. "I have brought you countless profitable ventures and steered you away from the disastrous ones."

"I taught you what to look for, what questions to ask. I showed you how to ferret out the truth—"

"And I crawled through mines, studied sewers, inspected hellholes, even risked jail to learn what you needed." He grabbed a tiny sandwich and ate it in measured, steady bites. "Our association has been fruitful."

"For us both."

More so for her, but he counted his education as a significant benefit. "Do not end it now just because I seek a little independence."

She waited as she sipped her tea, her expression demure. For a moment there, he thought he had won. He'd given up his valet, frequented a different tailor, even moved to smaller rooms all so that he could cut any string between them. What remained was shared interest and mutual respect. She had a keen mind when she did not obsess over petty slights. He hoped that was enough to keep her well disposed toward him since she was still more powerful than he among the financial set.

"No," she said, her tone taking on the cadence of a command. "I require your money in my canals."

So much for mutual respect and shared interests. "Isabelle," he chided. "You overstep."

"I will add my voice to your sister's come-out. She'll be married within a month."

It was a fair offer if she could accomplish it. Then she sweetened the offer.

"I will even help with all three of your sisters, not just the eldest." She smiled at him. "That's quite a commitment from me given that I know nothing about their talents. Come now. I've drawn up papers." She pulled an envelope out of a writing desk set close at hand. From it, she withdrew an investment contract and pushed it toward him. "You won't get a better offer."

That was likely true. But he did not like bargaining with vague things such as "help." She could shade that any way she wanted. And yet he couldn't resist looking through the papers. It didn't take him long to see the flaw.

"This will not give me control of anything. I will slave on the repairs and get—"

"A handsome profit."

"Assuming it is managed satisfactorily."

She arched a brow. "I have done excellently so far."

It was true. With his help, she had turned a significant profit. But she had not invested in the maintenance in her canals much less any improvements. And now she needed money that should have been spent years ago.

"Sell me these two and we have a bargain." He pointed at the documentation of her two most problematic canals. He'd done the math. If a certain engineering design worked out as he hoped, he could have a steady source of income with minimal investment.

She shook her head. "I did not get to where I am by selling my assets."

He had expected as much. "Then I'm afraid I cannot invest in your canals."

"Then your sisters might as well marry Lincolnshire yokels, for they'll find no one in London who will have them." Her smile widened. "I'll see to it."

And here he saw Isabelle's greatest strength and flaw combined in one statement. She was a smart woman with a focused mind who had accomplished impressive things. But she fixated on petty slights, refused to relinquish control, and wielded her single weapon—gossip—to devastating effect. The woman could have been a shining example of female independence. Instead, she obsessed on stupid things, all in the endless pursuit of control.

No matter what she threatened, he would work for her no longer.

"You would destroy my sisters simply because I wish to find my own business opportunity?"

"Yes."

He sighed. "So be it." There were worthy gentlemen outside of the London *ton*. He would find a way. He rose from his seat. "Good day—"

"I believe I shall attend your masquerade ball tomorrow night."

Her voice cut through his departure, and though he didn't sit down again, he did raise his brows in surprise. "You hate masquerades. You've called them crass invitations to debauchery by boring people."

"I have," she said. "If putting on a mask is all it takes to excite your imagination, then that is a failure of imagination."

"Then why attend?" he pressed.

"Because last year's event was the talk of the Season."

Last year had seen an attempted murder. "I doubt anything so exciting will happen this year."

"Then why have it? I'm sure the expense is exorbitant."

He dismissed her question with a casual wave. "As you said, last year's was so successful. Aaron wanted to do it again." That wasn't the whole truth. Jackson wanted to cement his standing as the host of one of society's most talked about events. It would help when launching his eldest sister next year. Even better, a masquerade allowed for a relaxed guest list. He could invite people who were wealthy investors but weren't part of the *ton*. The rich got to mix with the peerage, and he got to rub elbows with both. It was good business. Especially as he had a business concept that he wanted to explore with a few of them.

"I should like to attend," she said firmly. "I should like to watch boring people with no imagination."

Damnation, that was the last thing he wanted. Isabelle had a way of cocking up other people's plans for her benefit. "You are welcome, of course, though I fear you will be disappointed in the plebian affair."

"Perhaps I will find something to interest me." Her gaze narrowed. "People who need to be warned against supporting your mad ideas."

He grimaced. She intended to turn investors against him. It was a significant threat, but maybe not as dangerous as she wanted him to believe. Her patronage had opened doors for him, but he was the one who had walked through and established himself among the moneyed *ton*. He suspected that this afternoon's show was to cover a position that was weaker than she wanted him to believe.

Still, it was painful to feel her betrayal.

"You will do as you wish," he said with heavy accents. "Always."

"You are nothing without me."

He shrugged. "That may be true. Nevertheless, I must try." He set his feet firmly and gave her his most honest assessment. "Are you willing to make me your enemy? When we have been so successful as friends?"

He watched her gaze waver just for a moment. A brief flash as intelligence warred with jealousy. "Get out of my sight," she snapped. "You have until your ridiculous masquerade to change your mind."

"I won't," he declared.

"Then I will take great pleasure in ending you by the midnight unveiling."

CHAPTER TWO

"WHY ARE YOU staring at those children?"

Gwendolyn Rees jolted as her mother's voice cut through her thoughts. A lie sprang quickly to her lips, an automatic reaction begun at the age of fourteen in response to any question from her mother.

"I'm drawing the Paeonia Lactiflora," she said. She lifted up the barest outline of the white wing peonies in her journal. Fortunately, she was a terrible artist and her design didn't look anything like the true flower. Her mother would never guess that the plants were actually several feet to the right of the children.

"Well, someone ought to look at those children because their nanny definitely isn't."

No, the nanny was flirting with a footman. She was leaning alluringly against a tree while he stepped close enough to speak into her ear. Gwen could hear the woman's laugh in reaction to whatever he said. The sound was high and nervous as her cheeks pinked. And all the while, the two children were playing with fallen cherry tree branches. The boy used his as a sword, of course, but the girl was looking closely at something on the branch. A flower, most likely, though it might be an irregular bump or a broken leaf. One never knew with children. Adults, on the other hand, always looked at the pretty things.

Her mother was no different as she turned her face to the sunshine. "Look at all those cherry blossoms. No wonder you came here today. They're beautiful."

She came to the park every morning. She liked getting out of the house before her mother woke. It allowed her to dress without criticism and read or sketch without interruption. And—for the last month—it allowed her to look at the children and question her life choices.

"Where is your bonnet?" her mother asked. "You're going to increase your freckles."

"You're up and about early, Mother. What brings you outdoors today?"

"You, of course." She settled herself onto the bench beside Gwen. And once she finished twitching her skirts into place, she took a moment to adjust her daughter's. Gwen suffered the attention simply because her gaze had gone back to the children.

The little girl had straightened up, her arm held stiffly out as an insect crawled up her wrist. Far from being upset, the child studied it with fierce concentration while Gwen wanted to shout, Bravo! How wonderful for a girl to want to learn about creeping crawly things. Except at that moment, the nanny woke to her duty. Rushing forward, the woman swatted the beetle aside which flew away in a low trajectory into the nearest bush. The child exclaimed in dismay and was scolded for her outrage. In such a way, another girl was taught that interest in the natural world was wrong.

"Disgraceful," Gwen's mother exclaimed.

Gwen heartily agreed.

"Now the girl must be bathed in harsh soap to prevent disease."

Gwen heartily disagreed.

"It was just a beetle," she said.

"When it comes to children, one must be ever vigilant."

That was her mother summed up in one sentence. The woman devoted herself to making sure her children lived the lives she chose for them. No effort was too large, no tactic too heinous in the campaign to force her children into a future she considered appropriate. Which was why Gwen spent much of her life trying to avoid a single moment with her mother. She had never fit any of her mother's plans, and so was ever vigilant in thwarting the woman.

Until recently, that is, when she discovered she might agree with one of her mother's plans.

"Perhaps we should discuss the Season," Gwen offered. The parties were about to start, her mother's pre-Season planning had finished with the delivery of several new gowns, and now that Elliott had found a bride, Gwen knew she would become the brunt of her mother's matrimonial schemes. She was therefore steeled to negotiate what she would and would not do in the coming weeks.

"Not yet," her mother said, proving that her mother still had the capacity to surprise her.

Gwen dropped her charcoal in shock. "What?"

Her mother folded her hands atop a wrapped package and lifted her chin. She didn't quite meet Gwen's eyes, but focused on her cheek instead. "I should like to give you your birthday present first."

"Thank you, Mother. But wouldn't you prefer to wait until—"

"I got up at this ridiculously early hour to do this now. So no, I would not like to wait another moment, if you please."

Gwen buttoned her lip. Her mother waited a moment to be sure that Gwen would not interrupt, and then she began to speak with all the gravitas of a Shakespearean tragedy.

"Today is your twenty-eighth birthday. On this day, I have come to tell you that you are a fully grown adult." There was a long pause where Gwen wondered if she should say something. There was no easy way to explain that her mother's pronouncement came years too late. Gwen had viewed herself as an adult for a long while. Fortunately, her mother didn't remain silent. "You are no longer my child," she declared.

Gwen gasped, horrified. Was she being cast out? Disinherited?

"No, no," her mother rushed to say. "Not like that. I mean you are no longer *a* child." She gestured vaguely toward where the nanny was now ushering her charges away. "I cannot be vigilant with you anymore. It gains nothing and sets us constantly at odds."

"I have grown weary of our battles," Gwen offered.

"Don't interrupt," her mother admonished, then she frowned. "And yes, I am tired of them, too."

Gwen acknowledged the statement with a nod but knew better than to say anything more. It was a tedious thing, though. Usually her mother wouldn't shut up and Gwen was able to easily ignore whatever was said. But this slow, halting speech was strange and therefore captured her attention. As did the way her mother's eyes sheened with tears that she refused to shed. Her mother always enjoyed her tears. She let them flow with dramatic effect. Except, apparently, this morning.

"Mother, you begin to alarm me."

"Well," she said, "it is an alarming thing what I am about to say." Then true to her contrary nature, the woman didn't say anything, but shoved the package into Gwen's hands.

"What is this?"

"Yours," her mother said. "They're sketching charcoals. I know how much you enjoy it." She sniffed. "You're an adult now."

She kept saying that word—adult—as if it were something terrible. But rather than address her mother's illogic, Gwen gently unwrapped the paper around a beautiful package of new charcoals. "Thank you, Mama," she said, completely mystified. Of course, she enjoyed sketching, though in truth she was bad at it.

"You may draw whatever you like now. I won't pester you to sketch appropriate things."

"Thank you—"

"You never listened to me anyway." She blew out a breath as she looked away to the sky. "In ten years of seasons, you never listened to me. Ten years, hundreds of dances, and three offers. Many more if you'd given the slightest encouragement."

"They were idiots."

"They were wealthy. Two were titled, and they would have taken care of you."

Maybe. But Gwen had found she could care for herself just as well. "Our children would have been stupid. I could not abide—"

"So you've said!" her mother snapped. Then she caught her breath and modulated her tone. "It's done now. I have failed to ensure your future." She gripped her fingers together. "If only you hadn't fought me so hard!"

Gwen stared at her mother, old fury boiling up. "Then you would have married me to someone I hated as you did to Diana. I would have been trapped, just like Diana. I would have—"

"Diana is blissfully happy now!"

It was true. Her older sister had finally married someone of her choosing. But that came after twelve years of marriage to someone of her mother's choosing. A man who'd been nearly three times her age and had finally died the year before. His death freed Diana to find love with someone who honored and respected her.

"When a woman is able to choose for herself," Gwen said firmly, "she often chooses brilliantly. As Diana has now."

Her mother shot her an angry glare. "I have not forced you to marry anyone," she said. "I don't know why you hold Diana's marriage against me when it wasn't you who had to marry Dunnamore."

But her mother would have forced her into any one of those other marriages if Gwen hadn't fought tooth and nail against them. Despite her mother's threats and myriad coercion techniques, Gwen had told the gentlemen "no" and watched in satisfaction as they left her alone. Not so her mother, who then turned her sights on different gentlemen, different marital prospects, despite Gwen's absolute declaration that she had no interest in a husband.

But rather than argue old territory, Gwen lifted her chin and said, "Thank you for the birthday present."

"You're welcome. I've decided it's best if we try to get along. We'll be living together for a very long time now."

Gwen frowned. "We've been living together my entire life, Mama."

"Yes, but I've recently looked to our future. Elliott and Amber will happily house us, of course, but I cannot think a newlywed couple would want us bumping elbows with them. We'll need to retire to the dower cottage. It's small but should serve our needs."

Live with her mother forever? The thought horrified Gwen. The two of them could barely speak more than ten minutes without arguing. The idea of aging alongside one another in the tiny cottage equated to Gwen's image of Hell.

"Mother..." she began, but she didn't know what to say. Her future suddenly reared up in all its hideous lack of possibility. Which is when Gwen finally understood what the term "adult" actually meant. "You don't mean that I'm no longer a child. You mean that I'm *on the shelf.*"

Her mother pursed her lips. "You are twenty-eight today, and we both know men prefer the dewy ones."

"I'm not exactly wilting on the vine!" Gwen exclaimed.

"And you've done nothing but disdain every party, read at all hours until you are cross-eyed, and you ignore your bonnet such that your freckles grow to the size of pies! Face it, Gwen, I have tried and tried to keep you as fresh as a sixteen-year-old, but you have thwarted me at every turn. So now we are here. You are an adult, and I cannot fight you anymore."

"You mean I'm a spinster."

"Yes." Finally, her mother let her tears slip free. Big fat droplets quivered on her lashes until they trailed down her cheeks. She wiped them away with as if she were on the stage mourning the death of a fictional child. "I tried, Gwen. I did everything I know how to do, but you wouldn't listen."

Good Lord, once again her mother had made something as simple as a birthday into a drama of epic proportions. And worse, Gwen was hard-pressed to argue. It would be a disaster for them to live together in a tiny cottage. The only reason they got along now was because they had a buffer between them. It was unusual, to be sure, but her father's by-blow Lilah had been raised in her family since her birth mother died over twenty years before. She was the youngest sister in the Rees family, and the sweetest, kindest person on the planet.

"Lilah will keep us from killing one another," Gwen said. Though what a burden to put on her half-sister.

"No!" her mother gasped. "I cannot fail her as well. I won't!"

"But—" Her words were cut off as her mother grabbed Gwen's hands.

"You must help me with her. She's not too old yet."

No, but she was a by-blow. Not many bastard girls got selected in the Marriage Mart.

"You're going to take her to parties this Season. Go without me because it's always so awkward when I'm there with her."

True enough. It wasn't unheard of for a man to acknowledge a bastard child, but his wife was always viewed as an object of pity whenever that happened. And though her mother had never treated Lilah as anything but one of her own, society viewed things very differently.

"Of course, I will help. I want her to be happy."

"You must act as her chaperone. It's proper now."

Now that she was *on the shelf* and therefore no longer in need of constant supervision.

"She's been talking about that masquerade party. I know it was a disaster last year, but it's a good place for her to catch a man's eye. You go as chaperone, but don't be too strict with her. We need Lilah to entice someone and a masquerade is the perfect place. Anyone who attends one of those will be improper enough to make advances but elevated enough to be a good catch for her. You understand?"

Gwen nodded. She did understand. Her mother thought Gwen too old to be improper and Lilah too stupid to manage herself. Which was rich because Lilah had been managing the two of them since she'd first joined their home.

Gwen smiled, though the expression felt brittle. "I will do everything I can for Lilah." Then she frowned. "But aren't you afraid that I shall become improper at a masquerade?"

Her mother threw up her hands in disgust. "If only! You are more likely to inspect some rare bit of shrubbery than dance with someone even remotely interesting."

"That's because shrubbery usually is more interesting than any man."

"Oh Gwen," her mother said as she wiped away another tear. "That is exactly why I have failed you. Not once in ten Seasons was there a man who could drag your attention away from the greenery."

"I think that's the men's failing, not mine."

Her mother continued as if she hadn't spoken. "But I thought—I prayed—that if God had made you, then certainly He would have made someone to interest you." She blew out a breath. "Well, if that man exists, I certainly don't see him."

And at that moment, Gwen finally spoke her truth. She said the words that had been pushing forward with more and more urgency of late. "Perhaps I am the one who should be looking for a husband, not you on my behalf."

Her mother stared at her. "Yes, but you never did. And now you're too old."

Gwen winced, but she didn't argue. She very much feared her

mother was right. Lately she'd felt a yearning for connection, but she was a soul perpetually on the outside. She did not comprehend how people worked, and so she always said the wrong thing, did the wrong thing, or just stood there feeling stupid while other people turned away. It was a lonely existence.

"Mother, I'm sorry," she said. She was trying to find words to heal the divide between them, but as usual her words were wholly inadequate. Meanwhile, her mother pushed to her feet.

"I believe I shall go back to bed. This sun is surely going to dry my skin to the bone. Happy Birthday."

Gwen watched her mother's brisk steps as she fled the sun. When the lady was gone from sight, she looked down at the charcoals still in her lap, then up to yet another nanny strolling through the park with her charges. Inevitably her thoughts returned to where they'd been before her mother interrupted her musing. Though she stared at different children and a different nanny, the question returned, circling over and over through her mind.

Taking her pencil, she opened her journal. She skipped over the horrid doodle she'd made earlier and began at the top of a fresh page. On it she wrote,

> *On the 28th anniversary of my birth, I have decided I want to have children. Specifically, I want to raise a girl in the way she ought to be reared—with respect for her mind and a willingness to indulge her curiosity wherever it might lead. Therefore, as of today, I shall endeavor to find a man capable of siring a smart girl child.*

She stared at her words for a long time. She re-read it a dozen times. In the end, she forced herself to make a single correction. She changed the word "man" to "husband."

She would find a husband this Season.

"On the shelf, be damned," she muttered.

Chapter Three

JACKSON FELT RIDICULOUS. He stood next to the orchestra at Vauxhall in furred breeches meant to resemble goat legs. That was bad enough, but he hadn't wanted to spend the money for a specially fashioned shirt. The price of a goat horned mask had been ridiculous enough. So he'd sacrificed one of his few waistcoats to his Lord Satyr costume. He dirtied it and wore it unbuttoned over his bare chest as all the best goat-men did. Then he added a cape to cover up when the situation warranted. Which was right now, he realized, as he saw Mr. Brayden Murphy walk up the path with his new, young wife.

"Welcome to the festivities," said Jackson as he twitched the cape around his shoulders to cover the bulk of his nakedness. Then, to amuse Mrs. Murphy, he performed a goat leap in her direction before bowing deeply before them. "I am pleased you could attend. Tell me of your desire, and I shall see it fulfilled forthwith."

Mrs. Murphy giggled like a schoolgirl. "Lord Satyr, I presume?" she trilled.

"The very same. And you must be fair Titania with your Oberon." He gestured to her fairy costume and her husband's much more restrained attire.

"Oh, no one so grand," the lady said. "I am Peasbottom, and he is Cobweb."

"*A Midnight Summer's Dream* is a favorite of mine."

"Mine, too!" she cried.

"And if I might be so bold, a few more of the fair folk have found seats at the box just there."

Mrs. Murphy followed the line of his gesture and let out a gasp of delight. "I knew Anna would pick the red gown. I told her the blue was much better suited for her hair, but she would insist." She glanced at her husband. "You don't mind, do you darling, if I go have a word with her?"

"Not in the least, my dear," Mr. Murphy said and then smiled with fond infatuation as she pranced across the way to her friends. "Mark my words, Sayres," he said. "A young wife brings life back into the home. Her amusements are trivial and easily satisfied, and she has not had time to grow bitter."

Jackson quirked his brow. "I think that depends on the young wife, but it seems you have found a delightful one."

"I have indeed," the man said with a grin. "You should think of joining the matrimonial estate."

Not bloody likely. He had enough women in his life with Isabelle causing problems and his three sisters at home waiting for him to bring them to London. He could not see what could possibly be gained by adding another female to his life. But he didn't say that. Instead, he chuckled heartily as if he agreed, then spoke about what really interested him.

"If it please you," Jackson said, "I have saved back some excellent claret in the hopes that you would accept my invitation. I should like to discuss—"

Murphy held up his hand. "Save your breath, Sayres. I know what you want, and I cannot comply."

"I cry foul! You cannot know what—"

"You want to invest in my coal venture. I don't know how you heard about it, but it doesn't matter. I cannot run foul of Lady Meunier. She can be vindictive, as I'm sure you're learning."

True on all counts. Far from giving him until the masquerade to change his mind, Isabelle had waited a single day before she set about ruining him. Thanks to years of economy, he had a tidy sum to invest in the right venture, but now no one would take his money. He had spent the last weeks casting further and wider for someone who would risk annoying the lady. Mr. Murphy was his last hope.

"You despise her," Jackson pressed. "You hate her methods, have called her a viper, and—"

"I still use her canals."

Everyone used them. They were a main thoroughfare for goods coming into London. The irony was that Jackson had been instrumental in securing Isabelle's monopoly. "I have a way around that," he said.

Murphy's brows lifted. "How?"

"Horses, primarily—"

"Too expensive and slow. The canals work, which is why she was so smart to secure them."

"I was the one who did that," he grumbled.

"And now you know why she will not let you go. You've made her too much money." Murphy blew out a breath as he rocked back on his heels. "You should have been smarter when you first started to work with her. Should have negotiated a better situation or saved more money—"

"I was nineteen. What did I know about negotiation?" She'd brought him into her bedroom, and he'd been too stupid to realize the trap. It didn't matter that he'd left her bed soon afterwards, he'd remained in her employ and had made himself indispensable. "I was an idiot."

"We're all idiots at that age."

"So help me get free. Let me—"

"I cannot. I'm sorry, but I wish you well."

Jackson would have argued more. He had plenty of tools of persuasion, but the last few days had taught him when he was beaten.

Murphy was not going to change his mind, and so he bowed to the man and still sent a waiter for the good claret. At least Murphy had been kind with his words. So many others had been cruel.

Which left him with his choice of last resort. He needed a business venture of his own, one that he could make profitable quickly and with as small a use of funds as possible. One that remained far distant from Isabelle's influence. Unfortunately, he was fresh out of brilliant ideas. He knew all the ways to evaluate an existing business, but he had no clever thoughts for a fresh one.

Now he felt glum and stupid. Not the best frame of mind in which to host a party, but he'd promised Aaron and Lucas, and so would do his best. He had seen the Byrn party arrive while he'd been speaking with Mr. Murphy. Elliott and his wife Amber had led the way, followed by Diana and her new husband Lucas, who played the part of Lord Lucifer. The two younger sisters trailed behind. They had the favored box, set near the orchestra pit, and now that they were here, the ball could begin in earnest.

While Lucas brought his wife to the floor, Jackson selected his partner for the opening dance. She was the daughter of a man rumored to need investors in an African gold mine. The girl was nice enough and an acceptable dance partner, but she was three years younger than his youngest sister. He would not marry her even if it meant gaining part of an African gold mine. So he brought her back to her parents as soon as he could and tried to make inroads with the father. It didn't work. The man rebuffed any attempts at discourse.

Normally he would have taken the hint and withdrawn, but he was becoming desperate. He pushed the matter only to hear what everyone else had told him. "I have no investments available for you. None at any price."

Damnation. He didn't know what Isabelle had done to discredit him so thoroughly, but the noose was tightening around his neck. A smart man would give in to the inevitable and invest in her damned canals, but he was angry now. At this moment, he would rather spend the rest of his life slopping pigs in Lincolnshire than give one penny to Isabelle for any reason.

That fury sustained him for another two hours, but eventually it dulled to exhaustion and a frustrated kind of numbness. He tried to appear carefree, especially since he was supposed to be Lord Satyr, an entertaining goat of a man, but he could not force himself to prance one more step and he greatly feared his face had frozen into a distasteful grimace. Which was a lucky thing, because just then he happened to see a woman whose expression matched his mood for misery. She wore a costume of a dog of indeterminate breed as she sat alone in the Rees' box. He knew that Lord Byrn and his new wife Amber were still dancing, Lucas had been last seen wandering down the Dark Path with his lady wife, and the other sister Lilah was being entertained by Aaron. This woman, then, was Gwendolyn, the bluestocking who looked like she wanted to rip apart the daffodils he had set there with his own hand.

"If you're going to dismember my flowers, at least give me the chance to assist you."

The lady jolted where she sat, and her eyes widened over the long doggy nose of her mask. "I beg your pardon," she said as she straightened up.

"No, it is I who must beg pardon," he said. "I am feeling tired and particularly violent toward the shrubbery. Please, do kill the flowers while I consider hacking at the ivy."

She frowned. "That's not ivy. It's Common Amelanchier."

He turned back to her. "Do you have an interest in botany?"

"I do," she said as she lifted her chin. It was a challenging look belied by the way her shoulders tightened. "I have studied a great deal of the natural world and its mysteries."

"Then I bow to your greater knowledge. I have spent my time studying man's mysteries, and I hope you have had better luck answering your questions than I have with mine."

She arched her brow. "I have solved a few. Which mysteries have stumped you?"

He looked at her for a moment then abruptly leaned forward. "Shall I make a bargain with you?" he asked. But in this, he erred. As he leaned toward her, the sides of his waistcoat fell apart and her eyes abruptly widened at the sight of his bare chest. Jackson was not a vain man, but neither was he unaware of his physical attributes. And since he carefully conserved his money, his form was lean enough to show off a chest strong with muscle. Clearly, Lady Gwen was unused to seeing such a thing.

For a woman who claimed to have studied several natural mysteries, she was certainly flustered at the sight of a man's body. It really was adorable the way her cheeks turned pink and her mouth went slack. He was about to think her a complete innocent when her gaze abruptly sharpened. Her mouth closed and her brow furrowed. She even tilted her head slightly as she inspected his torso.

"Lady Gwen?"

"What? Oh!" She jerked back while her blush deepened to crimson. "I'm terribly sorry. I was, um, distracted."

It was only human to be pleased that his body intrigued enough that she forgot the conversation. A gentleman would cover up so as to not tease her delicate sensibilities, but he was Lord Satyr tonight, a man-goat fairy who was usually drawn naked. He shrugged enough that his waistcoat gaped completely open, then he gave her his most charming smile.

"I was offering you a bargain."

"Of what sort?" Her gaze remained fixed upon his face as if she had to force herself to not look any lower.

"I shall share why I feel murderous toward the shrubbery, if you would explain why you wish to decapitate the daffodils."

She shook her head. "I am afraid you are making a bad bargain. My sulks are truly not that interesting."

"Neither are mine, so we are a pair. And since misery loves company, pray will you tell me what is amiss?"

She grimaced and dropped her chin on her hand, and suddenly she did not seem so interested in his naked torso. It was quite lowering to realize she could dismiss it so quickly.

"I have discovered that I want a husband." And though he didn't say anything, her tone turned sharp. "I know I am incredibly old for this realization. Most girls discover it at a very young age, but I have been content with my books on botany and..." Her cheeks pinked. "And my other books. But then a few weeks ago I realized there are distinct advantages to having a husband."

"And several drawbacks, I should think. What appeals to you specifically?"

"I do not wish to live forever with my mother, for one." She sighed. "There is not enough money for me to set up my own residence."

"Then the problem is not so much the lack of a husband as the lack of funds. And in that, I fear, we have the same difficulty."

She arched a brow at him. "You don't wish to live with your mother?" He could tell she was teasing him, and he answered in kind.

"My mother is several years gone, I'm afraid. I have no wish to live with my three younger sisters who hope to find husbands of their own after a Season of hunting in London."

"Three sisters? One Season is expensive enough. Three would be—"

"Astronomical."

She leaned back and gave him a smile. "Numbers alone would suggest that you win."

"Win?" he asked.

"Three sisters to one mother suggests that you have the more difficult problem. But I submit to you that my mother could indeed be the match of three biddable girls. Indeed, I submit to you that she could make them miserable in the morning and still have time to poke at me."

"Goodness. I had no idea Lady Byrn was such a harridan."

Lady Gwen snorted. It would have been an inelegant sound except that somehow it matched her costume and charmed him instead. "Mama is not a harridan to anyone else. It is merely to me that she shows her worst qualities." She flashed him a rueful smile. "And I to her, I'm afraid. We have been at odds as long as I can remember."

"It shows good character that you can admit your part in your disagreements."

She shrugged. "Well, she has the larger blame, of course, being older. Isn't one's parent supposed to indulge the offspring?"

"That has not been my experience," he said dryly.

"Nor mine," she echoed in an equally glum tone. Then she lifted her gaze back to his face. "So that is my tale of misery. What is yours?"

"I told you. Three sisters who want Seasons in London."

"But you are a charming, intelligent man. Surely you can find—"

"Land to magically drop money into my open palms?"

She shook her head. "No, silly. Land is expensive and generational. Use your popularity."

He stared at her. He didn't know why he was conversing about money with a woman. She might be delightful, but he was the one who had studied the ins and outs of commerce these last ten years. And yet, she intrigued him, this woman in a mismatched dog costume. He pushed her for an explanation.

"I'm afraid I'm not as intelligent as one could hope. How, exactly, am I to use my popularity to get money? I assure you, it is a lot harder to wed an heiress than one might think."

"At least as difficult as it is for me to find a husband, I should think."

There was no polite way to respond to that. In truth, with a little help—and a total change of her wardrobe—he thought Lady Gwen could do well on the Marriage Mart.

"Then how should I—"

"It's fairly simple. Make something you own popular. You have the charm to make that happen. Whatever it is, make every hostess want to display it and every gentleman want to set it upon his desk. Do you recall when everyone was desperate to wear Prussian blue? Mama searched all of London for a dress that color, but a single swath of blue cloth cost the earth. She had to settle for blue embroidery on the bodice of one gown. She called it the calamity of the Season."

"I begin to see why you and your mother do not suit." Any woman who would wear a dog costume would not be one to follow the ebbs and flows of fashion. And she certainly wouldn't call blue embroidery a calamity.

"Quite right," she said with admirable restraint. "But to my point. The dyer who created Prussian blue made a fortune. Still does, I shouldn't wonder. What do you control that could become popular?"

Nothing. That was the exact problem. He had spent all his time finding ways to build Isabelle's fortune, not his. And all the contacts he'd made, all the gentlemen in finance he thought would be eager to help him, were all too cowardly to risk Isabelle's wrath. That left him with nothing.

"I'm afraid all I have are poorly producing lands in Lincolnshire and myself. And though I have worked these last years to make myself popular, I cannot sell myself. At least not for a high enough price to help my sisters."

He didn't think she would understand his off-color joke, but her pink ears told him she did. Strangely enough, she didn't seem nearly as discomforted by it as she had his bare chest. Which, he now realized, she gave no more attention to. And here he'd been flashing it at her just to keep her color high. But rather than stare at him, her gaze riveted upon the bright yellow daffodil with unusual intensity.

"Lady Gwen?"

"Did you say Lincolnshire?"

"I did. That is where my family hails from."

"And did you perhaps bring these flowers from there? These are Lincolnshire daffodils, are they not?"

She certainly knew her plants. "They were a favorite of my mother's and she kept a small garden filled with them. As I returned home from there just yesterday, I brought a few along to set at the tables tonight."

"They're very pretty."

He nodded because it was true.

"They're not common in London. At least they aren't right now."

"They grow primarily in Lincolnshire. Hence the name."

She nodded. "So do you think you could grow a lot of them on your poorly producing lands? And do you think you could make them popular here in London?"

He looked at her for a long moment, shock and inspiration hitting at the exact same moment. Not his inspiration, obviously. It was hers, and it was *brilliant!* "You think I could make the daffodil popular. Make it the flower of the Season and be the one to supply it as well."

"That is the usual way of things, isn't it? The one who supplies what is most sought after can make enough money to outfit three sisters for their Season."

He grinned, his mind scrambling with the possibilities. "I have spent my life figuring ways to move things from one place to another. It is the essence of commerce. Flowers can't be that different. This could work."

"Well," she said, her tone dampening. "It could work if you figure out how to transport the flowers. You cannot simply cut them in Lincolnshire and sell them an hour later in London. It's a day's travel at least."

"Closer to two," he said. "I cut an entire basket and these few are the only ones that survived."

She nodded. "Did you place them in water? Keep them sheltered from the sun? How old were they?" She adroitly lifted one of the blossoms from the vase and inspected the stem. "And you didn't cut these in the best way for them to last."

He leaned forward. "Could you teach me? Could you train others to do the same?"

"I'm not sure," Lady Gwen said, her words slow as she inspected the bloom. "I would have to do some studying. I should think your gardener would know more."

"Gardener!" he scoffed. "We have no such person. And I can assure you, my tenants are farmers who only care about pigs and oats. They know nothing about posies for girls."

Lady Gwen finally turned her gaze back to him. "I could figure it out, to be sure. A few experiments would make it clear. But would you be able to make the flower popular? Will the London hostesses take your lead?"

"I'm popular, aren't I? You said so yourself."

"And I am a student of botany."

He held out his hand. "What do you say, Lady Gwen? Have we a bargain? You will figure out how to best cultivate and transport my flower to London, and I shall make the blossom the most sought-after accessory of every *ton* party."

She looked at him, her brows narrowed in thought. "And what shall be my recompense?"

"I shall show you the accounting from the very beginning. And we shall split the profits fifty-fifty."

Her eyes widened. "An even split with a woman? Sir, you surprise me."

Did she think he would take her expertise as worthless? "I have no difficulty believing a woman can be an equal partner." He'd spent years being taught that by Isabelle. "We each have our skills, and together I believe we can make enough blunt to rid ourselves of one difficult mother—"

"And launch three expensive sisters."

Lady Gwen abruptly grabbed his hand, shaking it while her smile transformed her face into one of startling beauty. Her features didn't change, but suddenly they were animated with joy and that was a wonderous sight indeed.

"We have a bargain, my lord," she said.

"We have a bargain," he echoed. And to hell with Lady Meunier and her machinations.

Which was a fine thought until he spotted the damned woman walking steadily up the path and headed straight for him.

Chapter Four

Gwen saw Lord Satyr abruptly stiffen. It was hard not to, given the expanse of sculpted male flesh on display. Certainly she'd seen men without shirts before—farmers and laborers—but never so close or so tantalizingly like the anatomical drawings she'd studied. She was so busy trying *not* to watch the ripple of muscles that she nearly missed his next words.

"Don't speak of our plan to anyone. You understand? We need to keep it—"

"Good evening Lord Satyr," a woman interrupted. She and the two gentlemen flanking her stepped straight into the box as if they had been invited. "I see your costume panders to the lowest form of entertainment. Are your guests amused?"

Well that was rude. Lord Satyr co-hosted this event, which likely cost the earth for one night's entertainment. To criticize his attire was to show a level of ingratitude that was just mean. And if there was one thing Gwen despised, it was meanness. So while Lord Satyr was busy bowing to the shrew as a true gentleman would, Gwen pushed to her feet.

"If your host's attire offends you, perhaps you should refund him the price of your admission and return to a location better to your liking."

The woman's attention had been centered on the theatrical way Lord Satyr had been bowing. It involved a goat-like prance and a bleating sort of hello. Gwen thought it very clever, but the woman was unimpressed. Worse, at Gwen's words, she turned her hard gaze onto her. And then her eyes abruptly widened.

"Gwendolyn, whatever are you wearing?"

Oh damnation. She knew that voice. Worse, she knew those exact words spoken in just that particular tone of disapproval. She'd heard it often enough throughout her childhood.

"Aunt Isabelle? I had not expected to see you here."

The woman shook her head. "And I thought you were the clever one."

Gwen grimaced. She'd never been good with faces, but now that she looked closely, she saw her mistake. The woman in front of her wore a black lace domino like it was a fitted glove. Her mask did little to obscure her face, and yet still added to the woman's allure. In short, she looked elegant, darkly beautiful, and had a tongue sharp enough to slice wounds.

Of course, this was her mother's closest relative. Which meant Gwen would have to make nice or suffer months of her mother's desperate attempts to force her to mend fences.

"Forgive my mistake," Gwen said. "I have found my wit lacking of late."

Meanwhile, Lord Satyr straightened up from his bow with a startled expression. "You two are acquainted?"

Gwen nodded. "Lady Meunier and my mother are cousins. She has graced our home often throughout the years. It was my father who suggested I call her aunt rather than suffer through the explanation of cousin once removed—"

"By marriage," Aunt Isabelle inserted.

"Er, yes." Gwen decided to leave it at that rather than ramble on about the intricacies of who married whom in her family. She always found that sort of discourse boring. Then she looked past the lady to the young men hovering two steps back and to either side of Isabelle's shoulders. They were like brackets of silent handsomeness since neither stepped forward to greet them. And now that she thought about it, Aunt Isabelle had always had at least one pretty young man companion whenever she'd visited. Which brought her to the obvious question. "How are you two acquainted, Lord Satyr?"

"Old friends," her aunt answered though the question had not been directed at her. "Lately turned absent." Then her words slowed down as her tone dropped to a huskier level. "Though I am prepared to forgive all and invite you to a meeting of sorts. Early tomorrow morning with several bankers of my acquaintance."

Early tomorrow morning after a hosting a party that would go well into the wee hours of the morning? It would be exhausting for anyone to attend, which was exactly what Lord Satyr said.

"I am terribly sorry, my lady, but I fear my duties tonight will preclude me from your most generous offer."

Too bad that. He would need capital to make a go of his business idea and that meant working with bankers. Having Lady Meunier introduce him could make things so much easier, but he was right to decline. Bankers could be fussy with their money, and no one appeared to advantage after a full night spent entertaining people.

However, that wouldn't be a problem for her. She was generally an early riser. "Might I go instead?" she asked. It was forward of her, but if she were to venture into business with his lordship, then one of them ought to take advantage of the opportunity. If it couldn't be him, it might as well be her.

Lord Satyr jolted in surprise, turning to look at her with his eyes alarmingly wide. "I don't think—"

"What an interesting idea," Aunt Isabelle purred. "But I thought you had no interest in money matters."

Gwen shrugged. "My curiosity drags me in several directions. I have wondered about banking, but Mama thought finance inappropriate for a girl in search of a husband."

"Men do get touchy when faced with a woman of means," Aunt Isabelle agreed.

"But Mama informs me that I am now a spinster. Therefore, she cannot worry if I interest myself in more masculine pursuits."

Her aunt rolled her eyes. "Your mother does have a singular vision for your future."

"One in which I have been a resounding disappointment." She pulled off her ill-chosen face mask and stared glumly at it. That had been a significant error in judgment.

"Oh listen," Lord Satyr said suddenly. "The orchestra is beginning another set. Please, Lady Gwen, would you do me the distinct honor of joining me for a dance?"

Gwen looked to the crowded dance floor. The last thing she wanted was to display her lack of dancing ability among that many people. She was likely to cause a disaster the first time she forgot a step. "I'm afraid I have always been clumsy on the dance floor."

"Never fear. I am quite capable of seeing you safely through the experience."

His smile was mesmerizing when he spoke, especially when coupled with his nearly naked torso. Gwen found herself allowing him to grasp her hand, but she stiffened when her aunt pressed her own darkly gloved hand a top both of theirs.

"What he means, Gwendolyn, is that he does not think it appropriate for you to learn the basics of how to survive in a masculine world, and he means to distract you. Such is ever the way with men. They think they know our minds better than we do, and they have succeeded in breaking the wills of women like your mother. She cannot see that a woman has value outside of marriage, but you and I know differently, do we not?"

Well, that was certainly true. Mama saw no purpose to any female beyond marrying a titled, wealthy man and bearing him the next generation of arrogant men and obedient women.

"I assure you," Lord Satyr said, "I have no such thoughts in mind." He gently lifted off Aunt Isabelle's hand, but the damage was done. She was well aware of the tension in the man. He did not like her talking with her aunt, and that alone set up her back.

"And I assure you," Gwen returned, "that when you realize how badly I dance, you will be thankful I declined your offer." She took her hand out of his and turned to address her aunt. "Would you like to stroll about the gardens with me? I fear my family has wandered to the four corners and I have been left as a burden to Lord Satyr."

"On the contrary," Lord Satyr began, but Aunt Isabelle didn't give him the chance.

"You have ever been the niece with the most promise," she said. "I should be delighted to wander with you, provided you leave that dreadful mask behind. Whyever would you chose such a terrible costume?"

"It was an error in logic, I'm afraid. I thought if I wanted a husband, I should dress as something they adore. I could not come as a horse—that would invite all sorts of ridicule, not to mention the expense."

"So you came as a dog?"

"Of indeterminate breed. I thought it would allow the gentlemen to pick out the characteristics they most enjoyed—"

"And dance with you?"

"And speak with me," she corrected. "I thought to engage them in scintillating conversation."

Lady Isabelle arched a brow. "And the error in logic was what?"

Gwen shrugged. "Two-fold. The first is that men are not interested in marrying their dogs."

"Very true. And the second?"

It was embarrassing to confess, but Aunt Isabelle had always rewarded honest confessions. "I could not find any scintillating conversation topics to entice them."

"Entirely their fault," inserted Lord Satyr, which was kind of him. And then Aunt Isabelle delighted her by reinforcing the sentiment.

"On that we agree. Now come along, Gwendolyn. I should like to hear everything about what is happening at home. It has been too long since I visited your mother."

Gwen smiled and was about to fall into step with her aunt, except that Lord Satyr was abruptly between them, offering an arm to both women. "Pray allow me to show you the sights. I can think of nothing more delightful than to wander about the grounds with two beautiful ladies upon my arm. Indeed, one might say it's distinctly Satyr-like."

"As long as you do not expect me to dance about you like a nymph," Gwen said, "I should enjoy your company." It was her way of saying that she did not harbor any ill will toward him for trying to stop her from meeting with the bankers tomorrow. Aunt Isabelle, however, was not so kindly inclined.

"I should think you have other things to do," she said tartly. "Lady Gwen and I are quite able to entertain ourselves."

"But that would leave me at the mercy of several other less interesting ladies," he returned smoothly. Gwen had already taken his right arm, and they both waited to see if Aunt Isabelle would take his left.

She did, but with the barest tips of her fingers. Then before they could begin their stroll, Aunt Isabelle looked back at the two men behind her. "Go learn something interesting," she ordered.

They each gave her a deep bow and departed, which left the three of them to begin a leisurely stroll about the grounds. Lord Satyr was the perfect companion. He chatted amiably about the pleasure garden, brought others into their conversation when they were greeted, and listened with every appearance of attention. She felt relaxed by his side, and no one stared at her oddly. That might be because he listened when she spoke and didn't force her to participate when she had nothing to say. That allowed the conversation to flow easily which rarely happened when she was around. For the first time in a very long time, she felt part of the discourse without being an awkward barnacle hanging around to no purpose.

What a wonder that was. At least until she realized that he had an agenda.

He meant to keep her from being private with her aunt. In return, Aunt Isabelle seemed equally determined to find some secret conversation with Gwen. That led to a constant conversational jockeying between them. Lady Isabelle would ask about her family and try to draw her aside, but Lord Satyr would ask a pertinent question about her relations and he was once again in the thick of things.

Gwen didn't know what to make of it. She didn't understand the tension and she became more uncomfortable as the walk continued. And yet, during the forty minutes they took to promenade the gardens, she discovered Lord Satyr was well versed on a variety of different subjects which gave her a very favorable impression of his intelligence. Others seemed to agree as they picked up several more people during their wandering, expanding their group to nine.

In short, Lord Satyr exuded charm and set her at ease while Aunt Isabelle grew more irritated. Gwen saw her mouth tighten and her lower jaw thrust out more than once. Whatever their relationship had been, Lord Satyr was clearly on the outs with her aunt. But the lady contained her emotions beneath a superior smile and a sarcastic wit. A funny sarcasm, to be sure, but there was a cruel edge to her jokes that made Gwen uncomfortable. Unfortunately, she seemed to be the only one discomfited. Everyone else laughed with good cheer, and so Gwen smiled as if she agreed. But by the end of forty minutes, she wanted to return to her family, most especially her sister Lilah, who never had an unkind word to say about anyone.

They had just started back toward the box when a servant came running up to their party. The waiter looked uneasy as he drew Lord Satyr aside. Sadly, there was a great deal of noise, and she could not hear the conversation. She could only note that it looked very dire, especially when his gaze landed heavy upon her face.

When the waiter bowed and rushed away, Aunt Isabelle demanded answers. "You're frightening us," she said sharply. "What has happened?"

He didn't respond to her aunt, but instead turned to look to her. "Apparently there's been an altercation. Nothing to worry about—"

"Accident?" one of the men of their party said with a snort. "I heard 'attack.'"

"Attack?" Gwen gasped.

"An exaggeration, I assure you," Lord Satyr said with a hard glance at the speaker. "A few gentlemen in their cups."

The glare was unimportant to Gwen. She was done with socializing anyway. This evening had been a disaster in finding a husband and in figuring out what was between her aunt and Lord Satyr. In truth, she was done with the whole affair and would rather go back to her books. Or more relevant, she wanted to find out the perfect way to cultivate daffodils. "I will find my brother," she began. "He will want to go home soon, I'm sure."

"I will accompany you to Elliott—" Lord Satyr said, but Aunt Isabelle interrupted him.

"Don't be ridiculous. I'm her aunt. I'll take you home." She grabbed a nearby waiter. "Pray inform Lord Byrn that I will see Lady Gwendolyn home." Then she turned her hard glare on Lord Satyr. "I should have known that a masquerade at Vauxhall was an idiotic idea. Goodness, that's twice this has happened at your party. Come along, Gwendolyn."

She could tell that Lord Satyr wanted to argue. His hands twitched as if he wanted to physically drag her away from her aunt, but that would be impolite. Plus he needed to deal with whatever disaster had happened. Arguing would only slow that process.

"Do not worry about me," she urged him. "I find myself fatigued anyway."

In the end, he gave her a clipped nod and strode away while Aunt Isabelle pulled her in the opposite direction.

"Come along, Gwendolyn," Aunt Isabelle commanded. "It's time to remove ourselves from this disgraceful event."

"Of course, Aunt," she said, doing her best to keep up. She thought she spotted her sister Lilah as they hurried past the orchestra, but her aunt would not slow and Gwen hadn't the breath to call out. It wasn't until they were finally in her aunt's carriage that the woman slowed enough to speak.

"Finally, we have a moment to think clearly." She took out a breath. "Now tell me everything you and Sayres were discussing before I arrived."

"What?"

"You looked quite animated as I walked up. I insist you tell me everything."

CHAPTER FIVE

JACKSON FELT EXHAUSTION drag at him like a too heavy coat, but excitement pulsed through him nonetheless. It was because he finally had hope, thanks to the inventive Lady Gwen. Despite managing the masquerade singlehandedly—his co-hosts having both mysteriously disappeared—he hadn't been able to stop thinking about making the Lincolnshire daffodils popular. If it were possible, then he could save not only his family's fortune, but revitalize the entire region. And it all came because of a casual idea from Lady Gwen.

He couldn't wait to see her. Ideas were bursting through him along with a very big list of things to do before the concept became feasible. He wanted to talk them all through with her, but first he had to make things clear to Isabelle. He knew now that she had engineered the "attack" last night. One of her pretty boys had goaded two inebriated gentlemen into a spectacle of a fistfight. Sadly, it had taken some time to sort through the resulting mess and to do his best to quash any gossip.

It wouldn't help his reputation in business if he could not host a party without some disaster.

The hackney dropped him off in front of Lady Meunier's home. If he'd timed it right, then breakfast with the bankers was nearing its end and Isabelle was about to hit them with her newest investment idea. She probably wanted funds to upgrade the flash locks on her canals to the much easier pound locks. It was an excellent idea, but he'd much rather they loan him the cash to convert several oat fields into a daffodil farm. The two projects weren't mutually exclusive, but he knew if he didn't get his name in front of the bankers now, it would be ten times harder to gain an appointment tomorrow.

He sounded the knocker with an echoing clap.

He was known to Isabelle's butler, so the door was opened quickly. But he was also known to be persona non grata since his falling out with her, which meant he had to push past the large servant and rush through. "I won't be but a moment," he said as he hurried past. Fortunately, the man was large, not fast, and Jackson made it inside. That wouldn't last long, but hopefully he could make an impact in that short time.

He moved quickly into the dining room, skirting the servants poised to serve eggs, scones, or an excellent wine. Isabelle, he saw, was at the top of the table. She always liked to sit as a reigning queen, but then he jolted in shock.

Lady Gwen sat beside Isabelle. She wore a borrowed gown that did not fit her well, but served to display her bosom to a nearly scandalous amount. The three bankers sat nearby with full bellies and happy smiles.

What the hell was Lady Gwen doing here? And what had Isabelle said to her?

He recovered quickly, though, and he breathed with mock dismay. "Oh dear," he said as he entered the room. "I see I've mistimed my visit and you are still at table."

Everyone turned to him with varying states of surprise. Isabelle's expression darkened to fury, but she quickly covered. He performed his bow to her and Lady Gwen, even as he smiled at the three gentlemen.

"Misters Marshall, Brown, and Barker, pray forgive my intrusion. I have a mission here, and it won't take but a moment."

"Not at all, my lord. I quite understand," said Mr. Barker in a hearty tone. "Lady Meunier was telling us of your masquerade last night. Quite the frightening dealings, what?"

He blinked as if distracted. "What? Nothing frightening occurred unless you count fireworks as disturbing." Then he flashed them a smile. "Oh, and two gentlemen in their cups enjoying themselves in a boisterous manner. But then, ladies get frightened so easily, you know. They haven't the nerves for truly difficult things."

He nearly choked on the words as they came out of his mouth. If his sisters ever found out he said something so outrageous, they would punish him for sure. But given that Isabelle had just tried to discredit him in front of these men and the whole *ton*, he felt justified in returning the favor. Unfortunately, he was too tired to examine his words carefully. Instead of suggesting Isabelle specifically had been frightened, he used the word "ladies." Lady Gwen, of course, took umbrage at that statement.

"That's hardly true, my lord," she said. "Countless women have faced terrors that would leave us weak at the knees. And I promise you, it was not the fireworks that had me depart your masquerade so quickly." She arched her brows. "And I find it odd that an inebriated gentleman is called overly boisterous, but a woman in her cups is described in much uglier terms."

Oh hell. Lady Gwen was in a quarrelsome mood. That did not bode well for today's tasks. He smiled at her. "I apologize. I'm afraid I've had a long night of it. As you can see, I'm still in my costume." He gestured down at his ridiculous attire. He'd managed to button up his shirt, but there was nothing he could do about the goat-like breeches.

"Was it an exciting evening, then?" asked Mr. Barker. "If you're just now finishing up."

"I am and it was," Jackson answered, turning his back on the large footmen coming to drag him out of the room. "I should be delighted to tell you all about it, but sadly, I haven't the time right now. Tomorrow, perhaps? We'll meet at your club." He already knew the men frequented the same club and would enjoy hosting a man with gossip.

"A capital idea!" crowed Mr. Marshall.

He grinned as if he had salacious stories to tell. He did, but not from the party. Still, he'd always been good at enlivening a tale when needed. It was all in how he modulated his voice. All three men looked very excited at the prospect, which meant he had accomplished his task with them. Next came his message to Isabelle. He would have to hurry because the servants were gathering behind him to grab him and toss him unceremoniously out the door. Fortunately, Isabelle did not wish to make a scene in front of the bankers and so had waved them back, but that would not last long.

"I came here direct, Lady Meunier, to acquaint you with the particulars of the nasty intention of your companions."

Her eyes widened. "My companions?" she asked. "I have no such—"

"You arrived at Vauxhall in the company of two gentlemen. I'm afraid they were attempting to maneuver several gentlemen into compromising positions in order to blackmail them later."

Isabelle's eyes narrowed in fury for all that her voice sounded innocent. "That can't possibly be true. I can't imagine it! Do you have proof?"

None that he cared to share, though he knew it was true. "I will not sully the victims' names by involving them further in this. Be assured that I have verified it to my satisfaction." He raised his hand to his heart. "Upon my honor it is the truth."

He wasn't lying. Her companions had tried to compromise several gentlemen and one young lady with too much drink. The gentlemen had been smart enough to imbibe without spilling secrets best kept quiet. The lady had not, and that was going far beyond the pale for Jackson. "They had best not cross my path again," he said darkly. "I nearly called one out for what he planned for a young woman." The man who had been leading the lady down the dark path received a thorough drubbing. "It is because of my respect for you that he did not die from pistols at dawn."

She frowned, clearly troubled. "Surely you exaggerate."

"No, I do not."

His words landed hard and cold. He did not know if Isabelle had pushed her men to act in so dishonorable a fashion or if they'd done it on their own. He didn't care. She had drawn the battle lines the minute she began discrediting Jackson with the financial set. He was making it clear that she had a reputation to lose as well, and he would not hesitate to destroy it if she continued to cut at his.

She took a breath. "I will cut them from my association immediately."

He nodded. It appeared that mutual destruction would keep the worst of her tendencies in check. "Thank you," he began, but he had not counted on Lady Gwendolyn.

"That seems rather harsh, doesn't it? To cut the men off without even speaking with them?"

"I assure you, I spoke with them extensively—" he began.

"Not you," she said as she turned to her aunt. "You know these men," she said simply. "Did you think them capable of such a thing?"

"Of course not!"

"Then you should talk to them. I'm sure Lord Sayres did his best, but there might be something of which he is unaware."

Isabelle arched her brow as she all but sneered at him. "I assure you, there is a great deal of which he is unaware."

"All the more reason to speak with your friends."

Lady Gwen stared at her aunt, clearly confused by the illogic of the situation. Especially as Isabelle turned hard eyes onto her niece. "Gwendolyn, you appear overwrought. I was afraid that the party last night and this morning's early hour would be too much for you."

Far from being insulted, Lady Gwen smiled as if she had just been given a lifeline. She benignly addressed the bankers. "I fear my aunt is correct. I do feel somewhat tired, but I am very pleased to make your gentlemen's acquaintance. It would give me great pleasure to visit with you again sometime."

All three bankers pushed up from their chairs, bowing graciously. They said all the proper things, as did Jackson, before Lady Gwen bussed her aunt's cheek. "Thank you so much for a wonderful time, Aunt. I am very grateful."

Isabelle allowed the kiss with supreme indifference as she waved her hand at Gwen. "Wait in your room. I'll attend to you after I am—"

"Goodness no," Gwendolyn gasped. "I'll walk home on my own. It's a lovely morning."

"Don't be ridiculous," Isabelle said, her irritation plain. "It's too far to walk."

"I am a hearty country girl, aunt. I shall be fine."

Jackson grinned. Here was the exact opportunity he'd been looking for. "And I shall accompany you."

"Looking like that?" Isabelle cried, as she curled her lip at his Lord Satyr costume. "You'll be a laughingstock, as will my niece for being in your company. I shan't allow it."

Lady Gwen was moving toward the door, her expression amused as she got a full look at his attire. "She has a point, my lord. You do look unusual in the daylight."

He bowed as if he agreed, but then he flashed her a smile. "The secret to hosting the party of the Season is to have people discuss it long after the event is over. You would help me in this by giving me an excuse to remind people of the event by daylight."

He watched the lady consider his words, her delectable mouth pursed as she thought. "That does carry some logic, however—"

"Popularity has its own peculiar rules. Trust me on this." He held out his hand to her and was delighted when she set her fingers in his. And though Jackson heard Isabelle abruptly order her carriage to be brought around, he was too busy studying the intriguing color of Lady Gwen's eyes. They were the darkest blue he'd ever seen without being brown. And at the edges of the iris was the faintest hint of gold. Like sunlight touching the edges of a petal.

And wasn't that poetic of him? Truthfully, it was an extremely odd thought, but he couldn't stop himself from staring while they exited the room.

"I'll just be a moment," she said without withdrawing her fingertips from his.

He pressed a kiss to the back of her hand. "Please hurry," he whispered as he straightened. "I doubt Isabelle will let me loiter for long."

She nodded and rushed upstairs. Meanwhile, behind him, he heard the three bankers taking their leave over Isabelle's objections. Clearly, she hadn't had a chance to press them for money to upgrade her locks. Damnation, Lady Gwen was going to take too much time upstairs. Very soon Isabelle would be free of the bankers and then who knew what mischief she would perpetrate between him and Lady Gwen? But in this he was surprised.

Lady Gwen came down the stairs faster than he could believe. Behind her trailed a maid he recognized. Her name was Lucy. She was a smart woman with sharp ears and a penchant for snooping around places she didn't belong, and she had little love for Jackson.

"My lady," Lucy exclaimed. "It isn't proper for you to go alone and outside—"

"Piffle," Lady Gwen said, her long legs eating up the distance between the stairs and the front door where he waited.

"Lady Gwendolyn," the butler said, stepping in front of her. "The carriage will be brought around in a moment. If you would but wait—"

"Oh no need for that," she said, as she neatly ducked around the large man. "You can send on my things from last night. Good day!"

Jackson reached out his hand and she grabbed it like she was running from a storm. Behind them, he heard Lucy exclaim in dismay while the bankers confused matters by asking for their hats and canes. Together he and Lady Gwen practically flew down the front steps. Looking down the street, he saw Isabelle's carriage making its way toward them, so he turned in the opposite direction.

"This way," he said as he pulled her down an alleyway. She pivoted quickly, her steps nimble as they ducked out of sight. He wouldn't put it past Isabelle to send a footman to chase after them both. He shortened his stride for her but was then surprised again. She kept pace without losing breath as he took them quickly down another street, another alley, and several blocks beyond that.

Eventually he slowed. Once he was sure they were clear, he stopped to look at her flushed cheeks and wide grin. Apparently, the woman had found their mad dash exciting! She rose in his esteem.

"We can hail a hackney now, if you like," he offered.

"Why? It's a glorious day!"

It really wasn't. The sky was a dull grey, and the wind had a chill, but she shook her head at his bemused expression.

"I am always up walking at this hour. Any day without rain is a lovely day."

He grinned. She truly was a delightful woman. "As I am rarely awake at this time, I bow to your greater experience."

She cast him an admonishing look. "You should have told me you knew those bankers. It would have saved me from that interminable meal, then I could be at the park now and you in bed." She tugged at the bodice of her gown, pulling it up to cover her better. It was a futile effort. He now recognized the thing as one of Isabelle's cast-off gowns cut much too low even if the thing had fit.

"Would you like my coat?" he offered, even though it would leave him chest mostly bared to the wind.

She looked at him a moment, her eyes widening at the thought. And if he wasn't mistaken, her cheeks pinked as well, and not from the exertion. "I think your attire is scandalous enough, don't you?"

With that reaction, how could he resist? He shrugged off his coat and wrapped it around her shoulders, thereby exposing himself to the wind and covering up the distraction of her low bodice. He hoped God noticed how virtuous he was being. Her bosom was a magnificent sight.

But then, to his disappointment, she took a deep breath and appeared to focus her thoughts. "Very well," she said. "Out with it. What is your plan?"

CHAPTER SIX

GWEN FOLDED HER arms across her overly plumped bodice and began walking in the direction of her home rather than ogle the man she now knew was Lord Sayres. She hadn't realized his true identity last night and, truthfully, wouldn't have cared. But after she'd told Aunt Isabelle—ad nauseum—about her failed attempts to lure a husband, the woman had detailed Lord Sayres' vast sexual exploits as a way of dissuading Gwen from considering the man as a potential husband. According to Aunt Isabelle, he was not only unsuitable to know, his time was completely absorbed in orgies that would put the Romans to shame.

It was the first time in her life that she thought Aunt Isabelle lacking in wits. No man had the stamina to do what she claimed. Though glancing at him now—still in his Lord Satyr costume—she was forced to acknowledge his continued virility. Even after a night spent in revels, he appeared as attractive in daylight as he had under the stars. He had her thoughts wandering in surprisingly sexual directions which flustered her. She'd never fantasized about kissing a man before, and yet suddenly she was thinking about all sorts of erotic things. And much more than kissing!

It made her skin hot and her breath short. So she made her voice stern as a way to distract herself from looking at his bared chest.

"I should like to know your plan to make our venture successful."

"My plan?"

"Yes," she said. "Any endeavor requires careful planning. I had thought you were up to that task. Was I mistaken?"

He was silent for a bit, his long strides easily matching hers, but eventually he spoke and she found his gaze disconcertingly direct. Especially since she was doing her best not to look at him.

"You sound as if you have tried this before with someone who has disappointed you," he said.

Might as well tell him the truth. "I have thought of various schemes over the years to gain funds. I learned early that many activities were barred from me because of my gender, so I gave my ideas to my male family members."

"Did they listen?"

"Two did. They thought my ideas were excellent concepts though both had to do with farm innovations."

"What happened?"

She shrugged. "One was swindled out of every penny because he hadn't the foresight to talk to his steward first. The other failed because he didn't want to test the design." She stopped walking to look straight at him. "I have given up asking men to think of the details of gardening or cultivation. I can see to that, but I have no ability to make it popular. I should like to know your plans for that."

He tilted his head. "You know how best to transport it to London?"

She grimaced. "Not yet, though I have been ruminating on it. You cannot expect to cut the stems in the morning and sell them in London within the hour. Worse, it might be very difficult to move them in large enough volume for popularity."

"Scarcer things are more valuable."

She shook her head. "You cannot price a flower as if it were a diamond. There can only be a little profit with every sale. In order to make significant money, you will have to have significant sales."

He smiled at her. "You have been thinking about this."

"What else was I to do while Aunt Isabelle relayed tales of yet another one of your orgies?"

"*Another* orgy?" he gasped. "I submit that I have never been in a single one."

"Then I submit that she vastly overestimated your virility." She folded her arms across her annoying plump bosom and carefully looked anywhere but at his chest. "Why does my aunt want to dissuade me from you?"

"Isabelle and I have a long history."

"Yes, she told me she taught you everything you know." And promised to teach it to Gwen as well, assuming Gwen managed to get her dowry from her brother and invested it in the woman's canals.

"She taught me a great deal," he said with a wink. "And only some of it would be worthwhile at an orgy."

Gwen never knew how to respond when someone winked. She knew that it added meaning, but she never understood what. So she did what she always did. She looked away and pretended not to see. Normally that wouldn't bother her, but she truly wanted to understand what Lord Sayres meant by his wink.

Meanwhile, he must have seen her discomfort. "Lady Gwen?" he asked with a soft tone. And then he touched her arm which naturally caused her to jerk away. She hadn't seen his touch coming and that always startled her. "My apologies. I've upset you."

"Please," she said as she schooled her features. "I prefer plain speaking."

He nodded, his expression grave. "Isabelle enjoys telling people what they may and may not do. I accepted her tutelage for many years, but now our partnership has ended. She dislikes my quest for independence."

That didn't make sense. Slavery was outlawed in Britain, and Lord Sayres did not seem like someone who could be controlled. "You're a man. How can she tell you what to do?"

He didn't answer, but she could read the expression on his face well enough. He wore that male attitude of resigned arrogance. One that said he couldn't begin to fathom a woman's illogic. Unfortunately, it did not illuminate the situation. It might be that Aunt Isabelle was being ridiculously pig-headed in her hatred of him. She certainly enjoyed ordering Gwen around. Or it could be that he had offended her in some serious fashion and—in his blind male way—he could not comprehend his error.

Gwen did not feel she could ferret out the truth this moment. Which meant she would use her own judgment to evaluate Lord Sayres. So far, his actions had been completely acceptable if one discounted the nakedness of his costume. Which, to be honest, she enjoyed.

She began walking again. "If you could bring me a few of the flowers—potted if you please—then I shall begin experiments on the best way to transport them."

"I will send for them, but that is just the beginning of my plan."

So he did have a plan. Good. "What is the rest?"

"The only way to make the flower popular is to make a lady who wears it popular."

She supposed that was one path, but surely there were others. "Why go to the work of making a person popular? Surely you have friends who have already accomplished the task. You should make them adopt the flower."

He shook his head. "I don't think they can do enough. Not to make the kind of stir I need. I want my daffodil to become the choice for every debutante in London for years to come."

"An excellent goal, my lord, but rather ambitious, don't you think?"

He continued as if she had not spoken. "In order to make my flower popular, I have to make the woman who wears them a sensation."

"I am not persuaded that is the best path."

"It is," he said emphatically. "Especially if we link her with the flowers. Everyone will mimic her." He touched her arm. It was just the most passing touch, but she had been unprepared and flinched again. "We will claim that the daffodils have special magic in them."

She pulled her arm back, feeling the heat where his body had touched her, and she rubbed her hand over it. What was she feeling? Why did it tingle? "Magic is illogical," she stated firmly.

"But very marketable."

She understood his meaning. Just because she would never believe in magic transformations didn't mean others felt the same. Indeed, if he could find the right woman to do it, then he would indeed make his flower the most wanted bloom in all of England.

"You truly think that is the best approach?"

"I do."

As this was his area of expertise, she had to defer to him, though she found it all very strange. "You need to find the woman and apprise her of your plans immediately. She must agree."

"Absolutely," he said, his expression grave. "Do you agree?"

He was looking at her so pointedly that she shied backwards a step. She was not used to such direct attention from gentlemen, especially one wearing a waistcoat with no shirt beneath. "What?"

"Will you let me make you popular?"

She stared at him a moment as she repeated his question three times in her head. And when that was done, she reversed her thoughts all the way back to the moment when they'd first met, re-evaluating everything he'd said.

"Lady Gwen?"

"Are you flirting? Is this some Roman form of seduction—"

"What?" He looked and sounded appalled. "Of course not! I am in earnest. I think you are the perfect woman to promote my flower."

She stared at him, doing her best to read his expression. He did not seem to be teasing her.

"You are in earnest?" she asked.

"Most certainly."

She saw no lie in him, but she could not credit his words. If this was not a bad attempt at seduction, then his wits were lacking. There was no other explanation.

"Oh dear," she finally said. "I'm afraid you have failed."

"What?"

"An intelligence test, my lord. Do try to do better or I shall think this venture is not at all worth my time."

He rocked back on his heels, but he didn't seem offended so much as amused. "I see. And how have I failed?"

"Your chosen woman would need style, grace, and a hidden beauty that can be exploited to best effect."

He nodded, his expression excruciatingly bland. "Yes, I know."

Clearly, he didn't know. She began walking again. They were very close to her front steps and she sped up rather than further this incredibly awkward conversation. "She will need to be extraordinarily special because those are the qualities which you want associated with your daffodils."

"I completely agree." His tone was matter-of-fact, but when she glanced sideways at him, she saw his lips curve in a slow smile.

The slowness of the motion confused her, especially when coupled with such a direct gaze. There was meaning here that she did not fully understand, and yet she liked it. She enjoyed the way he looked at her.

"Lady Gwen?"

"I do not qualify," she stated firmly as she wrenched her mind back to the topic at hand. "I've spent the last three weeks of my life determining my assets in the Marriage Mart."

"You have?"

She blew out a breath. "They have been the most dismally uncomfortable three weeks of my life. Having decided I wanted children, I resolved to get married. Having resolved for a husband, I wrote down how I might be appealing on the Marriage Mart."

His brows rose but rather than confess the rest while facing him, she began walking and each step brought yet another one of her so-called attributes to light. "My looks are average at best. Men hate that. I am forthright in speech. Men and women alike hate that. What is special about me is my intelligence, and everyone hates that including—at times—myself."

"You hate your intelligence?"

"Believe me, my life would go so much more smoothly if I didn't realize how stupid people are." She glanced at him, batted her eyes, and spoke in a sing-song quality. "Oh my, sir, you quite astound me with your brilliant deduction that the earth is round, the sun heats the land, and we would all starve if it was always night!"

Laughter burst from him, filling the street with the warm sound. "Surely no one ever—"

"Surely they did. Or rather he did. My third and final suitor." She sighed as she began walking again. "I believe he offered for my hand because he was too stupid to realize I thought him an idiot."

He snapped his fingers. "I remember now. You're talking about Lord McCray and his fascination with astronomy. I cannot believe you entertained his suit."

"I didn't. Mama did." She mimicked her mother's most strident tones. "He has a title, adequate wealth, and a fascination with scholarly things. You suit one another perfectly!" Gwen rolled her eyes. "She didn't understand that he isn't really scholarly. He's in love with reciting obscure facts while silly women clap."

"Well, thank God you saw through him," he drawled.

"Even his dogs saw through him! He complained that they never listened when he addressed them."

Lord Sayres snorted, and his amusement made her smile. It moderated her ire enough that she addressed him directly and with total honesty. It helped that they were at last at the steps to her home and she could stop and face him.

"All my life, I have been out of step with everyone else. Even with my vast intelligence, I cannot find the right rhythm to match anyone else. I do not believe it is possible. Which means I cannot be brought into popularity."

"But of course you can," he returned. He was smiling warmly at her, and his eyes heated to a rich amber in the sunlight. Quite handsome, but not handsome enough to distract her from the discussion.

"I have tried, my lord, but—"

"You failed because you made an error in logic."

She felt her chin lift in automatic insult. She was not a woman who tolerated illogic, especially in herself.

"That is patently untrue," she said.

"The error is in that you tried to adjust yourself to everyone else. Lady Gwen, popular people set the tempo. Everyone else must march to *your* rhythm."

She stared at him a moment. She thought over his words and saw a certain type of reason in it. But she could not in any way see herself leading anything or anyone. "It's not possible."

"That is a failure of imagination," he chided.

She sniffed. "That is male arrogance. A better word is 'hubris.'" There. Let him ponder that. She didn't know ten gentlemen who recognized the word "hubris."

He shook his head. "I make no claim to be better than a god. And Arachne was a woman, so hubris is not unique to men."

She blinked, startled enough that she felt her jaw go slack. He knew the word? And the way in which it had been used? She couldn't credit it. "You're a student of Greek poetry?"

He shrugged. "Not really. The basics, at best."

She didn't know a single man on the *ton* who didn't preen a bit when he used scholarly words. Not a one would admit to knowing only the bare minimum of anything. They all pretended to more depth than they had, and it had become a game to her to pierce their veneer with a few well-placed questions. Needless to say, that did not endear her to them.

She was so shocked as to be silent. And in that space, he smiled at her, clearly knowing he had the advantage of surprise.

"I should like to change my clothes, Lady Gwen, and then return this afternoon so that we can discuss this more deeply."

She blinked. "Hubris?"

He chuckled. "Your transformation into a society leader."

That was ludicrous enough to jolt her out of her shock. "Impossible, my lord. Set your mind to finding a lady more suited to the task."

She nodded to him by way of good-bye, then began climbing the stairs in front of her home. Her butler was just opening the front door when she heard his words.

"I shall call this afternoon, Lady Gwen."

She looked back and saw the most curious expression on his face. It was one of challenge and mischief, accompanied by an ancient gesture more appropriate to a medieval night than a mythical satyr. He mimed throwing down a large gauntlet at her feet.

"Consider it a challenge."

"You're daft," she said.

"Even so." Then he winked at her as if he truly were a satyr tempting her into all sorts of inappropriate behavior.

Well that just showed that he didn't know her very well. She was never one to pick up a task just because a handsome man offered it. And yet, there was something about that wink that got her thinking, thinking, thinking in the most ridiculous directions.

Chapter Seven

JACKSON HAD NEVER wanted sleep more, but his mind kept churning. He had a plan to rescue his finances and his brain had arranged all the pieces including the people he could recruit to his purpose. But it all depended on Lady Gwen's cooperation.

Logic told him that hinging his entire business on one woman was a ridiculous choice. No matter how smart she was, he needed to control his own fate. But he could not make a sensation out of himself. He was already as accepted as he was likely to get. He needed a special woman with hidden charm that he was uniquely positioned to bring into popularity.

He'd finished his toilette and now sat in his shirtsleeves and nothing else as he polished his own boots. It was a tedious task and he missed having a valet, but he could not afford the expense. So there he sat in his tiny room in a gentleman's boarding house and rubbed his footwear while his mind wandered. More thoughts, more plans, and the recurring sight of Lady Gwen as she stood shocked by his intellect.

He shouldn't be thrilled that he had bested her. God knew, she was likely ten times more knowledgeable than he, certainly in botany. But he did know the word "hubris" along with its antecedents, which was a good thing. Lady Gwen respected intelligence. It was probably the only thing she did respect. And so he had matched her education—in that respect—and had garnered another chance to bring her into his plans.

And he did relish the idea of bringing her enthusiastically into his plans. He was busy imagining just what he might do with her when a heavy knock disrupted his thoughts.

"Come in."

If his mind had been anywhere but on Lady Gwen, he'd have realized the knock was not a valet here to rescue him. But he wasn't paying attention which is why he was startled when the door burst open and a broad-shouldered man with angry emerald eyes stepped in. There was a crackle to the air that pulled Jackson fully into the moment, not to mention the way his intruder scanned the room, then dismissed it with a single contemptuous look.

"Lord Sayres?"

Jackson didn't answer beyond a quirk in his eyebrow and that made the man's eyes flash.

"You are Lord Sayres?" His gaze took in the polishing implements and showed some confusion. After all, how many members of the *ton* worked their own boots?

"Is that a question?" Jackson asked.

The man frowned and shook his head. "No, I know it's you," he said. "I just hadn't realized how far you'd fallen." His gaze encompassed the cramped room that no servant had cleaned in far too long. And given that Jackson had spent the last week preparing for the masquerade, his rooms were in a disheveled state.

"And you are…?" he asked though he'd already figured out who the man was. It was a measure of his exhaustion that he hadn't figured it out at the beginning.

"Lord Byrn," he said, his voice tight. "Lady Gwen's brother and guardian."

Normally Jackson would make some effort to be charming. He had turned the opinion of many fathers and brothers, especially when he emphasized that he had no intention of marrying the wealthy women under their care. But he was overtired and caught—literally—with his pants off. It set him on the offensive. "I hardly think so."

"What?" The word sounded like the crack of a tree breaking.

"You're not her guardian. She's long since entered her majority."

Lord Byrn's brows drew down. He didn't start ranting, which was a point in his favor, and in truth, the hard stare was intimidating. But Jackson had never been one to falter just because of an ugly look. He'd have been done in years ago if that were the case.

"Listen, Sayres, I haven't the time to mince words. I know you're a fortune hunter. You're pleasant enough and I don't begrudge you your status—"

"Kind of you not to begrudge my title," he drawled. They were of an equal rank, though Byrn had inherited a healthy estate and Sayres had not. But on the societal rung, they were of a pair.

"You know what I mean," the man snapped. "I'm not here to threaten your standing in society or any such nonsense."

"Then why are you here?"

The man took a breath, paused, then shrugged. "To threaten all that if you pursue my sister."

At least he seemed to recognize the ridiculousness of what he'd just said. "Thank you for not mincing words. I appreciate people who understand the value of my time. Pray shut the door on your way out."

He didn't expect Lord Byrn to take the dismissal, but he also didn't expect the man to draw up a chair and wearily drop into it. "Gwen's an odd duck, to be sure, but she's also brilliant and not one for social niceties. Whatever man marries her will need to be indulgent of her odd studies and immune to the thousands of ways she might embarrass him. For example, she has several microscopes in her possession which she uses until an indent develops around her eye and she is forced to rest."

Jackson didn't know which to be offended by most—that her own brother could describe Lady Gwen in such an unflattering way or that he could do it while clearly bent on trying to protect her. He stared at the man in silent horror which was clearly misinterpreted.

"I promise you I do not exaggerate. Her scientific investigations can be distasteful. She spent a full year in the study of mites, and she would share her thoughts on the subject at the dinner table." Lord Byrn rubbed a hand over his face. "I love my sister to distraction, but there is no arguing that she is strange." His gaze turned to Jackson's neatly folded piles of clothes. Though he had little quantity in clothing, each piece was excellently tailored and of good quality. "Any man who marries her would see his invitations decrease, his place in polite society damaged, and his circle of influence severely curtailed." Then Byrn took a deep breath. "And then there is the other thing."

Jackson waited, but the man didn't speak. It was a cheap oratory trick to hold the listener's attention, and so Jackson picked up the polishing cloth and returned to his boots. Unfortunately for all his apparent disinterest, his imagination was fully caught and held. What was the *other* thing that so plagued Lady Gwen? Did she have a secret deformity or bizarre vice? Had fairies cursed her to turn into a frog every night at midnight? The possibilities were endless.

And damn the man for seeing his weakness for a good story. "I know I have your attention," Lord Byrn said.

"But not my patience," Jackson returned. "You have come into my home to level threats. Pray finish insulting your own sister or leave."

"My sister is an incredible woman!" Lord Bryn cried, clearly incensed though he was the one who had been discounting her. "She is delightfully intelligent and has a wicked sense of humor. She deserves a man who can see that."

Jackson lifted his gaze to meet Lord Byrn's with a level of fury that he rarely let show. "And you think I don't see her value."

"I don't know if you see it," Byrn said coldly. "I don't think you're worthy of it."

Well that was putting it succinctly. And though the hit stung, Jackson answered it in the only way he could. "Perhaps I will change your mind."

"Or perhaps you will look for a bride elsewhere because Gwen's dowry is not what you think."

He doubted it. Lady Gwen's mother had made the exact amount abundantly clear over the years. And had, indeed, raised the number as the years passed. "Let me guess, you will cut her off if she were to choose me as her groom."

"I would. Without hesitation."

A lie. Only the most hardhearted family would turn their backs on a loved one in need, and it was clear that Byrn had true feelings for his sister. If she made an unfortunate choice in husband, her brother would do his best to help her.

"Is that the *other thing* you mentioned?"

"Yes."

How prosaic. Such a dramatic wind up for a simple monetary threat. "It does not occur to you that I could be interested in your sister simply because she is delightfully intelligent and has a wicked sense of humor?"

"Of course, you could be. You're accounted fairly smart."

"Thank you?"

"I am here to tell you that as a marriage prospect, my sister is out of your reach. And I'm definitely not giving her her money early just because you've turned her head."

"I've turned her head?" That was an interesting thought.

"She asked for her dowry just this afternoon."

Had she?

"She said she had an investment in mind."

"Mine?" The thought made his heart leap.

"Something about canals. Since that has nothing to do with greenery—"

"Isabelle." Damn it. The shrew was trying to get her niece to invest. "It won't work unless your sister wants to supervise the upgrade of the locks. Lady Meunier needs more than money. She needs someone to supervise the work. And it won't be Isabelle wading into the muck."

Lord Byrn stared at him, his brow furrowed in confusion. "Aunt Isabelle wants my sister's dowry?"

"Yes."

"But she said—"

"Don't!" Jackson interrupted. He was too tired to even ask which "she" Byrn was referring to. "If you insult me or your sister again, Byrn, I might lose my temper and—"

A heavy knock on his door interrupted his violent mood. Bloody hell, he could go weeks without a single visitor and now he suddenly had two in the space of ten minutes.

"Come," he snapped. Might as well see life's newest surprise.

The door opened as he was speaking. It was Lucas, who had played Lord Lucifer during last night's masquerade. He looked annoyed as he pushed through the door, but his eyes widened when he saw his brother-in-law here even as his attention was on Jackson.

"I see Lady Meunier has been busy," Lucas drawled.

Internally Jackson sighed, but outwardly he merely raised his brows, inviting Lucas to explain. Lord Byrn wasn't so restrained.

"What does that mean? What does Aunt Isabelle have to do with anything?"

"She advised Diana of Jackson's wicked ways. Diana, in turn, sent me here to find out your intentions."

"My wicked ways?" Jackson pressed.

"I believe she mentioned whips."

Jackson nearly choked at Isabelle's audacity, but it was nothing compared to the glower on Lord Byrn's face.

"The devil," Lord Byrn cursed.

"I don't even have a horse in town," Jackson said with disgust.

Lucas smiled, his eyes twinkling with a mirth that hadn't been there before Diana became part of his life. "I never said anything about a horse. Just the whip—"

"Stop it," Jackson snapped. "You know I don't—I never—" This was ridiculous and so he was going to say in clear terms. He took a breath to do just that but was forestalled by yet another knock on his door. He didn't have to answer. He knew the knock. Sure enough, a moment later the door burst open only to have Aaron, Lord Chambers, pull up at the sight of three people in the tiny room.

"Good lord," he said with alarm. "Something's afoot." He ran a distracted hand through his already disheveled hair. "How can I help?"

And wasn't that Aaron in a nutshell? On the scene and willing to help even though his mind was obviously torn in another direction entirely.

"What's wrong with you?" Jackson asked. Aaron *never* appeared disheveled. His political position meant he had to act in all ways composed, even when he wasn't.

"An unexpected development," he said as his gaze landed heavily on Lord Byrn. "But—um—that's not important now. Why are you here?"

Jackson went back to polishing his boots. "They're both here to threaten me away from marrying Lady Gwen."

Aaron blinked. "You don't want to marry her."

There went what little fun he'd had poking at Byrn.

Meanwhile, Byrn jolted in surprise. "You don't want to marry Gwen? Why not?"

Of all the ridiculous conversations. "You were just warning me off."

"She's special and valuable—"

"She is."

Byrn pursed his lips. "Perhaps I misjudged you—"

"You did—"

"And that's nothing to the point," interrupted Aaron. "Jackson, put on some clothes. It's decidedly odd to converse with an unclothed man. Lucas, has something happened with Lady Diana?"

"No, no. Well, there might be some happy news soon, but we don't know yet."

All the men looked up with varying degrees of shock. Lucas looked in alt at the possibility of starting a family when just a year ago his thoughts had been at the lowest place a man could go.

"Good God, man, that's wonderful!" Jackson said with a grin as he pulled on his cleanest pair of pants. The other two men echoed his sentiment, but Byrn was clearly torn between the happy news and the puzzle that was Jackson.

Typically, Lucas was quick to understand the situation. "Never mind him," Lucas said with impatience. "He's not going to ravish your sister. Despite his reputation, he's a perfect gentleman."

"That's not what Aunt Isabelle said," Byrn grumbled. "She claimed—"

"That I've had orgies with half the ladies in London," Jackson interrupted. "There was only one orgy, and she was the one who arranged it!"

The silence that greeted his words was like the drop of a guillotine blade. It cut sharp and swift through the fog of distraction that had clouded his thoughts. Normally he never would have said something so unpolished. And now all three men stared at him as if he'd admitted to being the horned goat he'd played last night.

"I didn't participate in it!" he cried. But he had been witness to it, and that had been sickening enough to have him end his romantic relationship with Isabelle for good. But rather than explain, he glared at each man in turn. "Was there another reason you all chose to invade my room? Or may I go back to my plans for the day?" Unable to resist, he looked straight at Lord Byrn. "I have an appointment with Lady Gwen."

To the man's credit, he didn't rise to the bait, but he did fix Jackson with a heavy glare. Then he stood up and headed for the door. "I'll walk you out, Lucas."

Lucas nodded, his expression still vaguely besotted. The man was definitely in love with his wife, and Jackson felt a moment's envy. His parents had looked at each other like that until his mother's death. And though his stepmother made his father happy enough, they didn't share the deep love that his parents had once had.

Unfortunately, Byrn couldn't leave without one last threat. He stopped at the door to pin Jackson with a heavy stare. "I will go to any lengths to protect my sisters," he said. "All of them!"

Jackson gave the man his most taunting brow raise. He would have enjoyed Bryn's scowl except beside him, he noticed Aaron's flinch. What the hell?

He was still wondering about that when Lucas rolled his eyes. "Don't worry. Lady Gwen is safe with him."

Byrn seemed to take that at face value. He gave Jackson a nod, another to Aaron, then left on Lucas's heels. The two could be heard talking in low tones as they descended the stairs. Which left Jackson to button his pants and question Aaron at the same time.

"So?" he pressed. "Why did you come here?"

The man blew out a heavy breath as he sank onto the edge of Jackson's bed. "I've done something hideous, and I don't know what to do about it."

"You?" He couldn't believe it. Aaron was the most boringly upright man in all of England. Honest to a fault, moderate in all his passions, and forever looking to the well-being of his fellow man. "What have you done? Overpaid your butler? Tripped over a napping bootblack?" He constantly teased his friend for having the laziest staff in London.

"I've ruined Byrn's sister."

Jackson's head snapped up. "You did what? To Gwen?" He

couldn't believe it.

"Not her. The other one. Lilah." And the way he half whispered the girl's name with awe showed that the man was in deep trouble indeed. "I need your help to delay things until after my resolution passes. Then I can marry her."

Jackson held up his hand. He needed specific details if he was to sort through Aaron's mess. "What exactly did you do?"

Aaron took a deep breath. "We walked together last night. I don't know what I was thinking except that she was sweet, funny, and her eyes were so pretty in the moonlight."

"That's it? You walked together?"

"She was funny! Don't you understand? She made me laugh."

That was a surprise. Given Aaron's particular family situation and his political passions, the man tended to be intensely serious. Jackson was his best friend and he could count on one hand the number of times Aaron had laughed. But that didn't exactly equate to ruination. "You just walked."

"Along the Dark Path," he said, "in the moonlight. It was very..."

"Romantic?" Though his friend would never admit it, Aaron did have a romantic heart. It was, in fact, what drove his political ambitions. He wanted to support the returning veterans, he wanted to fund doctors who researched cures for any number of diseases, and he wanted to do it all with money most of the government wanted to go into war and other types of spending. It was very noble of him, and Jackson supported him, but marriage to a beautiful and funny bastard was not going to help his political cause.

"I need specifics, Aaron. What *exactly* did you do with Lilah?"

Aaron looked up at the ceiling. His breath came out in a deep exhale that somehow managed to be both romantic and tragic at the same time. "I kissed her," he said.

"And?"

"And? And nothing! What do you take me for? I wasn't going to—"

"Ruin her?"

Aaron scowled at his friend. "I'm going to marry her. I've ruined her, and therefore it must be done."

"With a kiss?"

"But I have to wait until after the orphan resolution is passed. We need money for those children, and I will not allow my indiscretion—"

"What indiscretion?" Jackson interrupted. "It was just a kiss." He stared at his friend. They both knew the political repercussions from a relationship to an acknowledged bastard would be devastating for his career. Political men married political wives from politically advantageous families. That was the way of things. And yet, apparently, Aaron had fallen for the most impossible woman of all. After just one kiss, no less, and the man insisted that honor forced him to marry the girl. "You know everyone will think she manipulated you into marriage. Can't you just…" He didn't know what. Fall in love with someone else? That was never going to work for Aaron.

"She didn't manipulate me!" Aaron gasped. "I overpowered her! I took advantage of her innocent nature. I must pay."

"Overpowered her with a kiss?"

"Yes!"

"You want this woman, and you're asking me for the best way to minimize the damage politically."

Aaron grimaced. "I don't care about the damage. I just want to pass my orphans resolution first. I need you to help me get her to wait."

"Just ask her to wait."

He shook her head. "You know her mother. Any understanding between me and Lilah will be all over London within the hour."

That was true.

"And I cannot ask a woman to keep a secret from her mother. I just—"

"You can't risk it. I understand." And he did. Aaron had fallen for an inappropriate woman and his honorable nature had made it such that he would propose no matter what the consequences were. But he couldn't choose his own happiness over food and shelter for orphans, so he needed a delay.

Or he needed a best friend who would turn the lady elsewhere, thereby saving Aaron from himself.

"I understand completely," Jackson said. "You may rely on me."

Chapter Eight

GWEN WENT UPSTAIRS with her mind swirling in chaos. It didn't settle while changing her clothes. Indeed, even composing a letter to Mr. Wedgewood of the London Horticulture Society regarding the cultivation of daffodils barely occupied her for more than fifteen minutes. In the end, she could stand herself no longer and went to the one person who never failed to settle her thoughts: her half-sister Lilah.

She knocked gently on the door into the upstairs parlor and was bid enter. As she knew would happen, she saw Lilah seated at her escritoire as she decided on the next week's meals. Mama had long since declared that Lilah managed the staff much better than anyone else in the household and Lilah was all too willing to bring the servants in line. She had been doing the menus—as well as a host of other household duties—since her adolescence. Except today, when she was staring out into space with her pencil unmoving where it pressed against the foolscap.

"Lilah? Is something amiss?"

"What?" The woman jolted before giving her a dreamy smile. "No, I was just daydreaming."

Intrigued, Gwen pushed inside. "It looked like a very pleasant daydream."

"It was," her sister said, but then her expression fell. "But it was just a dream."

"About what...?" She pressed, but her sister was ever circumspect.

"Just a kiss with a handsome man. No one of importance."

Gwen dropped down on the settee beside her sister. "Which man? When? Tell me everything!"

Her sister focused on her. "Since when do you find my daydreams interesting?"

"Always. I just..." She shrugged. "I suppose I forget sometimes to ask. I get distracted and then—"

"And then everything else disappears from your mind." Her sister smiled as she spoke to show she was teasing. "How was your visit with Aunt Isabelle?"

Gwen wrinkled her nose. "She wants me to get control of my dowry now that I'm a spinster."

"You're hardly that."

"I'm definitely that, and I like the idea of being independent, at least a little."

Lilah nodded. "Then you should talk to Elliot."

"I already have. Aunt Isabelle made me write a letter to him last night. She didn't want me to tell him she needs investors in her canals, but I think that's what she really wants."

"I'm sure it is."

"She's offered to teach me things if I give the money to her."

Lilah straightened. "What things?"

Gwen didn't answer beyond a shrug. Aunt Isabelle was remarkably vague on that subject, and Gwen didn't like vagueness in anything. But rather than dwell on that, she focused on her half-sister, struck anew by how kind, how absolutely unassuming her sister was. If anyone deserved to become popular, it was her sister. The woman was always poised, always knew what to say, and never, ever blundered about like Gwen. Why, she was the perfect woman to bring the Lincolnshire daffodil into popularity! Indeed, she felt ashamed that she hadn't thought of it before.

"Never mind that," Gwen said as she began mentally dressing her sister in Lord Sayres's daffodil. How could she make the blossom thrive throughout a ball? It would need to be pinned somehow and in a way that wouldn't break the petals. Just how exuberant was Lilah when she danced?

"Gwen? What are you thinking?"

"Tell me about the masquerade. Did you dance a great deal?"

"I had a lovely time," her sister said. "And no, I didn't dance a great deal." Her eyes sparkled with sudden excitement. "But I did go for a walk and kiss a handsome man wearing a very dark cape."

Gwen's eyes abruptly widened. "You did? Who?"

Her sister's delighted expression faded. "Someone who cannot do more. Someone who will never marry a bastard."

"But you don't know that for sure—"

"No, Gwen. Do not press me further. He will not marry me."

Gwen pursed her lips and studied her half-sister. When Lilah took that tone, there was no swaying her. And in this case, it meant that whatever gentleman had made her look like a woman awash in love, he would not come up to scratch. At least, not with the way things stood at the moment.

"What if you suddenly became popular?" Gwen asked. "What if suddenly you became the Season's sensation? Do you think he would ask for your hand then?"

Lilah laughed, the sound light for all that her words were completely depressing. "It is not possible, Gwen. You of all people could not believe anything so fanciful. I will never—"

"Lord Sayres could make you a sensation. I'm sure of it."

Lilah's brows rose in surprise. "Lord Sayres? Why would he—"

"Because I'll ask him to. It'll be perfect. I can help from the background then." That was exactly where she wanted to be. Nearby, watching as Sayres worked his magic. She wanted to see him bring her shy sister into the light. It would be like watching a master painter at work, only his canvas was society.

"The background! Whatever are you saying," Lilah countered with a laugh. "If anyone should become a sensation—"

"Don't say it!"

"It should be you. Didn't you just tell me you want a husband?"

Gwen huffed. "I regret ever telling you that." She leaned forward, her expression as open as it could be. "I'm no good in society. I never have been. Just imagine the blunders I'd make." And that would be the end of his flower and the end of her dream of financial independence. She pressed a kiss to her sister's cheek. "Don't worry. I'll fix everything, I promise."

Lilah grabbed her hand, keeping her from rushing out of the room. "Gwen," she said softly. "Some things don't change. You know that as well as I do."

It was true. Lilah's illegitimate parentage wouldn't change. Neither would Gwen's awkward personality. "It doesn't matter," Gwen pressed. "I won't let you give up on your dreams. If you wish to be wed, then you shall be."

Lilah's eyes widened in shock. "When did you start talking about dreams?"

"When I realized that you will make my dream come true."

LORD SAYRES ARRIVED late for tea. It shouldn't have annoyed her. She never made it to tea on time, so she could hardly blame him. And yet she did. She'd purposely dressed in one of her most presentable gowns. It didn't have any dirt smears, ink stains, and only one tear newly repaired. She'd worn it and headed straight to tea expecting him to arrive as he'd promised. She wanted to discuss Lilah with him.

Honestly forced her to admit that he had only promised to call that afternoon. He had never specified a time, and yet she'd assumed he meant tea for no logical reason whatsoever. Which made her severely put out with herself because she was never, ever illogical.

Then suddenly he was stepping into the parlor and her heart leapt into her throat. He was here! And looking very handsome in charcoal gray as he bowed to her mother, then winked over her hand.

Another blasted wink. What did that mean?

"Lord Sayres," her mother said. "You are tardy for tea. Gwendolyn told me you would be here earlier."

Trust her mother to sound peevish when the man hadn't actually promised to be here at such a time. "Mama, I only said he might come." Did he look tired? There was a heaviness about his eyes that suggested such a thing, but his expression smoothed out before she could say definitively one way or another.

"Your thinking was correct," Lord Sayres said smoothly. "I had intended to be here well before time, truth be told, but I was detained."

Her mother arched her brows and said nothing. It was her silent way of putting a man in his place, letting him know without words that he was out of her good graces.

"If it helps, I come bearing an on-dit."

It did help. Mother adored anything resembling gossip, and so she dipped her chin as regally as any queen. "If you—"

"Never mind that," Gwen interrupted. "I wanted you specifically to meet Lilah. She's upstairs right now, but I thought we could all take a walk together and talk about..." Her voice trailed away as her mother shot daggers at her.

Oh dear. She'd skipped ahead when she wasn't supposed to do that. It was just that she often saw the pattern of what was to happen and grew impatient with the slowness of it all.

"I do beg your pardon," she said, doing her best to curb her impatience. "Lord Sayres, please relay the on-dit. Then mother can be happy while I get Lilah, and we shall all take a walk together. Is that acceptable?" She frowned. "Unless you really want tea. I suppose I could wait—"

"Gwendolyn!" her mother snapped. "You told me Lord Sayres was here specifically to see you." She leaned forward to pour the last of the tea, though it was likely tepid at best. "Cream, my lord?"

"Yes, thank you."

He took the tea as well as a selection of small sandwiches, eating them during pauses in his on-dit. It was a silly story about some poor girl who had made a cake of herself during a party. To Gwen's way of thinking, it was the same as every other on-dit that was ever spoken in London. Someone did something silly and everyone else had to laugh about it. Except, to her surprise, Lord Sayres took a different approach.

"I do think it was awful of the hostess to make such a commotion over spilled wine. She will forever be known as the hostess who was cruel to a girl so nervous she fumbled her drink. Haven't we all been awkward at some point?" he asked.

And what was Mother to say but, of course, everyone got nervous, especially girls straight out of the schoolroom.

"I declare that Mrs. Saunderson will have to work especially hard for me to visit her again," he continued. "She was unkind, and I cannot abide meanness. Isn't that right Lady Gwen?"

"What? Me?" She shook her head. It wasn't that she disagreed. In fact, she heartily agreed that Mrs. Saund-whomever had been cruel, but wasn't that *ton* all the time? And why was she abruptly tongue-tied?

"Gwen agrees. Of course she does. But it wouldn't do to offend Mrs. Saunderson," her mother inserted. "But of course you know that, my lord. You excel at sailing the seas of society."

He arched his brows at her mother, but his gaze remained on her. "I suppose I do," he said slowly. "And I have an idea I should like to discuss with your daughter. One that needs her cooperation." He tilted his head at her and smiled in a way that was ever so handsome. "What say you, Lady Gwen? Shall we take an afternoon stroll?"

Finally! "I shall just get Lilah—"

"Lilah!" her mother gasped. "But there's no need. She's busy doing the menu for this week."

Gwen frowned. "I thought she finished those this morning."

"Certainly not. I need to teach her something about her choices." She rolled her eyes at Lord Sayres. "Truly, it's a never-ending process teaching my girls. Thankfully Gwen excels at studying."

"Plants," Gwen said. "I study—"

"Hush!" her mother snapped. Then she smiled at Lord Sayres. "Pray enjoy the afternoon sunshine. I believe it's a most glorious day."

"An excellent suggestion," Lord Sayres said as he pushed to his feet then held out his hand. "What say you, Lady Gwen?"

What was she to say? Her mother clearly wished her to be tete-a-tete with his lordship. And was going to forestall any attempt to bring Lilah along. "Very well," she said slowly. "But I insist you meet Lilah upon our return."

"It should be my greatest delight," he returned.

Which left Gwen to step outside for the second time that day for a private stroll with the man. Fortunately, just like this morning, she had an agenda and wasted no time in beginning the discussion the moment they cleared the front steps.

"My lord, I've had the most exciting idea. My sister Lilah will be the perfect woman to bring into popularity. I'm sure you could do it."

He nodded, smiling warmly at a passing couple out for a similar stroll. "An interesting thought, but I will not do it. Say, would you care for an ice at Gunter's?"

Clearly, he meant to distract her from her purpose. That was not going to happen. She could be more determined than a dog with a bone when she wanted. And this time, she *wanted*.

CHAPTER NINE

JACKSON LOOKED LONG and hard at the damned confusing woman walking beside him. He needed her to agree! This morning he had everything laid out clearly in his head. So much so, he'd already begun the groundwork for her to be the Season's sensation. He'd been sure that with little pressure, a few charming smiles, she would blithely follow his suggestions, and everything would come out just as it ought.

Except the woman had been remarkably immune to his charms. Even when she'd been flustered by his bare chest, she'd held herself in check and accessed her brain instead of her desires. And now, damn it, he could not distract her with flattery or maneuver her into the place he wanted. Worse, she'd called him out on his tactics.

"Will you stop trying to manage me and find someone else?" she huffed.

"You are the best choice," he said firmly.

"The best choice is someone who agrees."

He couldn't argue with her there. He blew out his breath and steeled himself to use his last chance persuasive technique: brutal honesty. "I should like to explain my choice to you," he said calmly. "I should like to explain in very logical terms why you are the best and only person who can do what we require this Season. But I have no wish to hurt you, and the truth can be very painful sometimes."

She lifted her chin. "Have I ever given you reason to think I was overly emotional? That I wanted anything but the absolute truth?"

"No," he said. "But in this, most people think they want to hear it—"

"Enough," she said. "Either spit it out or we shall end this mad scheme once and for all." Her tone was as tight as her expression. She did not like being thwarted in her plans, but in this she would have to give way.

"Very well." He paused a moment not to give her time to steel herself, but for him to find the right phrasing. It eluded him, so he began in a backwards way hoping to figure out the right approach as he spoke.

"Your brother came to me this afternoon."

She jolted. "Elliott? Why?"

"He warned me off from you. It was the usual nonsense. I am a fortune hunter, he would cut you if we married, blah blah."

She gaped at him. "But you aren't trying to marry me! And even if you were, he should not have—"

"It doesn't bother me. I have had many such talks over the years." He touched her hand. They both wore gloves and yet she flinched back from him. "Elliott said you were delightfully intelligent and had a wicked sense of humor."

She steadied, but her eyes were still wary. "He is my brother. His love clouds his judgment."

"I wholeheartedly agree with his assessment. Why do you disagree?"

Her lips curved into a small smile that mocked herself. "My intelligence is the one thing I am known for," she said. Then at his continued stare, she huffed, "It's not an asset in a woman."

"I find intelligence the minimum of requirements in any of my associates, especially the women." He shifted to guide her away from the park. He had a destination in mind that was not filled with every aristocrat who went strolling during the fashionable hour.

"You are unusual then," she drawled. "As is my sense of humor. I assure you, I am the only one who laughs when I make a joke."

He smiled. "I cannot judge that as I have never heard you make a joke. I suspect you have learned to keep your amusements to yourself."

She frowned at him. "You are not persuading me to your cause. Nor are you insulting me. What is this honesty you fear to reveal?"

Jackson held her gaze to impress his next words on her. "Your brother called you an odd duck as if that were a bad thing." He shook his head. "I am sorry if this hurts you. I know you must love him, but truly, that was the stupidest thing I have heard in a very long time."

She frowned at him. "But I am an odd duck. And I assure you, I have been called worse."

"Why does everyone think different is bad? Good God, odd is the best thing in the world! It means you are unique, interesting, and incredibly valuable." He leaned forward. "Indeed, it will make you an Original."

She stared at him a moment, and then a strange sort of snort seemed to choke her. He thought at first she was choking, but soon realized she was trying to stifle her mirth. It wasn't a delicate sound. With the way she tried to swallow it down, the humor came out more as a snort than a giggle, and it was soon replaced with a coughing bray.

He smiled, though his tone when he spoke was excruciatingly dry. "The fact that you are laughing right now tells me you do have a sense of humor. And a wicked one at that, because you are laughing at me when I am being very serious."

"You are not!" she said, her eyes crinkling with her smile. "You suggest that you will make me an Original, the *ton's* highest appellation to any woman. The one name that is guaranteed to make the woman a sensation. You—"

"Yes!" he cried. "What is being an Original but being different? Lady Gwen, you already are that in spades! The reason you weren't a sensation before is because everyone else was too blind to see it. Even you! But that is where I come in. I shall show everyone what they were too stupid to notice."

"My lord, intelligence is not original. There are countless people—even women—who are believed to be overwhelmingly smart. They're called bluestockings, and I am the bluest of them all."

"I tell you, that is a good thing!" Then before she could repeat her objections, he stepped directly in front of her, forcing her to stop walking in the middle of the sidewalk. "Listen to me. I can help you with the little things. People's names, how to gain their attention, all of the simple things."

"Simple!" she cried.

"Yes, simple for me at least. You may have to do a bit of studying." He winked at her. "But that is your forte, is it not?"

"Why are you forever winking at me? What does that mean?" she cried out.

He stared at her for a moment, seeing her genuine distress, and he felt an equal confusion. Who needed an explanation of a wink? She did, apparently, and so he answered as honestly as he could. "I suppose it means that I like you."

She frowned as she considered his words. In the end, she shook her head. "I don't think that's what it always means."

"It does with me. When I wink at you, it means I like you." And now he had a clue as to why she hadn't taken before. She didn't seem to understand the usual cues. But that was something that could be learned. "Lady Gwen, if ever you don't understand something I'm doing, pray ask me to explain. I shall be all too happy to answer."

She stared at him, clearly thinking about it. "I will, if you will swear not to laugh at me."

And there he heard the pain of a woman who had been sneered at all her life. Unable to fit in, she had withdrawn and refused to shine for anyone else ever again. "I swear. Even more, I swear I shall make you appreciate your beautiful intelligence and your wicked sense of humor so you won't care what anyone else thinks. And once that happens, everyone will be so amazed that they will try to copy everything you do." His smile widened. "Even to the point of buying your signature flower from me at a grossly inflated price."

She stared at him with no more objections to voice—at least no new ones—and he held her gaze.

"I know you don't believe me," he said, "but this is where I excel. I promise it will work. Can you not trust me?"

She shook her head, the gesture too small for the misery in her eyes. "You cannot promise that. No one could."

"No man can promise the future, and yet I am still confident." And when she didn't speak, he pressed her further. "I am the expert on bringing things to popularity, am I not? You said so yourself."

"I did," she grudgingly admitted.

"I can do it," he said. "But you need to try with your whole heart, Lady Gwen."

She took a deep breath, one that lifted her bosom and momentarily distracted him. "I promise to do that provided I can bring Lilah with me everywhere. She needs to find a husband and—"

"Agreed!"

It startled Jackson that he was so happy to finally gain her agreement. Normally he looked for easy compliance in all his business endeavors. He knew what he was doing and anyone who questioned him merely wasted time and energy. But far from being exhausted by their battle, he felt strangely exhilarated. He guessed that Lady Gwen did not give her trust easily, and yet she had given it to him. That was a victory worthy of an epic poem.

Buoyed by his success, he pulled out a page of foolscap and showed it to her. "I have made some preliminary sketches for your wardrobe. I have no skill with a pen, but I hope you can make sense of these."

She took them and frowned, turning them slightly left and right.

"What are these? Ribbons?" she asked as she stepped around him to let the full light of the sun land on his ugly sketch.

"Only one here and here." He gestured to her hair and bodice on the paper. "I'd like to use them to tie in the flowers."

She frowned at the design. "The ribbons will have to be very large to hold and hide a small water vase to keep them fresh."

He hadn't thought about that. "Excellent suggestion. Perhaps we could discuss it in here?"

She looked up and frowned as if she hadn't realized how far they'd walked. "How did we get to Madame Juliette's?"

How lucky he was that Lady Gwen frequented the same modiste as Isabelle. Though he'd never had occasion to discuss Isabelle's wardrobe, he had been called upon to find various fabrics that were difficult to locate. He had excelled at that task, and Juliette had reason to be grateful to him. Hopefully that was enough for her to throw herself into this task.

He opened the modiste's door and set his hand to the small of her back as he ushered her in. You would think that his hands were made of ice given the way her back seemed to ripple at his touch and she all but leaped inside.

Clearly, the woman did not like his touch. That was going to be difficult if he were to help dress her in his flowers. Fortunately, he didn't have time to dwell on the problem as Madame Juliette rushed forward.

"Lord Sayres, I'm so glad you made it." The lady clapped her hands with enthusiasm. "How can I help you today?"

Jackson smiled. "I should like to make some changes to Lady Gwen's gowns. We have a possible design…" His voice trailed away as he reached for the foolscap still clutched in Lady Gwen's hands. She stepped back in confusion, her shoulders so tight they seemed to reach her ears.

"I don't understand," she said. "How do you know my modiste?"

"Oh la," Madame Juliette trilled. "He is a wizard at finding things that I need. He's been helping me find silks for your family for years."

Lady Gwen's mouth parted as she put the pieces together. "You mean for Aunt Isabelle."

Jackson huffed. "I have been living and working in London for the last decade. I have spent most of my time finding profitable enterprises for your aunt." He gestured to the modiste. "Madame Juliette is one of those businesses that enjoys increased trade because of supplies brought in at a discount through Isabelle's canals." In return, Isabelle took a cut out of Madame's profit. He knew. He was the one who had negotiated the bargain.

"Lord Sayres is a great friend," Madame Juliette said. "Now come. Tell me what it is you want."

And so the negotiations began. Madame took them to a large table where Lady Gwen lay the paper down. All three of them crowded together as they discussed the possibilities while Madame made notations or adjusted the sketch. Well, two of them crowded together. Lady Gwen set herself on the opposite side of the table, making comments though the image was upside down to her.

She was keeping herself apart for some reason, and he resolved to do everything he could to bring her into the discussion.

"The ribbons cannot be made that large. It will look hideous," Madame began.

"Lady Gwen said that's important so they can hold vases of flowers." He looked to her. "Correct?"

"Yes—"

"Vases! You are joking, aren't you?"

No, he wasn't. "Pin vases, I believe. What do you think, Lady Gwen?"

"I suppose that could—"

"You are mad," the dressmaker said.

Jackson was silent a moment, then he turned to the modiste. "Madame, if you interrupt my lady one more time, then we shall take our business elsewhere."

"Oh," gasped Lady Gwen. "It's not important. I would like to hear what she says."

"And I would like to hear what you say first," he countered. "I cannot abide rudeness in anyone. Even the lowest bootblack may speak his peace. It is common courtesy."

Gwen tilted her head in confusion. "You have been in Aunt Isabelle's company for ten years, and yet she interrupts at every turn."

"Which is one of the very many reasons we have gone our separate ways." He took a breath. "And I was in her employ, not her company." It wasn't something he would usually confess with a servant around. The *ton* took a dim view of anyone who worked for their supper. But he decided it was better to let everyone know he had been engaging in trade with Isabelle rather than whatever depravities she laid at his feet. Especially since she had quite the imagination when she set about destroying someone's reputation.

Meanwhile, Madame was all apologies. "I do beg your pardon, Lady Gwen. It will not happen again. What were you saying?"

"I—I don't...um..."

She had no idea what she'd been saying. He'd forgotten it as well because he was focused on the way she stammered as her cheeks turned bright pink. Damnation, the woman was so used to being ignored that she grew confused when people gave her the respect that ought to be her birthright. She was the daughter of an earl, after all, but he'd never met one so uncomfortable in her own skin.

"That's all right," he said as he tapped the design. "What material do you think for the gown?" he asked.

"Silk, of course," inserted Madame, but then she fell silent at his cold stare.

"Lady Gwen?" he prompted.

"I should like something more durable. And silk shows water spots."

"So it does," Jackson mused. "I should like you to appear like Hebe, the Greek goddess of spring. You should have light clothing with the flowers adorning you." He cocked his head toward Lady Gwen. Fortunately, Madame had learned her lesson and kept silent.

"I think I have too large a frame for light clothing. As if an oak tree was trying to dress all in lace."

He gaped at her. "I would bet you are echoing your mother's words. You do not resemble an oak tree."

She smiled at him. "I said the same thing to her, but she could not be more specific in her analogy."

Jackson looked at her shape and found nothing at all too heavy except the fabrics that seemed to weigh her down. She wasn't waif thin, but he preferred women who didn't look like they'd bowl over in a stiff wind. And he liked what he saw in her. "Your frame is perfect. Besides, spring has a great deal of work to do, what with birthing calves and causing shoots to break through hard packed soil."

"You've gone poetic," Lady Gwen countered as her eyes narrowed. "You are enjoying this."

"Of course, I am. I always like it when an idea begins to take shape."

"And I am that idea?"

He nodded. "Aren't you enjoying it?"

"I..." Her eyes abruptly widened. "I suppose I am. You make it fun. Nevertheless, the fabric must not show water stains. The flowers will be wet."

That was an excellent thought and required a full twenty more minutes of discussion. But in the end, they found a compromise. At least until Lady Gwen pointed to the bodice.

"You have cut the neckline high. May I ask why?"

"Do you wish it lower?"

"Goodness no! I just wonder why, is all."

Did she think he disliked her cleavage? "You have a glorious bosom," he said with a wink. Then he froze, waiting to see if she appreciated his gesture. She did, though it took a few seconds before her cheeks pinked and her lips curved in a shy smile. "Unfortunately," he continued happily, "the vases and flowers will be heavy, so the gown needs structure. Besides, I recall how often you tugged at Isabelle's gown."

She shuddered. "It was beyond annoying."

"Then we shall cover up your glorious asset in the name of not annoying you."

She titled her head. "Are you teasing me?" she asked, and her tone was serious.

"No," he responded truthfully. "I am in earnest." He leaned forward. "I could wink again, if you like."

Now her cheeks bloomed very bright, but she didn't avert her eyes. A victory, he believed, especially when she made an awkward wink back at him.

The gesture was so delightful that he nearly crowed out loud. He didn't, though. He simply echoed her gesture and waited to see her glorious smile grow even wider.

"So we are agreed on this design?" the modiste asked.

Lady Gwen recovered faster than he did. She blinked as she refocused on the sketch. "I agree."

"As do I," he said as Madame Juliette scooped up the design. But then he pulled out five more sheets of foolscap. "On to the next one."

And so they began it all again, on and on with each design until Lady Gwen had a full wardrobe. At one break in the discussion, he sent a message that her maid join them. He claimed it was for propriety, as it was growing dark. The two of them could not be about without a guardian of some sort watching them. But also because he wanted her dresser to know how to put flowers onto her gown and into her hair. But at that, Gwen held out her hand in refusal.

"Stop! We must discuss the vases first. Madame cannot make all the dresses unless we have tested it."

He nodded. "A sound argument, but do you have the vases available?"

"I have one," the dressmaker said as she pulled out a small bud vase. It was a wearable one, meant to be pinned onto a gentleman's lapel. She held it out to him, and he inspected it from every side.

"It looks serviceable enough."

But Lady Gwen shook her head. She'd been using a sharp pair of scissors to cut a piece of paper. When she held it up to the light, he saw that it was roughly the shape of a daffodil. "The blossom will be a great deal heavier, but this is the approximate size. Put it in the vase."

He tried. The stem didn't fit at all. She took it from his hand and quickly trimmed the width of the stem, but even he could see that it wouldn't serve. The weight of the blossom would have the whole thing tilting over. The blossom was too heavy for this gentleman's lapel pin. A lady's pin was supposed to be even more delicate.

This is why he needed her. He would not have thought of that himself. Until this moment, he thought all flower stems were the same size. "We shall require a larger vase pin."

"Do you know of any?"

He shook his head. "But I know someone who can fashion one." In fact, he knew several people. "Is there a design you would recommend?"

She nodded. "I would like to experiment, of course, but I think something like this…" She began to sketch, sliding around the table to his side as she worked.

"We should talk to the man who will fashion it," he said. "He may have suggestions."

She agreed just before she brought up another concern and another, each one well-reasoned. He realized, to his shock, that he should have discussed these things with her earlier before running pell-mell into creating gowns for her. He wasn't used to having someone as detail-oriented as he was. In truth, she was more so and that surprised him. In his experience, no one thought through ideas thoroughly. It was the primary reason he was able to find good investments over bad ones. But he had been so caught up in enthusiasm, he hadn't even checked to see if she knew more than he did.

And that was an embarrassing error.

He let his appreciation show in the warmth of his voice. "You have been thinking a great deal about this," he said. "And not just grand imaginings, but the finer details. I am impressed."

"Did you think me incapable?"

"No," he said. "Unwilling, perhaps."

She pulled back as if insulted. "If we are to make this venture successful, then we must see to even the finest detail."

"I agree."

"And in my experience—"

"No one looks closely enough or thinks thoroughly enough."

She bit her lip. "I meant no insult."

"None taken." He clasped her hands. "Lady Gwen, do you not see it? We are alike in this. Thorough, detailed, and committed to seeing a complete success of our venture." He was so excited, he clasped her hands. She didn't resist his touch and that made him happy enough to swing her in a circle. "I have never been more filled with hope in my entire life."

She laughed, and the sound was sweet because she did not try to stifle it. "We have only just begun. There are so many more—"

"Hush," he said. "We must enjoy the moment we have." And so saying, he drew in her in for a kiss. It wasn't a seductive kiss. Nothing so planned. It was an expression of joy because he had finally found someone who thought as quickly and as thoroughly as he did. Because she knew things he did not, and together, they could make a fortune.

But mostly it was because she was beautiful, and he was happy. He pressed his lips to hers. He tasted the tea that she'd been drinking, and smelled a flowery scent he couldn't identity. He felt the grip of her fingers in his, and the weight of her body as he drew it close.

Then he kissed her because that is what a man does with a woman who is smiling at him.

He felt her surprise. But he also felt the moment she gave into curiosity. She opened her mouth to him, she angled her head, and she teased him with her tongue.

Heat shot straight to his groin. His heart sped up and his mind was lost under the sudden need to deepen the kiss, to draw her harder against him, and to touch her in ways that weren't in the least bit appropriate. And yet at that moment, he didn't care. Not until he heard her maid cry out in alarm. Not until Madame Juliette poked him hard with a needle. And even then, he was dazed enough to ignore it.

It was the second stab that brought him back to reality. And the third had him shying sideways even as he drew Gwen with him as if to protect her from a demon seamstress.

Only then did he realized what he had done. He had kissed Lady Gwen! And he wanted to do it again and again, even though she was his partner in a business venture. Damnation, this was not a good thing, no matter how nicely she fit in his arms or how sweetly she was tucked against his shoulder.

Why was she tucked against his shoulder? Shouldn't she be shoving him aside with maidenly horror?

He turned to look at her, his expression apologetic. "Lady Gwen, I should not have—"

She pressed her fingers to his lips. "No," she said, her voice breathless. "You shouldn't have, but I don't care. I'm on the shelf, remember? I'm allowed a kiss every now and then, aren't I?"

He gaped at her. Did she truly think she was unmarriageable? He dislodged her fingers from his mouth, though there was a burning fire beneath his skin where she'd been. And he gently set her aside. "I was overcome," he finally said. "I beg your pardon."

He looked around at the angry women in the room. It wasn't just the maid and Madame Juliette. There were two other shop girls there, each with a pair of scissors clasped in their hands like daggers. Lady Gwen's maid rushed to her side with an imperious sniff.

"I believe there has been enough work for one afternoon," she said stiffly as she tugged her mistress further away from him.

Madame Juliette let out an equally loud huff. "I shall begin on the first dress tonight," she said imperiously. "Bring me the flower vases as soon as they are complete." She moved forward to grab the sketches off the table and "accidentally" shoved him further back as she went.

He didn't blame her. He was completely in the wrong, and yet he resented the further distance from Lady Gwen who was looking flushed, beautiful, and very much not insulted at all.

"Lady Gwen?" he pressed. "Do you want to end now?"

She frowned at him. "I still need to work on the pots to carry the flowers from Lincolnshire," she said, telling him that she was not nearly as flustered as he was. Her mind had gone straight back to work, which was almost insulting. Could she dismiss his kiss that easily? He'd just trifled with her! She should be furious with him and not thinking about any damned flowerpots. "Could you call on me tomorrow? I should like to discuss them with you."

"Of course. Just after luncheon, if that would be acceptable."

"Yes, erp—" Her maid shoved a bonnet on Lady Gwen's head and was tying the ribbons with furious movements. "Stop, stop!" she huffed at the woman. She grabbed hold of the ribbons and stepped back from her maid, but her eyes remained on him. "Tomorrow then, my lord. We have much to discuss."

"I shall be prompt," he said as he bowed to her. By the time he straightened up, she was already out the door and all he could see was the maid as she pushed Lady Gwen toward a waiting carriage. Behind him, the shopgirls and Madame Juliette sniffed loudly—again—then turned their backs on him.

He deserved that. He deserved all of that and more. And yet, he couldn't resist whistling as he gathered up his coat and headed for the door. Lady Gwen's color had been very high, and she had looked spectacularly beautiful. Perhaps he had just found a way to make her re-introduction into society even more incredible.

A well-timed kiss before she entered a ballroom, perhaps. Or a scandalous whisper into her ear. If she hadn't been offended today, then she would probably allow it then. And maybe even a bit more.

The idea was intriguing and the graphic images in his mind matched the pounding hunger in his blood. But he was not a man ruled by his passions. He used them judiciously. Carefully. And in this case, scandalously, if it meant that Lady Gwen would present his flower to the *ton* in the most spectacular way possible.

Chapter Ten

GWEN MADE IT home late for something her mother had scheduled. It didn't matter. She barely even waved at her sister before collapsing onto her bed, her clothes still on. She'd been taking off and putting on clothing far too much for one day, she would not do it again. Besides, she was exhausted. Also exhilarated, which was something she never experienced except in the throes of some new scientific passion.

She'd felt this way with her first microscope so many years ago. She spent every moment of the next month putting things on slides so she could look at them under magnification. She fell asleep next to it most nights, much to her nanny's consternation.

She'd felt this way when she first thought of her formula against sheep lice. She spent weeks that summer mixing and testing her creation. Butterflies captured her attention next. That was her nod to the traditionally beautiful creatures that all girls loved. She studied the process of making a cocoon and spent months trying to create a synthetic thread as strong. She'd failed in that, though she still held out hope that someday she'd figure it out.

She'd felt this particular exhilarated exhaustion many times in her twenty-eight years, but never, ever had it happened because a man kissed her.

She was just closing her eyes, determined to examine this bizarre aberration in her person when her bedroom door burst open and ended all thought of peaceful reflection.

"He kissed you and changed your dresses? What have you done?"

Her mother was out of breath and yet still able to be unfortunately loud. Instead of responding, Gwen shot an accusing glance at her maid. The woman sniffed loudly as she straightened her spine.

"He should not have done that," Webster said firmly. "It was my duty to tell your mother."

Gwen pursed her lips. "I am of age," she said sternly. "On the shelf," she shot at her mother. "There is no need to tell anyone about anything I do as it is not—"

"Do not cut up at Webster," her mother interrupted. Then she settled down on the edge of the bed as if they were the best of friends. But they had never had comfortable cozes together, and they would not start now. Gwen was about to tell her mother exactly that when Lilah drifted forward.

"Gwen, dear, we're just terribly confused. Did Lord Sayres attack you?"

There was true concern in her sister's voice, which was ridiculous. "Of course not!" Gwen said. "And any suggestion to the contrary is a blatant lie." She shot Webster a glare. In response, the woman curtsied with all appearance of respect, then left the room to no doubt regale everyone belowstairs with the tale.

"But did he kiss you?" her mother pressed, and Gwen had to sit up at the note of hope in the woman's voice.

"It was a mistake," she said as she studied her mother's face. "He apologized immediately afterwards."

"A mistake?" her mother scoffed. "Did he trip and fall on your lips? It's just as Isabelle said. He's a libertine and he's taking advantage of your naivete."

"He did nothing of the sort!" Gwen retorted. "He's not a libertine and he didn't trip. It was...we were celebrating. We'd been there for so long and there is so much more to do, but he said we should celebrate, and he spun me in a circle."

No one spoke for a moment, and Gwen realized that she'd done it again. She'd completely botched a simple explanation and now they were going to start pecking at her again. Typically, mother went first.

"And did he trip when he was spinning you around?"

"No one tripped," Gwen said miserably. How could they take a beautiful moment and make it sound so sordid?

"You mustn't go meeting men at your dressmaker's. And definitely not such an unseemly hour."

"It was half past four."

"Nevertheless." Her mother folded her hands together in her lap. "Why would you seek his advice on your dresses anyway? You've never cared one whit what you wore."

That wasn't true. She was very specific on the type of fabrics she could tolerate.

"Was he trying to compromise you? He's a fortune hunter, to be sure, but why do it at Madame Juliette's? Thank goodness Webster was sent round, otherwise you might now be forced to marry the man!" Was there a note regret in her voice? As if she wanted Gwen to be forced into matrimony?

"He sent for Webster." Gwen was not going to explain that they needed to figure out a new way to dress her hair, one that accommodated water vases for the daffodils. "And you may cease worrying. I am not going to marry Lord Sayres. We have come to a different arrangement."

If she were less tired, she would have been more careful with her words. She would have known that she could not declare such a thing and have anyone leave her in peace. Though for a sweet moment there was absolute silence. But then her mother and sister began speaking at once, the first in strident tones, the second in softer, gentler tones.

"An arrangement? I won't allow it! You as a demi-rep. It's insupportable! Is that why he was changing your clothes?"

"Oh my. Could you explain what you mean? It sounds quite alarming."

Gwen held up hands to silence everyone. They complied eventually, though her mother huffed in disgust.

"Why do you think demi-rep is the only possibility? A man and a woman can have many perfectly proper arrangements without anything scandalous at all."

"No, they can't," her mother responded tartly. "I should think you were old enough to know that. What has he convinced you to do?" That last sentence was uttered in dramatic accents.

"As to that," Gwen said, "it was my idea, but he has done so much more with it that I am rather impressed."

Her mother gasped, but Lilah placed a hand on the woman's shoulder, and she remained quiet while Lilah stepped closer. "Gwen, could you try to explain? You're making us very concerned. And I don't think we're going to leave until we have the full story." By which she meant that Mama wouldn't leave until it was all laid bare.

"But there's nothing to be worried about." She looked at her mother. "I am doing exactly what you asked me to. I am going to help Lilah find a husband." She smiled warmly at her half-sister. "Mama asked me to escort you about this Season, and Lord Sayres has agreed to help me."

"By kissing you?" her mother cried. She never stayed silent for long.

"By agreeing to escort me—us—about town this Season."

"In return for what?" Her mother's tone was strident.

"He has a flower he would like me to wear. Often. It's the Lincolnshire daffodil and it's quite lovely. He even calls it magical." She grabbed her sketch book off the escritoire, quickly flipping through the pages until she came upon her best drawing of the flower. "See how bright it is? Very sunny looking, I think—"

"But why you?" Mama interrupted, her tone strident.

"What she means, I think," Lilah said quickly, "is isn't Lord Sayres very well known among town? I'm sure he could get plenty of hostesses to display his flower."

"Scores, I should think," her mother returned dryly.

"I asked him that very same thing," Gwen responded.

"And what did he say?"

"That the ladies wouldn't pay for his flowers if they were doing him a favor. He needs them to want the flower and pay a very high price for them."

Mama's lips pursed in a very unflattering expression. "How much did you pay for them?" she asked.

"I didn't pay for them at all!" Though, she realized uncomfortably, she was likely going to have to pay for all those new gowns. Someone would also have to buy the vases that would hold the daffodils. She guessed he would carry the cost of transporting all those flowers to London. He'd need to find someplace to store the flowers and someone to care for them as well. The costs were mounting in her head and she wondered if he had already thought of those things. Did he have the money? She might when Elliott released her dowry to her.

"Gwen dear," Lilah said, "this all sounds very strange."

Did it? But it made sense to her.

"And you don't need to escort me about town," Lilah continued. "I am perfectly happy as things are."

And that, Gwen already knew, was a complete lie. Lilah wanted to be married and raise children. That's why she'd been daydreaming about a special kiss the night of the masquerade. But rather than argue that, Gwen focused on the one thing she knew her mother wanted.

"Lilah, you must accompany me to every single one of my engagements this Season. Every single one. I insist."

"But—" Lilah began.

"That is an excellent idea," her mother interrupted. And she would think so because it had initially been her idea. She turned to Lilah. "And you will make sure Lord Sayres no longer trips onto her lips ever again."

"Mama! He didn't—"

"Now I am late for Almack's. It shall be a dead bore without you there, Gwen, but I can see you're in no mood to join me."

It would be a dead bore with her there, and so she would have said if Lilah hadn't gestured her to silence. Gwen collapsed backward onto her pillows and said with absolute honesty, "I'm too tired tonight, Mama. Pray do enjoy it without me."

Her mother straightened up and headed to the door. "We shall go over the invitations tomorrow first thing," she said over her shoulder. "You will need a strategy if you intend to find Lilah a husband."

She didn't wait for a response but was soon heard calling for the carriage as she descended the stairs. That left Lilah in the room since she would never be allowed within the excruciatingly correct halls of Almack's.

"Webster shouldn't have said anything," Gwen groused.

"Hush. You know she had to. A kiss is a very big thing." Then Lilah leaned forward. "Was it at least a good one?"

Well, how was she to answer that? It happened so fast, and she hadn't had time to think about it properly. But if she were to analyze it now, she remembered that he had apologized immediately afterwards. If it were a good kiss, would he have done that? Would he have looked so very startled and possibly horrified?

"No," she said slowly. "At least he didn't seem to think so."

"I didn't mean him, silly. I meant you. How do you feel about it?"

"I don't know." That was the honest truth. She simply had not had the time to make any clear deductions. Fortunately, her sister was well used to her. She settled down at the far side of the bed and smiled warmly.

"Then let's talk about it, shall we? Tell me exactly what happened."

Gwen wasn't sure she wanted to. It was all so new and strange. But Lilah knew just what to say to get her to talk, especially since she spoke quietly without jostling the bed. That allowed Gwen to settle back onto her pillows, close her eyes, and speak as if discussing things with the darkness rather than a person. It made it so much easier to talk about confusing things. She began with the details of their business scheme, telling Lilah exactly what had happened in a linear progression. She started with their talk at the masquerade and progressed all the way through the kiss as a recitation of facts.

Lilah listened without interrupting and then she asked the one question she always asked. "And how does all that make you feel?"

Gwen's eyes shot open. "I have not decided!"

"One generally doesn't decide about feelings."

"Well, I do," she declared flatly. "Which you well know."

Lilah nodded because Lilah always nodded. She didn't quarrel with anyone. "Start with the business idea. Are you happy to work on it?"

Gwen pushed up from the bed. "I am terribly excited about that. I have begun notes on a study of the best soil and light for the daffodils. It will be terribly important for Lord Sayres to know that, don't you think?"

"I have no idea how to answer to that."

"Well, I do. And yes, he should be very interested indeed." Gwen said it more as the man *ought* to be interested rather than a prediction that he would.

"So you have found a new scientific inquiry. I can tell you enjoy that."

"Most definitely."

"And what of Lord Sayres? You said he's not a libertine—"

"Definitely not."

"But do you like him? I can tell that the idea of being in trade doesn't bother either of you, though Mama will cut up stiff about that."

"Mama hasn't a say in that." Which was true, but that never stopped her mother from voicing her opinions.

"Will you like working with him?"

That was a more serious question. There were several people she could tolerate for a while, but only a precious few could be in her presence for more than a quarter hour without becoming an annoyance. It was frustrating to be so uncomfortable with people when she longed to connect with them as she did Lilah.

"I was with Lord Sayres for nearly three hours today, and I didn't despise him once."

"Not once!" Her sister smiled, her eyes dancing in the candlelight. "Do you think that comfort with him will continue?"

"Probably not. But for now, I shall be grateful that he has not given me a disgust of his person." And that he didn't appear disgusted with her. "In fact," she confessed, "I really enjoyed his company."

"Now that is very interesting," Lilah said. "Let's hope it continues."

Well, that would be wonderful, but experience told her it wasn't likely. "If we are to make a great deal of money, I shall tolerate him. And even if we don't make any money, I shall be happy enough if you find a husband."

Lilah raised her hand as if to ward off the thoughts. "Let us leave the question of me for another day, hmm? Let's talk instead about that kiss."

Gwen squirmed on the bed, feeling both intrigued and disquieted by the memory, and that alone was cause for examination. She was usually clear on her emotions. Unless it was science, she usually had a negative response or none at all.

"He was laughing as he spun me around. And because he was so happy, I was too."

"You laughed?"

"Freely," she confessed. And it had been astonishing.

"Then he set you on your feet?"

Gwen nodded. "We were still looking at each other, and there was a moment…" She frowned. It was so hard to put into words. "I was still laughing, but I saw his head lower. It wasn't fast. I saw him do it."

"Did you know he was going to kiss you?"

"I did."

"And you didn't move away."

It was a statement, not a question, but Gwen nodded anyway. "It was so fast, and yet, I knew it would happen. I had time to run if I wanted to."

"But you didn't."

Gwen felt her lips tingle in memory, and she touched them. She felt her mouth curve into a smile. "I think he is a good kisser," she finally said.

"You look like you enjoyed it, at any rate."

"And it went on a very long time." She remembered the feel of his hands on her back, drawing her close. Her entire body had been pressed up against him. And his tongue had teased in past her lips before thrusting in and out.

She had allowed it. She had enjoyed it! And given that all her other kisses from gentlemen had been wet, hurried, and thoroughly repellent, that was a significant surprise.

"I think I shall enjoy being on the shelf," she said firmly.

"What nonsense!" Lilah exclaimed. "Isn't he planning on making you this Season's Original? That is not being on the shelf. That is being wonderfully available on the Marriage Mart."

"That's just the thing," Gwen countered. "Whatever he does with me is for his flowers. It is just a way to make people want his daffodils."

Lilah's forehead wrinkled as she looked at Gwen. Her expression was one of puzzlement, but Gwen could not understand it.

"It's simple," Gwen explained. "I am too old to compete with all the new girls. Let them have the men. I shall not be doing anything but showing off his flowers."

"I thought you wanted to get married so that you could have children."

"I should not have told you that," Gwen said.

"But you did. Have you given up your hunt for a husband?"

She had. Right after the masquerade when it became very clear she was very bad at husband hunting. "Making money is my plan now. And if I wish to teach little girls to explore their world and not be cowed by stupid people, then perhaps I shall open a school."

"I think a school is a very nice idea." Lilah leaned forward, a twinkle in her eye. "But I think a husband might be more fun."

"Now there is where you are wrong," Gwen said firmly. "A school will give me very many opportunities to teach young girls. A husband will be fun only for as long as he kisses like Lord Sayres. And even those kisses will get boring after a bit. I am sure of it."

Chapter Eleven

When Jackson finally found his bed, he collapsed into it with the exhaustion of a man who had been awake for two days. He counted the time well spent. He and Lady Gwen had made significant strides on their business plan, and he had every hope that they could continue working at extraordinary speeds. And so he slept with a smile on his face and woke uncomfortable thanks to incredibly erotic dreams featuring his business partner.

It didn't help that he remembered every second of their kiss, reliving it while he wondered what had happened for him to descend so quickly and so thoroughly into their embrace. Never before had a single kiss blocked out his environment to the point where he forgot that they were surrounded by several people. He was a man who valued discretion, and yet he had exposed Lady Gwen to the worst kind of gossip.

Fortunately, the witnesses were not predisposed to talk, thanks to a healthy bribe to Madame Juliette and a warning that, should gossip emanate from her place of business, he would make sure her other patrons knew they could not count on her discretion.

He had just finished his ablutions when a knock sounded on his door. When he answered, he was started to find his landlord there, his expression tight and his chin lifted in determination.

Damn. It never boded well when the normally passive Mr. Feit turned stubborn. "Good morning," Jackson said by way of greeting.

Instead of answering, the man held out a handful of coins.

Jackson took the coins because it was that or let them drop on the floor. "What's this for?"

"That's the remainder of this month's rent that I'm returning it to you. Me and Mrs. Feit run a quiet home for good gentlemen. I'm sorry to say that you can't remain here."

"Whyever not?"

"Lady Meunier told us wot you've been doing. We can't have that here. Now don't make a fuss. We'll let you take your things, but we need you out by this evening."

"This evening!" he gaped. Damnation, he did not have time for this. It was Isabelle, of course, putting more pressure on him to bend to her wishes. Well, if she thought losing his sparse rooms was enough to send him running back to her, she was sadly mistaken. He looked hard at his landlord. "What did she say?"

"Who?"

"Lady. Meunier. Whatever it was, she was lying."

"Well as to that, she said you and… that you've been…" Mr. Feit's face turned a mottled red and then he cleared his throat twice.

"You know it's not true. I haven't done any of it."

Mr. Feit looked down at his feet. "Well, as to that, no, I didn't rightly think you did."

"Then why—"

"Because she pays the bills."

Jackson's chin shot up. "The hell she does. I paid you—"

"Not yer bills. Ours. Lady Meunier bought the house couple years ago and pays me and the misses to run it. She's been right kind to us. This is the first time she's interfered with us, but I can't say no. She'd toss me and the missus out just like that. You know she would."

He did. After all, that's exactly what she was doing to him.

"I'm right sorry," his landlord continued. "I'm giving you back the extra rent when I didn't have to, but it's the decent thing to do."

Normally Jackson would have negotiated. The last thing he had time to do was move residences. But the Feits were kind people, and he knew what it was to be caught in Isabelle's grip. So he nodded. "I'll have my things gone by afternoon," he said, "but it would make matters so much faster if I could have one of Mrs. Feit's excellent meat pies while I pack."

The relief on his landlord's face told him more than anything else just how hard Isabelle had pushed the normally gentle man to get him to act. Which made the man's next words all the more worthwhile.

"You tell yer next landlord to come talk to me. I'll tell him you're a good man who pays his shot right on time. You send him here and I'll tell him that."

Jackson smiled his gratitude. He hadn't been afraid of finding new lodgings. He wasn't that poor, but he appreciated the offer nonetheless. So he said one last thing before Mr. Feit bowed away.

"It's not right, what she's doing."

"I know it, sir. You've been a good tenant—"

"Not that. I mean if you run the house, then you should have control over who stays and who doesn't. What if she told you to allow someone who really was having ladies over at all hours of the night? What would you do then?"

The man's eyes widened. "She wouldn't."

"I think she would. She certainly could, and that's not right."

"But wot can I do about it? She owns the house."

"You could re-negotiate. This has been Mr. and Mrs. Feit's Home for Upstanding Gentlemen for generations. That means something. And if she's to profit from it, then you should be compensated."

The man stared at him, obviously confused. That was the problem with so many people in business. They didn't understand what they could negotiate or how. But of course, that was one of his specialties.

"Talk it over with your wife," he said gently. "When you're ready to re-negotiate with Isabelle, come find me. I'll help you stand up to her. I don't know why you sold in the first place—"

"It was to help my daughter and her husband start their bakery. It was always her dream, and I couldn't say no."

He understood a father wanting to sacrifice for his daughter. "Does Isabelle own any part of the bake shop?"

"No, sir, she does not."

"Good. Keep it that way."

"I will. And I'll get you that meat pie right now. Plus a tart from Missy. And you let me know where you end up. I'll talk to my wife. She's never liked the way Lady Meunier acted anyway. Not since she bought the house from us."

Mr. Feit flashed a quick grin, then rushed downstairs while Jackson began the tedious task of packing up his belongings. His clothing didn't take long, but his books and papers did. He had boxes of notes on various business opportunities, articles on canal designs, and now a new book on horticulture techniques. He already knew where to send it. Aaron would let him store his things for a while, at least until he settled in new rooms. But he hated to add to the clutter of his friend's home. If ever a man needed a good housekeeper, it was Aaron.

But that was a thought for another day. Especially since packing up had taken too much of his morning. He needed to meet with a tinker he knew and then pay a visit to Lady Gwen. And then he had to convince her to run away with him to Lincolnshire.

Though God only knew what Isabelle would do to his reputation in his absence.

Chapter Twelve

GWEN WOKE WITH a clear head and an overwhelming sense of doom. She had been incredibly stupid. She wasn't sure how it had happened. Normally she never missed details like this, but somehow in the midst of Lord Sayres's enthusiasm, she had forgotten basic botany.

The daffodil's blooming season was at its peak now. Soon it would be over. It had only this moment dawned on her that Lord Sayres had been making plans for *this Season,* but they couldn't possibly get everything in place in time. They'd have to wait until next spring.

She would have to tell him as soon as he arrived this afternoon. She fretted about how she would give him the news even as she tried to focus on ways to make next year successful. It ate at her concentration and she was thoroughly put out with herself by the time the man arrived. She even heard the knocker sound from all the way up in her upstairs garden. But when she made it to the front parlor, she found the place empty.

Spinning around, she addressed their butler. "Mr. Parry, wherever is he?"

The man curled his lip. "Who, my lady?"

"Lord Sayres. As you know very well."

"I sent him to the kitchen, my lady."

She frowned. "The kitchen? Whatever for?"

"I thought it appropriate, my lady."

She arched a brow. "You thought it *appropriate* to put a future earl in the kitchen?"

"Indeed."

One word and a blank face. Well, something had obviously happened to put their normally sane butler into a stiff mood. She didn't try to understand but headed directly to the kitchen.

She heard the giggling well before she pushed through the door. Then when she did cross the threshold, she saw Lord Sayres nose to nose with an upstairs maid. And while she watched in shock, he bent down even closer to her. Was he kissing her servant in the middle of the kitchen? While everyone else watched? There were more than a half dozen people in here.

"My lord!" she snapped, her voice higher and more shrill in her outrage. It startled her because she couldn't remember ever hearing such a sound from her own mouth. It was a tone reserved for her mother. And yet, there was no ability to draw it back, especially as his chin jerked up in surprise while his cheeks tinged with red. But if he felt embarrassment, there was no trace of it in his voice or his sudden wide grin.

"Lady Gwen, you are here at last!"

At last? She'd only been told he was here two minutes ago. And yet, as she looked about the kitchen, she realized he must have been here for much longer. There was a large assortment of metal wares spread across the kitchen table. Several pots took up one side. The cook was carefully inspecting those. While the rest of the space was filled with smaller pieces, jewelry, and utensils. She saw every servant in the house except the butler all crowded around, inspecting things. And there, in the center, was Lord Sayres gesturing her to step into her own kitchen.

"Come take a look and give me your decision."

On his kisses? She stood there, her feet immobile as she scrambled for words—any words—but nothing made sense. And when nothing made sense to her mind, every part of her locked up.

Meanwhile, he looked back down at the maid, gave her an approving nod, then stepped back, gently guiding the young woman to stand beside a line of their other maids and kitchen staff, including the cook.

"Lady Gwen?" he asked as he extended a hand to her. "Let me show you what we've been doing."

"What?" she said, though the word was barely intelligible, especially as she spoke over another man who was in a boisterous conversation with the cook about a pot. There were so many people in here, she hadn't noticed him at first, but his voice was certainly hard to ignore now. Lord, he was so loud!

"Yorgos! Hush now," Lord Sayres admonished. "Sell your pots later. Lady Gwen is here to look at what you've done."

The large man looked up from his pot with a wide grin. "Welcome, Lady Gwen. Welcome!"

And here was another man welcoming her to her own kitchen. But she didn't have time to respond as Lord Sayres took her hand and gently tugged her forward.

"This is my friend, Mr. Yorgos Callatos."

"Greetings, sir," she said politely. Then she tried not to recoil as her grabbed her hand and kissed it with excessive enthusiasm. At least it felt excessive to her because she didn't know him, and she wasn't wearing gloves to blunt the feel of his calloused fingers.

"Stop that," Lord Sayres chided, as he gently moved her to the far side of him while forcing his friend to step back. "She's a lady who is not to be handled like one of your pots."

"On the contrary," the man said heartily. "I handle every one of my pieces as if it were a lady born. Such love I stroke into every peak and valley, such tender care—"

"As you strike it with your hammers," Lord Sayres interrupted. "My apologies, Lady Gwen. Some time ago, I searched for the best metal worker in London. Little did I realize that this loud-mouthed brute could work magic with silver."

"Not just with silver," Mr. Callatos returned. "These hands have wrought beauty out of iron, turned disasters into delight, and reaped grateful kisses from—"

"Your wife and children." Lord Sayres shot her a look. "He's a terrible flirt, but a good man with a very patient wife."

"She's a good woman, my Eugenia."

"But we're here for Lady Gwen's opinion." He gestured to the line of women. "What do you think? They're all so lovely, I can't think what would work best."

Think? She couldn't think, not with him standing so close and her shoulders creeping up to her ears. He crowded her with his body, and though she had certainly enjoyed it at the dressmakers, right now she felt as if there were too many people making too much noise and pressing too close. Lord Sayres stepped toward her and she cringed backwards. She didn't mean to, but it happened anyway, and she saw his brows shoot up in surprise.

He stayed back then, but he still seemed to herd her in the direction he wanted. Not by touching, but by leaning in enough that she adjusted back. And then, when she apparently stood where he wanted, he gestured to a line of her female staff who all looked rosy cheeked as they tittered.

He wanted her to pick one of her servants? For what purpose? After he'd already been kissing one in full view of everyone?

"I didn't have one of the flowers with me," he continued, "so I don't know about this one. Is it wide enough?" He gestured at Betsy, their kitchen maid. "And this is lovely, but perhaps too delicate." He pointed to the cook who was anything but delicate. "I think this one would take too much time to make, but we only need a few at first."

He was pointing down the row of women, gesturing to their bosoms in a most indelicate way. She had no idea what he was talking about, and it upset her to be so confused. So she dug in her feet and stepped away from his distracting presence. And when she was two full steps away from him, she drew herself up to her full height and spoke as calmly as she could manage.

"Please explain." Two words, and she meant no insult. She was overwhelmed by all the noise and commotion when she was already in an unsettled state from before. She didn't speak overly loud, and neither did she yell. But when she was done, an uncomfortable silence settled on the entire kitchen. The maids stopped giggling, Cook regarded her with a stern expression, and even the grinning Mr. Callatos stopped smiling. And worst of all, the footmen took the moment to step backwards out of the room. She was sure the women would have left too, but they were lined up in front of her and couldn't go anywhere.

The only one who didn't seem annoyed with her was Lord Sayres, whose brows arched with surprise, but his smile never faded. Instead, he dipped his chin.

"My apologies, Lady Gwen. I'm afraid I got so wrapped up in what we were doing that I didn't properly set the scene." He stepped even further back from her as he gestured to the wares on the kitchen table. Grabbing the smallest piece, he held aloft a dress pin vase. It was suitable for the tiniest posies as it might adorn a petite woman's dress. "Mr. Callatos fashions pins, among other things. I asked him if he had anything that might work for our daffodils."

Finally, something she could say. "That is too small."

"That is exactly what I thought." Then he turned to gesture to the women behind him. "I thought perhaps one of these might serve better."

She looked at her servants and abruptly realized she had missed that every single one wore a dress pin. All were empty except for one the upstairs maid Alice wore. It sported a poorly done paper cut of the daffodil. Good lord, was that the paper cut she had fashioned yesterday? She thought it was and was horrified by her own lack of skill.

"I thought this vase would work," he began.

"I am a terrible artist," she murmured, then she focused on the pin vase. "The petals are the right size, but not the right weight. The stem is—"

"Still too narrow?" he asked as he plucked the flower from the vase. Alice blushed a fiery red, but Gwen focused on the paper flower. He'd wrapped the stem in a scrap of rag to thicken it.

"The opposite," she responded. "It's too large now."

"Ah. Hmmm." He held out his hand to Mr. Callatos who passed him a pair of scissors and another sheet of foolscap and held them both out to her. "Would you make another one please?" he asked.

She frowned. "Paper cutting is not one of my skills."

"Nor mine, obviously. But you have a better eye than I do for botany."

She couldn't argue that, so she took the scissors and bent to her task. "A real flower would be better," she said as she began to cut.

"Just give me an idea of the size," he coaxed. "It doesn't need to be exact."

She hated things that were not exact. That was where problems always lurked. Inexact statements always led to inaccurate conclusions. But she didn't quarrel. She'd learned long ago that she was unique in that assessment, and so she did what she could to adjust his cutting. Then she handed it back and Alice plumped up her chest as he set the new flower in her pin. Unfortunately, it toppled sideways in the wider mouth of the vase.

"Oh dear," he said.

"That pin will not work," she said, stating the obvious. "Unless you wish to add other flowers or leaves to make it stand up more."

He shook his head. "I want it to be the daffodil alone."

She always thought that the simplest answer was the best. Meanwhile, she had to seal her mouth shut while he stepped down the row of women, dropping the paper cutting into each pin while the ladies pinked beneath his attention. She knew he was murmuring something to them. Cook even giggled. But the exact nature of his flirtatious behavior was hidden from her, for which she was both grateful and annoyed. What did she care if he whispered something scandalous to the parlor maid?

After each woman, he would step back and survey the picture. He complimented her looks—whichever *her* it was—but his eyes seemed to be on the pin and flowers. Each woman preened under his regard, Cook no less than the younger ladies, but in the end, he shook his head.

"I cannot think which shape is best," he said. "They all look lovely."

"Because you are not thinking about the use of the vase." She stepped over to a cold teapot and brandished it aloft.

The women all looked alarmed by her movement, probably because she was known for occasionally being so absorbed in a task (usually a book) that she poured tea into the saucer rather than the cup. Or onto the table all together. Rather than terrify them, she passed the cold pot to Lord Sayres.

"Would you please put water in the vases?"

He understood immediately. Brandishing the teapot, he headed for Alice but they both could see that the spout was much too large and the vase too narrow. "It will spill all down her front," he said. "Do you fill them first and pin them on later?"

He obviously had not worn one of these before. She had and had declared them useless, frustrating things. Even if she succeeded in getting a watered flower onto her dress, it nevertheless spilled when she sat down or stood up or walked across the room.

Webster knew just what to do. The woman might be too stiff in her idea of how a lady should act, but her maid was a genius when it came to dressing. Gwen gave her a nod, and the lady pulled out a bowl of water. She pulled the pin off herself and dropped it into the water to fill it up, then held her thumb over it to stopper it. His lordship watched with an interested look.

"A small piece of cork would work best, I should think," he said as he glanced back at Mr. Callatos. The man nodded even as he stepped around to watch Webster's work.

With her thumb over the top, she crossed to Gwen and pinned it on her just over her heart. The perfect place, her mother had once said, to accent the bosom. Then Webster pushed the paper flower into the waiting vase. That completely ruined the paper cut, but it wasn't worth saving anyway.

"Very clever," Lord Sayres said as he inspected the vase from every side. "I see why you wanted fabric that wouldn't show water stains. But how well can you move with it?"

Gwen breathed deeply, lifting the pin with every breath. It didn't spill.

"No, no," Lord Sayres said. "We need to see how it will work with you dancing." So saying, he grabbed her arm and set a hand on her waist. "Callatos, a waltz, if you please."

Immediately the tinker began to hum. He had a beautifully rich voice that la-dee-dum, la-dee-dummed a tune. Meanwhile, Lord Sayres held out his hand to her.

"May I?"

"There isn't room," she began, but at Webster's gesture, the staff quickly stepped back and even moved the kitchen table to the side. Lord Sayres arched a brow at her, his expression mischievous.

"Any other objections?" he asked.

Many, all crowding against her tongue. It was silly. Everyone was watching. The paper cut flower was a soggy mass drooping in the vase. But when she looked in his eyes, her anxieties faded. She nodded her head, and he immediately clasped her hand in his and set the other at her waist. She knew the dance. She'd been approved for the waltz since her first Season. But it was nothing compared to what they did now.

With so little room in the kitchen, he held her inappropriately tight. She tried to relax but she'd never been good at dancing. This close, she was likely to trip them both and knock someone unconscious on the stove.

"Trust me," he said as he smiled at her. "I'm strong enough to keep you safe." And then he winked at her.

Ridiculous that a simple wink could relax her, but it did. When it came from him, it certainly did. So she nodded and he began to move her left and right in an exhilarating kind of swoop.

He was right. His arms held her safely as they danced. In fact, she could feel the solid power in his muscles, so steady that she believed that if she did lose her footing, he would be able to hold her in place as if she weighed nothing.

Very well then, she thought, as she exhaled some of her fears. She could relax in his arms, let him take some of her weight in his supporting arm as she arched her back. And once she did that, he straightened even taller as they moved. Their knees didn't knock together once, and her feet landed on solid ground with every step.

Mr. Callatos speeded up the tempo. A waltz was often a sedate affair, but not with the tinker leading. Lord Sayres matched the beat, spinning her in tighter circles until she had no choice but to grip him tight and hope her feet went where they should. They did. And for a few breathless moments, she felt like she was flying.

It was so wonderful that she laughed in breathless delight.

Then the dance slowed. Her feet found a stable purchase, though her heart beat in rapid pulses at her throat. The staff was clapping, Mr. Callatos being the most enthusiastic, all while Lord Sayres held her gaze.

"I didn't trip us," she whispered.

"Of course not," he said, as if it had been her doing. It was all him, and she reluctantly stepped back when he released her waist. But he didn't let go of her right hand even as he stepped back to look at the flower vase. "Did it spill?"

She looked down at her dress. She was wearing one that would show water spots clearly, but it appeared that the vase had done its work without disaster. Or the wet paper had sufficiently clogged the top of the thing that it was one and the same. A real flower would do something similar since the stem would choke off many spills.

"I'm dry as well," he said as felt across his lapel. Then he flashed Callatos a grin. "Can you make more of these? With corks?"

"I can have a dozen by the end of the month!"

"No, no," Lord Sayres said as he looked at the vase. "We shall need them in two weeks. As many as you can fashion."

Mr. Callatos frowned, but he didn't argue. "I shall get straight to work."

It took Gwen a moment to bring her thoughts back to order. The dance had been so lovely that she'd completely lost track of what she had to say to the man. But a discussion of schedule brought it all back to her.

"A month will be plenty of time, Mr. Callatos," she said. And when Lord Sayres turned to frown at her, she felt her cheeks flush. "I'm afraid I have done a terrible miscalculation. I'm an idiot for it. I cannot tell you how terrible I feel about it." She took a breath. "My lord, our plans will not work for this Season. We must delay until next year."

His eyes widened, and his expression fell. Not into dismay as she expected, but into doubt. It was the look of a man who thought he knew best, and it never failed to raise her hackles.

"We have been moving so fast," she continued. "You surprised me last night and I was caught up in the enthusiasm, but it will not work this Season. I'm sorry."

He nodded. "I can see that you are serious, and we must discuss this then."

"Yes—"

"Will you take a walk with me then?"

"What?"

"Didn't you tell me that you often go to a park in the mornings?"

"Yes, to sketch."

"Then let us go there."

She was already nodding when she remembered. "Mama wanted to discuss this Season's schedule. She will be awake soon—"

"Then we must be away right now." He lifted their joined hands and pressed a kiss to her knuckles. "Doesn't that make sense?"

Nothing with him ever made sense. She felt as if she were always leaping and rushing to match him. Normally she became annoyed with the slow plod of other people's thoughts, but not his. His mind was quick, and she found it exhilarating to match him even when she had to slow him down.

"I shall change my shoes and be down in a flash."

He nodded. "And I shall help put the kitchen back to rights while I wait."

He would? Truly? "That is kind of you." She might have said more, but Webster was already between them as she shooed Gwen forward.

"You will need a wrap too," the woman said, and Gwen was forced to step quickly or be run over by her own maid on her way to yet another walk with Lord Sayres. The first had been through Vauxhall while he and Aunt Isabelle jockeyed for her attention. The second had led them to the dressmakers and her very first good kiss. She hardly dared wonder what would happen on this third excursion with him. And yet, she was very excited to find out.

Chapter Thirteen

JACKSON MOVED QUICKLY as he helped reset the kitchen. But even as he took his leave of Mr. Callatos, his mind remained on Lady Gwen and his very important deduction about her.

She did not like to be rushed.

Whereas most women in Jackson's circle preferred to be swept away, Lady Gwen liked to think about her words before she spoke. She didn't accept invitations without coming up with at least one way it would fail. And for the important things, she had at least a dozen objections.

He assumed that was the reason for her current statement that their business scheme would not work. It would be his job to soothe her fears and make sure things proceeded apace. Fortunately, he didn't have to wait long. By the time he made it to the front hallway, she was already pulling on her bonnet.

"Mama was calling for her morning chocolate. We had best be off if we want to avoid her."

He nodded and extended his arm to her. With any other woman, he would have clasped her hand and drew her forward instead of waiting for her to set her fingertips along his forearm. But that was the other thing he needed to remember.

She didn't like to be touched. At least not without warning.

That was unfortunate because he did love touching her. He loved the way her body started out tense but eventually relaxed as long as he was patient. He felt a heady rush whenever a woman gave her trust, and Lady Gwen let him experience that over and over. Which made him wonder, just what had happened to make her so prickly?

"The park is this way," she said as she gratified him by entwining her arm with his. It was a casual pose and one that he suspected was not given to many. They walked in silence a moment, but then she must have become self-conscious because she started to pull away from him.

"I need to tell you—" she began, but then stopped when he gripped her hand to prevent her from leaving his side. They both wore gloves, so it was not nearly as intimate as their waltz, but for now, he found himself loath to release her.

"Whatever it is, I am confident we can overcome it."

"No, we can't!" she huffed. "You cannot order flowers to grow when it is not the right season."

He turned and frowned at her. She sounded extremely irritated and he could not fathom why. "I think you need to explain."

She nodded. "I feel incredibly stupid for not thinking of it earlier, but I was so startled yesterday. I thought you already knew, but then you began ordering gowns for this Season." She stopped and took a deep breath. "Your flowers will all be gone in three weeks. They won't grow again until next spring. We cannot cover me in blooms that won't appear until next year."

He nodded because he already knew this. "We will cover you in some blooms and then take orders for next year."

She frowned at him. "I don't understand."

"Did you think me so stupid as to rush forward without even knowing when the blooms will be available?"

He could tell from her expression that she did.

"My mother adored daffodils. All through my childhood I sat with her at the window talking about when the snow would melt. We cheered as every tiny leaf broke through the cold ground. And we made bets on when this flower or that might bloom. I know we will have blossoms for only a couple more weeks at most."

"Then why are you rushing to change my gowns? To fashion vase pins for—"

"If we hurry, I think we can have you outfitted for the Cordington Ball."

She wrinkled her nose. "I hate their ball. She is nearly blind, and he is a pinchpenny, so they skimp on candles. Last time I attended I couldn't read my dance card because it was so dark."

He grinned. "Exactly. You shall be a vision in yellow with daffodils in your hair and upon your gown. You shall glow in an otherwise dark room and everyone will remark upon it."

"Especially if I trip and land on my nose."

"You must trust me," he said softly. "I have everything under control."

That was a mistake. At his words, she stopped walking, withdrew her arm from his, and turned such that she faced him eye to eye. "Why would I do that?" she asked.

"Because I am not an idiot when it comes to these ventures. I have been searching for a long time for a venture that Isabelle cannot touch. I will not let this chance pass by because of something stupid. Betting on a flower crop is risky enough. Everything else must be planned meticulously."

"And you have done that? In two days' time?"

He nodded.

"Without even talking to me? Am I to be your partner in this? We have not discussed anything and yet you ask me to trust you. I do not know what you are thinking, and you cannot know that I have done anything I promised."

He rubbed his chin, unaccountably annoyed. "Of course, you have done what you promised. You are working on a safe means of transport, as we discussed at the beginning."

"But you cannot know I have tested the ideas. That I have thought through temperature and expense, the wetness of the soil or any of a thousand different things."

He folded his arms. "Of course, I can. You are not a woman to be casual about her plants."

"I'm not a woman who is casual about anything," she snapped. "And you have been entirely too quick with your plans without discussing a word with me."

She was right. Hadn't he just told himself that she was not a woman to be rushed? And yet the whole thing annoyed him. He did not know a single woman who truly wanted to be involved in details. They always left the management to him because the particulars bored them. In truth, all they really wanted was his attention, and he did not have time to give it!

"I cannot wait to explain everything to you," he said, his voice tight. "There is too little time and too much to be done. But I promise you, once the idea is launched, I shall be at your disposal."

She stared at him a long moment, her mouth tightening into a very straight line. In the end, she blew out her breath. "I see we will not suit," she finally said. "I wish you luck in your endeavor, my lord. I hope it brings you everything you want."

It happened so very suddenly that he was momentarily thrown. When she turned away from the park to walk back toward her home, he grew downright panicked. He needed her! She could not possibly think to end this simply because he had not gone through every little thing ahead of time.

He scrambled to catch up to her, his longer legs serving him well in this. "Lady Gwen, please. We came out here to discuss things in private. We should do that."

She didn't slow her steps, but she did look him in the eye. "Why? You are not going to share your decisions with me, and I am not going to be comfortable blindly following your dictates."

He hadn't been dictating to her… much. "You have never before told me you wished to know the details. You appeared surprised every time I said I would call on you."

She shrugged. "I am always surprised when someone wishes to call on me. Most people avoid it."

He held out his hand in front of her. With any other woman, he would have pulled her to a stop, but with Lady Gwen, he knew better now. He held out his hand before her and she stopped rather than connect with his arm. It was rather lowering to realize how much she didn't want to touch him when he enjoyed every time they had brushed skin to skin.

"Lady Gwen, you accuse me of making precipitous decisions without discussing things with you. Are you not doing the exact same thing now?"

"You are aware, are you not, when your clothing pinches? When your cravat is too tight?"

Whatever was she talking about? "Of course."

"Well, you, my lord, pinch. And I do not like it. That doesn't require discussion, it requires removal."

"Or you could just ask me to relax my grip."

She stared at him, her lips softening then compressing again and again. She appeared as someone who wished to speak but was constantly choking off her words. And in her silence, he confessed something he just now understood.

"I believe we both have been disappointed often by people who do not do as they promise. Who will not listen to reason and who dismiss us as inconsequential."

"You are a man," she said with a touch of bitterness. "If you are dismissed, you can find a way to accomplish it on your own. All I can do is walk away."

His brows rose. "You overestimate the power of my gender." Then when she opened her mouth to argue, he raised his hands in surrender. "But I grant that I have resources you do not. Which is why we need to work together."

"Telling me what to do is not working together."

"Neither is walking away before I have had a chance to amend my behavior." Rather than reach for her, he folded his arm across his chest as they faced one another eye to eye. "Who taught you to expect the worst at every turn?"

"I don't," she said, though she didn't sound entirely sure. "I believed in our business idea from the very first. It is a sound idea."

He acknowledged the point. "Then it is not ideas that disappoint you, but people."

She swallowed. "You do not know me well enough to say such a thing."

"Then let us rectify that." He smiled at her. "Come with me to Lincolnshire. You can work directly with the plants there, I will have time to explain my thoughts in detail, and we can make decisions that will satisfy us both."

He could see that she was considering it, but he had to wade through her objections. The first was easily dispelled.

"It would not be proper."

"Bring your maid. That harridan is excellent protection from everything, especially for a woman so firmly on the shelf."

"Webster does like things proper." It sounded like she meant Webster made everything excruciatingly painful.

"My sisters will delight in making you comfortable," he countered.

Her eyes widened in alarm. "Your sisters! But they will want to talk to me about things, and I shall have no time to work with the daffodils."

"I promise you they will not. They have more hobbies than any ten women and are perfectly content pestering me. If I tell them to leave you alone, they will."

She didn't look like she believed him, and truthfully, he prayed he could convince his family to let Lady Gwen be. They would not mean to bother her, but—

"If they are pestering you, then we cannot get anything done."

"Do you know how to handle your mother such that she leaves you alone? What if Elliott knocks on your door, or Lilah?"

She nodded. "I have a great deal of experience in avoiding them."

"Then trust that I can handle my family as easily."

"It's not easy!"

Neither would it be with his. "But I can make sure everything will go as it ought."

She sniffed. "It seems I am to trust you in a great many things."

He shrugged. "What better way to find out if you can rely on me?"

He could see her thinking about it, but in the end, she nodded. "Very well. We can leave after the Season—"

"Today. This afternoon." He glanced at his pocket watch. "I need to secure the carriage and will be back for you in an hour—"

"Today!" she gasped. "You cannot be serious. I cannot up and fly to Lincolnshire as if I were popping around to the milliners."

He took a breath and released it with care. "My lady," he said slowly. "You must choose. Do you think our business idea a good one?"

She nodded. "I have said so."

"Then do you wish to do everything you can to make it a success?"

"Of course!"

"Then you cannot be forever walking away, saying no, and throwing up obstacles. Fortunes do not land in anyone's lap without discomfort and hard work."

"I am no stranger to hard work."

He didn't think she was. "But you work on your terms, in your way, and walk away from any who would disagree with you." He held out his hand. "I am asking you to agree to work with me no matter what. I swear to discuss things with you until you are satisfied, if you swear to persevere with the discomfort to talk to me about your worries and give me the chance to allay them." He stepped forward and turned his hand palm up before her. "Can you promise that, Lady Gwen?"

She took a moment, her gaze troubled as she looked at his hand and then his face. She seemed to study his expression in minute detail, and he had no idea what conclusion she drew. She gave nothing away while he did his best to remain strong beneath her heavy regard.

And what an odd feeling that was. He'd given that speech before. He'd had to gain others' commitments any number of times while pursuing Isabelle's business interests. He'd asked for trust, for work, for simple courtesy, and most had given it. Never before had he done such a thing with a woman. Nor had he ever waited so long for an answer.

"I want to trust you," she whispered.

"I want to earn your trust," he returned.

"You confuse me. I feel things when you are around that are unusual."

His throat closed up, and his heart sped up. Was she confessing to an attraction? The very idea sent his thoughts down a very different road. One he'd best avoid if they meant to work together. And yet he couldn't stop the hopeful note in his voice.

"Are these pleasant feelings?"

"Yes."

"And I have very pleasant feelings toward you," he admitted.

Her eyes searched his face. "Does that make this difficult for you? Does it make you question our business?"

"Absolutely not." Then he winked at her. "I like working with someone who gives me pleasant feelings. Don't you?"

She bit her lip. "Very well—"

Relief made his knees weak.

"—But do you truly mean to leave this afternoon?"

"And return in a week." He didn't want to tell her that he had no place to sleep tonight otherwise.

She blew out a breath. "Mama will be furious. And what shall I do about Lilah? I am to help her—"

"You cannot split your focus. Do you worry about your family or strive for your own independence?" Then because he saw her hesitate, he sweetened the offer. "Remember, once you are established with your own fortune, you can do a great deal for your half-sister. Perhaps next Season she will be the one wearing the flowers."

She nodded, and he could tell that she understood what he was asking. "Lilah has always been pushed off until next time, next Season, next something. Never now."

"You cannot help her until you are in a better position in society."

"Yes, I know," she said. "But I can still regret the necessity."

He had no argument. He understood forcing someone to wait until he was in a better position to help. It was what he had been doing to his sisters for nearly a decade.

"This can work," he said as much to himself as to Lady Gwen. "We will see to it."

Lady Gwen didn't speak. She merely slanted a glance his way as she took his arm. No hesitation, no barest tip of her fingers, but her whole hand and with it her commitment. The exhilaration of it was more drugging than the finest brandy.

CHAPTER FOURTEEN

TO SAY THAT her mother was displeased was like saying that plants wilted when set on fire. Gwen's mother was furious that she intended to abandon London at the beginning of the Season. Gwen could admit to herself that she had a secret thrill when she responded that a woman on the shelf could do as she pleased, even at the beginning of the Season. Less fun was telling Lilah that she was leaving. Her sister took the news as she took everything: with a calm understanding and a smile, even though she was being abandoned with Mama.

"But of course you must go. Lord Sayres sounds like he has a very exciting business idea. If it can restore his titular fortunes, you must help however you can."

"The business was my idea," Gwen complained. "And since when did you start using words like titular?"

Lilah grinned. "I have decided to broaden my education."

"You're very well educated. I couldn't tolerate you if you weren't."

Her sister shrugged. "I've decided to broaden my appearance of an education."

"Well, don't go overboard. You know Mama says that men hate smart women."

"You're smart and Lord Sayres doesn't seem to hate you."

Gwen looked out the window. "Lord Sayres is an exception. And we are not courting. We're trying to make a fortune."

Lilah didn't comment, except to refold an undergarment that Gwen had thrown into the portmanteau. Normally Webster would be doing it, but their maid was right then rushing to pack her own things for the two-week journey. And when Gwen grabbed her softest and most favorite gown, Lilah gently took it from her hand and put it back into the wardrobe.

"Bring the blue gown instead." When Gwen started to interrupt, her sister shook her head. "I know you like that one, but it has stains, rips, and looks like you're wearing a sack."

Gwen knew it was true. "It's still my favorite."

"Maybe the blue will become your new favorite."

Gwen chose to leave her clothing choices to her sister. Lilah cared much more about that sort of thing, and she always knew what to do. Gwen focused on gathering the books she would need, her sketchbook, and her notes.

"It really doesn't bother you then?" her sister asked, seemingly out of the blue.

"What?"

"Going into trade."

Gwen looked up to see her sister was speaking delicately, as if Lilah knew the words might upset her. They didn't. They just confused her.

"I want an independent fortune. If I cannot inherit it, then it must be found another way."

Lilah nodded as if that were the normal way of thinking which it was not. Even Gwen knew she was unusual in this.

"There's nothing wrong with you," her sister persisted. "You're perfect, titled, and have a good dowry. You could marry a man with money."

"After a dozen Seasons, I believe I've seen my options in that regard. An independent fortune is my choice."

"Of course, of course. But..." Lilah busied herself by placing the blue gown neatly into the portmanteau. "People will look down on you for it. It will damage your reputation. His as well."

She knew it was true. For some strange reason, the aristocracy seemed to prize lazy men who inherited their wealth and did nothing but enjoy it. And of course Lilah would be well aware of the *ton's* thoughts. She was constantly reminded that as a by-blow, she didn't measure up to their standards.

Gwen, on the other hand, thought the aristocracy remarkably stupid. She found Lord Sayres' industry attractive. His mind was constantly working—just as hers was—and that made him a man of action. Assuming they could find a way to communicate their ideas to one another, she had very high hopes for their business. She just had to accept the increased speed at which they were doing things.

Speaking of which, his lordship was due in fifteen minutes and Gwen had no desire to make him wait. She looked over at the carefully packed portmanteau. Lilah had done a much better job than Gwen ever would.

"You're perfect in every way too, you know," Gwen said softly. "I hate that I'm leaving you just when I said I'd—"

"Hush." Her sister came forward and clasped Gwen's hands. "You cannot solve my problems for me."

"Not without a fortune of my own."

"But you can change that hideous gown. Lord Sayres will be quite put off if he has to see you wearing that for the entire trip."

Gwen looked down at herself. "But it's my travelling gown. It's comfortable, it doesn't restrict—"

Lilah looked at her steadily. "Don't you want to be in your best looks for him?"

"Why? We are not showing off the flowers yet. He needs me for my knowledge of botany, not my gown."

"Because you like him. Because you kissed him—"

"By accident."

"Because he waltzed with you in the kitchen and you enjoyed it immensely."

Trust Lilah to know that already, for all that it happened barely more than an hour ago.

"Aren't you a little interested in Lord Sayres? In a romantic fashion?"

Gwen worked very hard to keep her expression calm. It was true that she had revisited the memory of their impromptu kiss several times, most especially at night. She relived it in every detail, re-examined what had led up to it, what they'd said and how she had felt in his arms. She touched her lips and wondered what it would be like to feel his mouth against hers again. She played with the memory like she played with her plant sketches. She analyzed them and wondered what would happen if the tiniest thing changed.

And she already knew that she'd do the same with the memory of their waltz. Hadn't she already spent several minutes examining the feel of his hand about her waist when she should have been sorting through her botany books?

Was that romance? Perhaps. For her part at least. But Lord Sayres was a notorious flirt. Even she knew that what a man considered romance was vastly different from a woman's dreams. And even if a fraction of what Aunt Isabelle said was true, then she would be well served to keep her heart and her fantasies to herself.

"I don't read too much into a single dance or any kiss, especially since he apologized directly afterwards. Isn't it the nature of some men to be free with their attentions?"

They both knew it was true and so Lilah nodded and closed up the portmanteau. But she was unable to keep silent. "I still wish you would consider him. He's upset your days and you've never seemed happier."

Gwen bit her lip and looked at her sister. "You know how hard it is for me to talk to people," she said. "You know how I have tried and tired, but they always laugh at me. They think I don't see it, but I do."

"Of course, I know," said Lilah as she grasped Gwen's hands.

"Lord Sayres is different. He doesn't laugh, and he explained about winking. I know it's a silly thing, but no one has ever explained it to me before."

Her sister smiled as she pressed a kiss into Gwen's hands. "That sounds like you like him."

"Of course, I like him. I wouldn't be going to Lincolnshire if I didn't. But..."

"But what?" Lilah squeezed Gwen's fingers. "Come now, tell me everything."

"But is that romance?" she said. "Or am I merely happy to have someone new who will talk with me? Someone who understands and does not laugh?"

Lilah was silent. Gwen could not read her expression, but then Lilah always kept her thoughts to herself. In the end, she pulled Gwen into an impulsive hug.

"You will make the right choice, Gwen. You're the smartest person I've ever known."

"But I'm not smart with people."

"You're smart enough," Lilah said. "You just need more time in his company."

Gwen wasn't sure, but there wasn't time to argue as they both heard a carriage ride up to the house. Lilah's eyes widened as she quickly tugged on Gwen's gown.

"Hurry. Let me help you change out of that awful dress."

"But—"

"Do it for me, since I shall not be wearing a pretty dress anywhere without you to accompany me."

It was guilt that made her agree, but it was worth it when she saw the gleam in Lord Sayres's eyes as she descended the stairs. He was probably happy that she was ready and would not make him late.

They had a very long way to go. But she imagined that he thought she looked very fine and that lifted her spirits. Which was very uncharacteristic of her, though she refused to examine the feeling. There were plenty of other things with which to occupy her thoughts.

First was the loading up of the carriage and the unfamiliar crest on the side door. It was not Lord Sayres's emblem, she was sure. He must have noticed her looking because he answered without her having to ask.

"I borrowed Aaron's carriage."

She frowned. "Lord Ares from the masquerade?"

"The very same. He lends me the use of his conveyance and in return I give him excellent advice on where to invest his money."

She arched her brows. "And will he be buying daffodils?"

"Goodness no! Aaron prefers a solid, boring investment. Flowers would be much too risky for him. Going without an umbrella on a sunny day is an uncomfortable stretch for him." He chuckled as he spoke, and she heard affection in his voice. "Besides," he added as he held open the carriage door for her, "I want to keep all the profits for us."

After her conversation with Lilah, she should have been excited about the pile of money they were about to make. About how flowers were a difficult product, but that they would find a way to see it work. Instead, she was thinking about how the sunlight hit his hair and turned it into a bronze halo about his face. About how he never smelled rank and that she'd noticed an ink stain on his shirtsleeve. Far from dissuading her from him, the dark spot made her smile. All of her dresses sported ink stains, and she thought that made them two of a kind.

Better yet, after Webster climbed into the carriage, Lord Sayres surprised her by joining them inside the well-appointed interior. It made sense. There wasn't another horse around for him to use. Where else would he sit? It was just that her brother always chose to ride postilion rather than sit in a stuffy carriage all day with the women. She couldn't stop herself from smiling when he dropped down on the seat across from her.

"You look remarkably happy for a woman about to spend nearly two days in a carriage," he commented.

She felt her cheeks flush, but didn't wish to admit that the idea of such close quarters with Lord Sayres was indeed stirring her imagination. She knew that they might hate each other by the end of their travels. But at the moment, the prospect of time with the man set her heart to pumping. Whatever would they discuss? All Mama wanted to talk about was fashion and parties. And Lilah would never force anything on anyone, much less a change of topic. What would his lordship want to discuss?

The carriage started with a jerk and their journey began. Gwen had her sketchbooks handy, as well as a favorite tome on botany that she would read until the motion of the carriage gave her a headache. But for the moment, she was filled with curiosity about how Lord Sayres would spend the intervening hours between London and Lincolnshire.

She didn't wait in suspense for long. As soon as they were moving, he leaned back against the squabs with a sigh and let his eyes drift shut.

Gwen gasped. "You're going to sleep?"

"No," he said, though his eyes remained closed. "Though it has been an enormous strain getting everything set in motion so quickly. I am merely relishing a moment of rest." He blew out a breath. "You would never guess the difficulties I have had just this morning."

"Beyond finding Mr. Callatos?"

He arched his brows, though again, without opening his eyes. "Pietro was the easiest of my problems." He exhaled in a long slow sigh. The kind that usually prefaced a long, snoring nap.

He was going to sleep. Disappointment cut at her, and she grabbed her book with an irritated grumble. She must have made more noise than she intended because when she looked up, he was watching her with an amused expression.

"Did that tome offend you in some way?"

"What? The book?"

"You seemed remarkably displeased with it."

"It's a book. How could it bother me? If I didn't like it, I wouldn't have brought it."

"Very sensible of you." There was a lightness in his tone that bothered her, and she glared at him. He responded by raising his brows in an unspoken question.

"You're teasing me," she said. "And I don't like it."

"You don't like being teased?"

"No, I don't." Even she could hear the childish petulance in her voice, and so she changed her words. "What I mean is, I don't like being teased when I don't understand it."

"Ah, well that is different. I don't suppose anyone would enjoy that."

"My brother and sisters often laughed at something I said or did. It never made any sense to me."

"And no one explained?"

"Lilah did eventually. And even then, I thought their reasons remarkably stupid."

"Truly? What were they?"

"It usually was because I wanted to share an interest of mine with them. Insects, plants, even gardening, anything but fashion. They found my comments funny."

"Well I shall be happy to listen to all manner of botany discussions…later."

"You needn't bother. I know there are few people who share my interests." She waved at him, prepared to be magnanimous. "You must be terribly fatigued. I won't mind if you sleep."

"Thank you," he said. "But I have things I would like to discuss with you, if you are amenable."

Finally! Intelligent discussion! She sat up straighter. "Please, I have a passing understanding of a variety of subjects and detailed knowledge of several more. Though I warn you, I have some very specific opinions regarding female education. I do not think our current method serves anyone very well."

"My goodness, that does sound intriguing. But for the moment, I have something else in mind."

"Yes?"

He grinned at her. "Fashion."

She gaped at him. She could hardly believe he had just said such a thing to her. And as she stared at him, he burst out laughing.

"My word, but you should see your face."

She pressed her hands to her cheeks and was hard put not to curl them into fists. Of all the nerve. To think that he could laugh at her—

"Don't be upset, Lady Gwen. Perhaps I was teasing you a little, but only a little. My fashion question has to do with our daffodils. I wished to ask you about colors. Our flowers are yellow upon yellow, meaning yellow petals—"

"And a yellow trumpet," she finished for him. "Of the exact same color. Or nearly the same."

"Exactly. But there are a few different varieties it seems, some blooming later than others."

She nodded. She had gleaned that much from her studies. Daffodils did come in a variety of colors, but she thought the Lincolnshire daffodils were the brightest of the lot.

"I had thought to order a silk in pale yellow for you. As if your gown was a further expansion of the flower, but I begin to think that so much yellow would be overpowering."

"And horrifying," she said. "No matter how beautiful the fabric, it cannot compete with the natural beauty of a living thing." She tilted her head. "What time of day did you find the flowers most beautiful?"

"I beg your pardon?"

"When you were a boy with your mother. Did she never speak of her favorite time to wander in her garden? Was it at dawn? The heat of the afternoon? Anything like that?"

He looked off to the side as he searched his memory. "Once, when was I boy, I wanted to hunt ghosts." His lips curved into a smile. "One of the village boys told me that the woods near our home were haunted. I thought it was his older brother making scary noises."

She had no trouble imagining him running around the woods in search of larger, scarier boys. He seemed completely fearless to her. "Was it one of the older boys?"

He laughed. "I have no idea. My mother caught me outside. It was a beautiful night, and she was walking."

"So she enjoyed the moonlight?"

"That night she did, and we walked together through the daffodils. It was like they glowed. The moonlight made it seem as if the sun had settled in her flowerbed and we walked upon its surface."

"How old were you?"

He shook his head. "Eight, maybe? I'm not sure. It was before I went away to school and before she got sick." There was a moment when his expression turned sad, but it quickly passed. Then he focused on her. "You have the right of it," he said firmly. "A dark dress, say midnight blue, will truly show the flower. And every time I look at you, I shall think of walking at midnight through the blossoms."

She smiled. "I hadn't been thinking so poetically. But it sounds good to me."

He echoed her expression. "I suppose you have brought out the poet in me." Then he leaned back onto the squabs. "Now it is your turn."

"What?"

"Come come, I wager you have sketched the transport boxes in several different designs. Don't you want to discuss them with me? I'm afraid I have been too scattered to give them proper attention. But we have the sunlight and a very long trip ahead of us." He made a grasping gesture with his near hand. "Hand them over."

He had the right of it. She had wanted to discuss her thoughts with him from the beginning, but she hadn't expected him to want to see her sketches. "They're not a finished design."

"Of course not. We haven't discussed them yet."

She nodded and opened her sketchbook. She knew from experience to only show the best design. People got bored afterwards. So she opened to the appropriate page and turned it to him.

"I think that will be best for carrying cut blooms to London."

She watched as his face tightened and he studied the design from all angles. "Is this the only design?"

"There are many more, but not—"

"May I see?"

He had his hand poised, ready to turn the page, but he waited until she agreed. She appreciated that he didn't just paw through her sketchbook without waiting for her permission. So she agreed.

"You may look, but remember, these are only ideas—"

"I understand."

She doubted it, but in this she erred. He flipped backwards through the pages and began asking questions. Why this over that? Did she consider such a thing? Oh yes, he could see that she had. But what about this? Oh, that's clever.

On and on, and he never seemed to tire. And while her considerations had simply been for the flowers themselves, he thought about the workers assembling the crates, the ease with which they could lift and carry them. A dozen ideas discussed, sketched, and discarded again. It was awkward trying to talk to him across the carriage with him facing and her trying to see things upside down. Besides, Webster had fallen asleep and was pushing her knees into Gwen as she sank on the squabs.

"Give me your hand please," Gwen said at one point.

Lord Sayres looked up from the current sketch with a frown. "What? Oh, certainly."

He extended his hand and she gripped it tight, pulling herself upright such that she could spin around and drop down beside him. It was a tight maneuver, but it was necessary, especially as she wanted to see what he had written along the edge of the latest design thoughts.

She landed with an "umph," then had to adjust her skirt from where it had twisted beneath her. Eventually she had it set and she blew out a sigh of relief. Webster was no longer pressing her knee hard into her thigh. No, instead she had the whole of Lord Sayres's thigh hot against hers. His arm and shoulder knocked against hers until he shifted such that his arm lay behind her on the squabs. Indeed, given the confines of the carriage, they pressed rather intimately together.

"Is that better?" he asked.

"If you're uncomfortable, I can go back," she said. "I just thought this would be easier than trying to look upside down at the page."

"I am most comfortable," he drawled. "And you?"

She was hot because her cheeks were burning from the flirtatious look he gave her. It flustered her. Certainly gentlemen had flirted with her before, but this was the first time such a smoldering look had ever affected her. It was an invitation to things she'd been thinking about already. How could she not? The last time they were this close together, they'd been dancing. Or kissing.

Fortunately, he didn't press closer or even keep his gaze on her for long. Within a few moments, he turned back to the sketchbook and she was able to breathe again. Which was a relief and a disappointment all at once.

He began asking questions again and before long they were deep in discussion. They finished on the design, proceeded next to his plans for this Season, then the next year's Season, then the one beyond that. He had ideas for the next five to ten years depending on how quickly and how popular their business became. It was enough to fill the time through two changes of horses and supper. Her head was swimming by the time she climbed into the carriage after their third change of horses, but it was only after his explanation of the Dutch tulip market of the 1600s that she cried done.

She could take no more discussion, no more money talk, and certainly no more sketching because the light was gone. He was better than she at all of this business stuff, and all she wished to do was climb into a bed in absolute silence with only the smell of her plants to disturb her.

He chuckled. "Then it is a good thing that we will be stopping soon. I declare that we have made good progress this day on all counts."

They certainly had in all but one. After today, she wanted absolutely nothing to do with the business of flowers ever again. But she couldn't say that. She'd committed herself to this venture after all, but he had exhausted her.

"I think, my lord, that I shall rest my eyes until our last stop."

"An excellent suggestion," he agreed. "I think I shall do the same."

And so he stretched out his long legs, and she was forced to tilt toward him for that was the only room left to her.

"Would it upset you if I put my arm here?" he asked as he extended it behind her head.

"I don't mind," she said. It wasn't a proper position, but Webster was napping again. She wouldn't see to object. And Gwen did like smelling his scent.

"Close your eyes," he said. "I shall catch you if you fall."

He adjusted until she was all but laying in his arms. Definitely not proper.

"Don't forget," he mused softly near her ear. "You're on the shelf now and your harridan of a maid is right here to protect you. This has been a long day and we'll have another one tomorrow. Whatever position we land in is perfectly proper."

"That's not exactly true."

"It's not exactly wrong either."

She acknowledged his point in the only way possible. She shut her eyes and relaxed against him. His body felt strong beneath her, and she felt very safe. Her very last thought was, if one day together had brought a waltz and now a nap tucked against him, what would tomorrow bring?

It was the wrong thought. She should have been wondering about when they stopped for the night. But she didn't realize her error until long after they'd settled into an inn. Indeed, she didn't think about much of anything until she was wide awake at midnight with a dozen conflicting feelings crashing about in her thoughts.

There was no hope for it. When this happened to her in the country, her only solution was to head outdoors and walk the feelings away. And so she donned her half boots and a cloak. Five minutes later, she had escaped into a gorgeous night in an unfamiliar village. But oh, it was so wonderful to be outside and alone with her thoughts.

Chapter Fifteen

WHAT THE HELL was wrong with him?

Jackson kicked at a stone outside the inn and cursed when he realized it was an immovable tree root and not something he could fling far away from him. The jolt up his spine increased his ire and he leaned against the tree to stare out at the village in moonlight.

Pretty. But not as pretty as Lady Gwen.

He inhaled, trying to overwhelm the scent of her body pressed against his. Her hair had sported a lemony scent that remained in his memory even as he absorbed the smells coming from the nearby mews.

He wandered away from the stable in search of quiet. He'd already burned through his plans for their business and was frankly, heartily sick of the details. He was sick of it, except that he couldn't stop himself from remembering the way she had argued with him passionately about the way to harvest daffodil bulbs for sale. He hadn't the slightest information on what was best and would follow her advice to the letter. But he hadn't been able to resist poking at her, questioning her decisions, all while watching the animation on her face and feeling the strength in her body as she moved against him.

She'd merely been gesturing to add emphasis to her words, but they'd been so close together in the carriage that lust had surged forward with every shift of her body. And that was nothing compared to what happened when she relaxed against him in sleep. As she had relaxed, her body had sunk against his and he had cradled her as he might a newborn babe. He kept his hands scrupulously honest. He did no more than pull her hair from her face when a lock slipped down over her luscious mouth. But in his thoughts, he had done so many things with her.

In his mind's eye, he had caressed her breasts, pinched her nipples, and drew sounds of delight from her mouth. He had kissed her face, her breasts, and between her thighs. And then he had spread her open and lost himself in her sweetness while she welcomed him with cries of delight and hands that pulled him closer, harder, faster.

Such fantasies had tortured him while he kept himself from even the smallest caress. He knew if he once touched her, he would take more and more.

He was not a man who indulged his appetites. Not since Isabelle had shown him how depraved people could become. He enjoyed physical release as well as any man. But he was not one to let such a thing overpower his reason.

Until Lady Gwen. He wanted her with a hunger that stunned him. It was a need that drew him from his bed to pace the dark countryside as a way to prevent him from sneaking into her bedroom and taking her to a place where he could indulge his fantasies until they were both sated. It made no sense to him. She was not the type of woman to attract him. He liked soft-spoken women who were easy to be around and who were content to let him do as he willed, whatever he willed. Obviously, he preferred quiet, biddable women of leisure and Lady Gwen was the polar opposite to that.

And right there was a problem. Lady Gwen would not be ignored. She challenged, she questioned, she forced him to think about things he'd only assumed. She exhilarated him, and when he won against her it was a true victory. She listened to reason, accepted logic, and forced him to do the same.

They matched mind for mind, and he desperately wanted to see if they matched body to body. Which was why it was a terribly bad thing for him to turn back toward the inn only to see her step outside.

She was dressed in a sackcloth. That was his only word for it. A large dark thing that gave no idea as to the shape of the woman underneath. It didn't matter. He'd felt her curves as she leaned against him, he'd seen her being fitted for gowns, and he'd undressed her in his mind's eye a thousand times. That ugly dress was simply a tease. Like the wrapping on a birthday present just for him.

He stepped out of the shadows to go to her. She shouldn't be out alone this late at night. Two steps closer, and he heard her cry out in surprise.

"Get away or I'll cut you!"

He jerked backwards not from the knife but from the woman's voice. It wasn't Lady Gwen, and he felt ridiculous thinking that any woman coming out of the inn would be her. No, now that he was near enough for the breeze to carry her scent, he couldn't believe he hadn't seen the dark curls about her face or the fearful twist of her expression.

"My apologies," he murmured. "I thought you were someone else."

"I'm not," she spat, then she rushed by him. He kept moving back, giving the unknown woman as much room as she wanted. And as he moved, he rubbed a hand over his face. He really needed to get Lady Gwen out of his mind.

Then he turned and saw her leaning against that same tree he had accidently kicked when he'd started his rambling. He told himself it could be any woman. Hadn't he just learned that? Except as he watched, the woman tilted her head as if examining a knob on a tree branch. Only Lady Gwen tilted her head just so when looking at a tree. And only she stood with both feet planted as if she expected the world to tilt beneath her.

He came closer, his gaze roving over the shape of her gown. It was the same thing she wore earlier, flowing loosely over her curves but still giving shape to her figure. Normally he noticed her full bosom, but from this angle he could appreciate the length of her legs and the shape of her bottom, especially as a breeze momentarily flattened her gown against her.

"Lady Gwen?"

She gasped and spun around, then she tilted her head again, this time as she inspected him. "Lord Sayres? What are you doing up and about so late?"

"I was about to ask you the same thing."

She shrugged. "I blame it on the nap. I am not usually so sedentary and find myself strangely restless now."

"I was thinking exactly the same thing," he said. Then he extended his arm. "Care for a walk?"

"Only if you swear not to tell Webster that we did. She'll have my ears for wandering around at night."

"Are you prone to nighttime rambles?"

She shrugged. "Only in the country. I am not so bold in London."

"Your secret is safe with me." Her secret, yes. But her person? Her virtue? Maybe not, because as she took his arm, his lust surged again. What things he could do to her in the moonlight. And yet, he held himself back. He was an honorable man who would not take advantage of her just because desire pounded in his veins.

"Mind the rock there," he said as he steered her away from what looked to be a large flat stone. "It's actually a tree root, and I bruised my toes kicking it."

"Do you often kick stones?"

"Only when I can't sleep."

"Then you should be used to bruised toes."

He chuckled, his insides settling at just being with her. He didn't know why. She did not seem like a restful person, but then, neither was he. Their minds churned too fast. But after their heated discussions earlier, it was nice to know they could simply enjoy a moonlit walk together without poking at one another.

After a minute or so in silence, she spoke softly, her words filling the night air with the cadence of her voice. "Are you worried about our daffodils?"

He liked the way she called them "our daffodils." It showed him she was committing to their venture. "No worries, and I am done with making plans for now."

She blew out a breath. "Good. I confess I am tired of the discussion as well. For now."

"So is it the moonlight that draws you outside? Or something else?"

She wrinkled her nose in the most adorable way. "I don't know," she finally said. "I have found myself focusing on all manner of strange things lately. It's unsettling."

Now he was definitely intrigued. He thought her mind was consumed by science and botany. "What strange things?" he prompted when she fell silent.

"Well," she said slowly, "you recall that when we first met, I was in search for a husband."

He nodded. "But you have given that up in favor of making an independent fortune."

"Yes," she agreed slowly. "But I have been imagining myself in five years. I have been pretending what it will be like when our flowers make enough income that my sister and I can live independently."

He'd barely given that idea any thought. His focus had been on establishing a profitable business now. He'd planned out this year and the next. He'd certainly touched on five years and ten, but that had been in the far-off future. He had more than enough to do now.

"What is your conclusion?"

She laughed. "So very many. For example, I should need to buy a home in Lincolnshire, I think. If I am to be of continued use in our venture, then I need to supervise the growing of the flowers, the cutting and the like. We will need a steady crop."

He liked the idea of her in his home village. "Very practical. I applaud this idea."

"I think I could enjoy the challenge. There are several different types of daffodils. I should like to experiment with other kinds, perhaps find some other rare ones. We could sell them all."

They had touched on this in the carriage. "I believe that is an excellent place to expand in the future."

"Yessss," she said slowly and without much conviction.

"You don't sound like that appeals to you."

"It does. I assure you, it definitely does."

"But?" There was certainly hesitation in her voice.

She blew out a breath. "But I find myself still unsettled. That future holds everything I could want in life. Useful work, a lovely home, opportunities to further my interest in botany, but..." Her voice trailed away on a frustrated note. He echoed it. What was bothering her?

"But what? You must tell me. I cannot build a five-year plan for our business without knowing."

She didn't answer. They were walking into a light wood well back from the inn, and she reached up to push a branch out of the way, but she didn't step beneath it. Instead, she looked up at the moon now revealed in the gap between the leaves.

"I am not of a poetical bent, my lord. I think about practical things, about science and how the natural world works. I have even dabbled in astronomy." She lifted her hand from his arm and pointed at the moon. "I know the scientific reasons for the phases of the moon and can cite the differences between a planet and a star in the night sky."

"I know very little about that," he confessed. "As a boy I only thought of the things here on Earth." And as he grew older, the most he thought about the moon was how he could get a beautiful woman naked beneath it.

She looked around them, seeming to inspect every tree branch, every leaf as it was lined in white light. But in the end, she faced him. "My thoughts tonight are not scientific. I am thinking about waltzes and kisses, and I find myself plagued by a single question."

His body tightened with the way she looked at him. Her eyes were wide, and her shoulders slightly hunched. She looked vulnerable and yet hopeful. "What is the question?" he whispered.

"Did our waltz seem…different to you? I know our kiss was an accident borne of enthusiasm, and I have so little to compare it to, but I have waltzed several times. It seemed different to me, and I wondered—"

"If I felt the same?"

She looked up at him and now it was her face touched with silver. Her lips turned dark, and yet he could see every curve. But most of all he saw that her eyes held a magical glow.

"Did it feel special to you?" she whispered.

Desire pounded in his veins, and he pulsed with the need to possess her. He held himself back. He didn't want to frighten her, especially since she was so careful with whom she touched. But how could he resist a woman who asked such a thing? Especially when the answer was so clear.

"Yes," he said, his voice husky. "Yes, it was different. Yes, Lady Gwen, you are special. And yes, I should very much like to kiss you again."

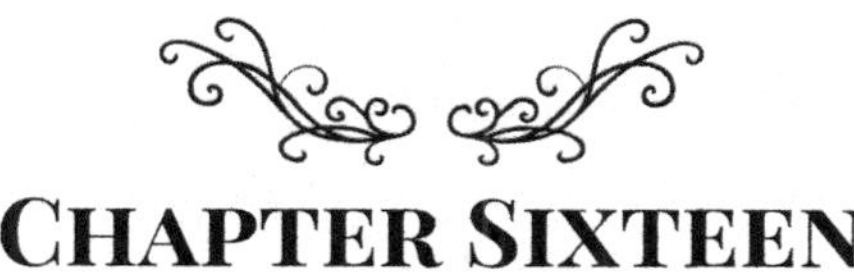

CHAPTER SIXTEEN

GWEN HAD BEEN kissed before. She'd had men come at her too fast. She'd felt their thick lips press against hers as they grabbed her body and pressed against her with too much force, too many smells, and far too much of them coming at her. She knew she was supposed to like it. Girls tittered about their first kisses, and Aunt Isabelle had talked candidly with her about the pleasures of the flesh.

She thought herself singularly odd that she'd never really enjoyed a kiss until Lord Sayres had impulsively kissed her at the dressmakers. She had been happy and already swinging about in his arms. For the first time in her life, she'd seen the kiss coming and hadn't tensed up.

She wanted to repeat that experience exactly to see if it was a fluke. But she wasn't feeling giddy right now, and in the darkness, she was well aware of his larger size and the tension in his body. She heard desire in his voice and felt her pulse increase as he held her gaze.

"Lady Gwen? What are you thinking?"

How did she answer such a question? "I—" Her voice cracked on the word and she had to clear her throat. "You said you want to kiss me again."

"I did."

"You are waiting for my permission?"

"I am."

He could overpower her in a second. He could press her against the tree right here and do whatever he wanted. But he waited, his gaze on her face, his eyes barely illuminated by the moonlight, and yet she felt the intensity as he looked at her.

Her breath shortened and her belly tightened. She felt her toes curl in her half boots, and her mind splintered. She tilted her head back and she wet her lower lip as she thought and thought and thought about everything that was happening. It was as if every one of her senses were sharply alert, and her mind spun from one to another to another in a whirlwind of excitement.

He was leaning closer to her, so close that she smelled the faded scent of his cologne and the sharper musk of his own body. And also her own scent, she realized, as interesting as his.

She wanted him to close the final distance between their mouths, to sweep her up in his emotions as he had before, but they weren't dancing now. They seemed poised in an almost touch, and her lips tingled from his nearness.

This was becoming unbearable. She wanted him to kiss her if only to end the frantic spinning in her thoughts.

"I should like you to kiss me," she said. Then she rushed the next words before he could act. "But quickly, not too hard."

His brows rose but his chin dipped in a slow nod. "A quick, light kiss."

"Yes."

He smiled. "My favorite word."

He leaned in until, at last, their lips touched. She felt his breath mingling with hers as he brushed across her mouth, back and forth and barely there. Her breath caught at the feel, and just when she would have pressed forward for more, he pulled away.

"Like that?" he asked.

"Yes," she said. And no, because she wanted him to do that again, only longer this time.

"Would you like another?"

"Yes."

"Anything different?"

It was as if he'd read her mind, but there was a note in his voice that she'd heard before, and it soured the experience. "Are you making fun of me?"

He pulled back as if shocked. "Of course not!"

His outrage sounded real, but she had a great deal of experience with people laughing at her when they seemed to be saying nice things. She looked away, her gut clenching now as her shoulders hunched. She had done this all wrong.

She started to move away from him, but he held up his hand. He didn't touch her, but it was enough to make her stop.

"Lady Gwen," he said softly, "I was not making fun at all. I like that you can be so specific about your desires. I'm grateful because it makes it easier for me to please you."

"Why?" she whispered.

"Because clear direction makes—"

"Not why is it easier," she huffed. "Why do you want to please me?"

He rocked back on his heels. "That is the purpose of kissing, isn't it? To please one another?"

She frowned. "I thought it was an imitation of the sexual act as a prelude to true intercourse."

"Um, well, I had never thought of it that way before."

Then he held up his elbow, inviting her to take his arm in the most formal of poses. She did, but slowly. Were they to walk again? When her knees still felt week and she could still feel her pulse low in her belly.

"I suppose," he finally said, "that kisses can be both. A prelude to intercourse and an activity enjoyable all on its own."

So she had imagined. They began walking and he kept his steps short to match hers. In the silence, she found the courage to be bold. "Do you mind talking to me frankly about these things? I have many questions, and I can only find a limited amount of information at the lending library."

"I should think so." Then he tilted his head toward her. "What do you wish to know?"

So many things, but she wasn't bold enough to talk about all of it. She would just start with kisses. "Have you ever felt repulsed by a kiss?" That was uppermost in her mind because no one had ever spoken of such a thing to her. She needed to know if she was unusual.

"Certainly, I have," he answered, to her intense relief. "That is a sure sign that you should run away from the perpetrator and never be alone with him again." He paused a moment as he slanted his gaze at her. "Did—"

"Not yours," she rushed to say.

He nodded. "I am relieved to hear it."

She chuckled. He was speaking in the same tone as he might say, *I am relieved that it is not snowing today.* She found it exceedingly helpful, and she relaxed more as they continued to walk.

"I should like to know the correct way to kiss," she ventured. "When the man's tongue intrudes, am I to push back? Should I open my mouth as wide as possible and allow it?"

"I believe gentlemen prefer enthusiasm during kissing."

She nodded as if that made sense. "But what *exactly* does enthusiasm entail? What should I do so as to demonstrate it?"

"I don't really know. I have never thought of it that way before." He turned to look at her more closely. "Do you analyze all of your actions like this? How to *appear* enthusiastic? Happy? Sad? Don't you just feel them?"

"I do feel them," she said. "But I don't seem to respond as most people expect. So I have to learn what others expect so as to—"

"Mimic it?" He shook his head. "I don't want you to mimic anything with me. Ever. I want you to react however you feel, no matter if you think I might be offended or not."

She stepped back from him, both startled and pleased by his emphatic statement. "You are very kind, my lord, but truly, this is not unusual for me. I do not know how others learn to act normally, but it has always required specific study for me. It is still hard sometimes to know when and how to laugh, for example."

"Is that why you keep to yourself so much? Why you are so against being the one to wear our flower?"

"Yes." Hard to say that one word, but the darkness helped. It hid her burning cheeks.

"Lady Gwen—" he began, but she cut him off. Best to confess it all while she felt brave enough to say so.

"I am incredibly intelligent," she said. "Everyone says so."

"Of course, you are."

"It is because I have had to learn how to study and memorize. I watch what everyone else does, and I repeat it." She took a deep breath. "It's my darkest secret. I'm afraid I'm not even remotely smart. I can't do what everyone else does naturally. I don't laugh right, I don't speak correctly."

"That must make society very hard."

"There are ways to cover. Sometimes I am bold and laugh about my oddities. Other times, I am just—"

"Tired of working so hard all the time?"

She looked up at him in surprise. "Yes. How did you know?"

"We all have difficulties of one form or another. And society is unforgiving of the slightest mistake. I may not understand how hard it has been for you, but I certainly know how exhausting it is to constantly monitor my words and actions so as to maintain a place in society."

"But you're a man, and a confident one at that."

"I wasn't born an adult man. I have made mistakes and had to learn just like everyone else."

It wasn't the same. It was ten times harder for a woman than a man. And for her, sometimes life seemed like an insurmountable mountain where even the smallest step became too much.

He stopped walking and turned to face her directly. "I can see you don't believe me."

"But I do," she said. At least she knew he believed his words.

He smiled at her. "I thought we agreed you wouldn't lie about anything with me."

"That goes both ways, my lord. Do you honestly think you struggle to move about in society? That it is hard for you?"

He opened his mouth to argue, and then shut it with an audible click. In time, he shrugged. "You are the smartest person I have ever met, even if you don't know when to laugh or how to kiss."

"But I should like to learn," she said, hope creeping into her voice. Then she dared touch his hand. "Would you teach me?"

"How to kiss?"

"Yes." Then when he did not answer, she rushed to calm what was likely his biggest obstacle. "I am on the shelf, you know, and if we can walk about after dark together, then we can certainly engage in a little bit of scandalous behavior. If neither of us tells, then we should be able to keep my reputation safe." She stopped, trying to read his expression. She couldn't. It was as blank to her as a new piece of paper. "You needn't fear my being upset if I fail to learn. I practice things a great deal before I am proficient at anything. I won't blame you." Again she stopped and tried to guess at his thoughts. He was watching her carefully. His face wasn't pinched in displeasure, but neither was it relaxing as if reassured. "My lord—"

"Lady Gwen," he interrupted, and she fell silent. "Do you like lemon ices?"

She blinked. "What?"

"Do you like lemon ices? They serve them at Gunter's. Have you ever had them?"

She didn't know what that had to do with anything, but she answered nonetheless. "Yes, I do."

"Is there a sweet that you prefer to that? A tart, perhaps, or a pie?"

She frowned. "I prefer apple pie, one hour out of the oven with cinnamon on top."

"Did you have to study to know that?"

"No. I just tasted a variety of sweets and picked my favorite." If he wanted, she could detail that she preferred hot to cold. She liked the crunch of the crust over the melt of the ices. And sometimes—when it was very hot—she preferred an ice to a pie, but she didn't want to over-answer his question, so she kept her thoughts to herself.

"Are you categorizing the things you prefer in pie over an ice?"

He was so perceptive. "Yes."

"Then perhaps you don't need to learn how to kiss. You merely need to experience a wide variety of kisses and pick the kind you like."

She pursed her lips, considering this possibility. "Is that how you did it?"

"I believe it is how everyone does it."

It made sense. "Pity that women aren't generally allowed that kind of exploration."

"But now that you are on the shelf—"

"You will let me learn?"

"I shall do my poor best." There was a dryness in his tone, but she wasn't offended. Indeed, it made her tease him back. A little.

"You are accounted very experienced. I have every confidence you will be up to the task."

He grinned. "Perhaps, but I get the feeling you will be a very exacting student."

Chapter Seventeen

His teasing set Gwen at ease, and so when they came to the next tree, she reached up and grabbed a branch. It was a sturdy oak—though somewhat young—and she used it to stop their forward momentum. Or perhaps just to have something solid to grip. And then she turned to face him.

"Will you kiss me now?"

He seemed to contemplate that for a minute. "I'm trying to decide which would be the best to start."

"What did you conclude?"

"We'll start as you asked. Quick and light."

She nodded, her lips already tingling in readiness. He leaned forward—just his head—and she held up a hand. "But I suppose we have already tried that. Perhaps you could try a little longer this time."

"An excellent suggestion," he said, and she detected no mockery in his words. But rather than close the distance between their mouths, he held up his hand. "I should like to touch your face too. Would that be allowed?"

She shook her head. "The best scientific method requires changing one variable at a time. So the first kiss can be of longer duration. The second one can add touching."

"A sound decision." Then he smiled, and before she could question his expression, he said, "I am not teasing you. I am finding this a great deal of fun."

"Really? But we have not even begun." Though, she had to admit, she was feeling very energized.

"Even so." Then he straightened. "First test. Or second if you count the earlier kiss."

She did, but she didn't have time to say that. He leaned down and she stretched up. Their lips touched and tingles seemed to shoot from their point of connection straight into her blood. He kept the pressure light as he moved across her mouth. Their shared breath seemed to heat the space between them, and she was grateful for the cooler air when he finally pulled back. Grateful, and also sad, because that had been fun.

Thankfully, she still had a grip on the branch because her body swayed toward him as he pulled back. He took a deep breath as he looked at her, and she struggled to catalogue her own reactions while also wondering what he thought.

"Did you like that?" he asked, his voice rough.

"Yes," she said, her mind spinning again as she realized her heart was beating fast and her breasts felt heavy.

"Are you ready for the next test?" he asked as he raised his hand.

She smiled. "Yes."

He did not wear a glove, and so she felt the callouses in his fingertips as he stroked her cheek and along her jaw. His touch was very gentle, and she was surprised to feel her head moving deeper into his caress. Before long he was cupping her jaw as his mouth descended. The caress of his lips was exquisite this time, and she leaned into it despite her plan to keep the kiss light. Not only that, but she opened her mouth to his.

He drew back, though his hand remained on her cheek. She noted that he breathed quickly, as did she. And her grip on the branch had loosened, though she pulled strongly on it now to keep herself from swaying into him.

"How far do you want to go with this?" he rasped. "I would like to use my tongue now."

She swallowed and nodded but worry had her pulling back. "What do I do when you…?"

"How about this? I shall go slow and you can test what you like. That way you can do nothing at all or whatever you want?"

That was not a good scientific method. Clear tests with beginnings and endings were her general preference, but she appreciated the efficiency of his suggestion. Not to mention that her mind was a bit unfocused right then. She didn't much care for clear delineation in his kisses. She knew only that she wanted more.

But instead of proceeding, he reached up and gently disentangled her hand from the branch. And when she started to ask, he coaxed her deeper into the shadows.

"This way you can touch me if you want," he said. "And if you lean back against the tree trunk—"

"I won't worry about my balance."

He nodded. "I was going to say you would be more comfortable, but I suppose it is one and the same."

She agreed and she happily rested her spine along the tree trunk. "Where can I touch you?"

His smile was wide as he answered. "Wherever you want."

"But—"

He drew her hand up to his lips, kissing the tips of her fingers. "Wherever you want," he repeated. "And may I…" He swallowed, then shook his head. "I will keep my caresses to your face."

"You want to touch more," she said. She was not completely ignorant. Aunt Isabelle had described the sexual act in detail. The lady had claimed that certain areas of the body were very sensitive to stimulation.

He blew out a breath. "I want to do everything with you." His voice was heavy, and he kneaded her palm where he still held her hand. She felt the strength in his grip, and it added to the sizzle in her blood.

Suddenly, she realized that she wanted it. She wanted to try these things with him. She wanted to feel his hands everywhere and to let his organ penetrate her. All those things that Aunt Isabelle had described held far more interest, now that she thought of Lord Sayres as the man who would do those things to her. With her. She was dizzy with the thoughts that spun through her mind.

"I will not," he rasped. "Don't be afraid. I won't harm you, I swear."

She smiled. Was this the first time he hadn't read her thoughts? "I'm not afraid." Then she took a moment to truly process that thought. She wasn't cringing away from him. She wasn't measuring her actions while constantly watching to see if he reacted badly. "You have never laughed at me." Odd how freeing that statement was. "You and Lilah are the only two."

He frowned. "Surely the rest of your family has been kind."

She shrugged. "Children are often cruel, brothers and sisters especially."

"Well, yes. I suppose I was terrible to my sisters at times."

"They haven't been mean to me in years."

"And your parents?"

"They love me, and my father was more tolerant of my oddities than anyone else. But Mama especially has tried to teach me how to go on in society. It has made our relationship difficult."

"I'm sorry," he said.

"Thank you," she responded. "But my life is much easier than most. And they all love me, so I have found contentment." Or she had, until his kisses had set her to wanting more. She tilted her face up to his. And now that the tree supported her, she could touch his face as he had hers. She explored the rough texture of his cheek, the hard cut of his jaw, and she rolled her thumb over his lips. The texture was uneven, the shape interesting. Then he abruptly caught her thumb between his teeth and bit lightly down before his tongue teased the pad of her thumb.

She gasped in surprise, but she did not draw back. Indeed, he pursed his lips and sucked gently while her belly clenched in reaction.

"I think I would like you to touch more than my face."

He licked her thumb one last time before releasing it. And then he leaned in close, with one arm braced above her head. "I will stop whenever you want. You have only to say so."

"And you to me," she said as she let her hand trail over his chest and up to his shoulders.

He grinned. "Are you ready?"

Yes, yes, and yes! But rather than speak too enthusiastically, she simply nodded her head and waited with growing anticipation as he leaned down to her.

He started lightly, as he had all the other times. She was the one who opened her mouth to him, and she leaned into his kiss because she liked the pressure on her lips. She felt his free hand stroke her jaw and the length of her neck, flattening out over her shoulder before trailing down her arm. But it was his tongue that consumed her thoughts. He pushed into her mouth slightly at first before withdrawing. And then further and deeper in.

She tried to remain still. She wanted to start by simply receiving his attentions and observing her reactions. But that lasted a very short time. Soon she was pushing against his tongue. She wanted to try pushing forward and back as he did, but she couldn't keep a steady rhythm in mind. It was all tongue and teeth and angling her head.

And then he pulled away, his breath quick. Hers was faster, her chest lifting and lowering as she inhaled. Her mouth felt swollen and wet, and then suddenly, there was a lightning shock that burst from her nipple to her whole body.

His hand was on her breast, she realized, and the play of his thumb across the peak had everything clenching to his rhythm.

She looked down at what he was doing as if mesmerized. She felt his mouth at her temple.

"Too much?"

"No."

"Too little?"

"I don't know."

He widened his fingers until he cupped her full breast. Then he shifted his stance such that he had both hands free. He cupped them both then, while she breathed deep enough to press her chest into his hands. Her head dropped back against the tree trunk and she felt herself arch even further into his hold.

"Too much?" he asked again.

"No." It felt so good. Never had she experienced such wonderful sensations. She stretched her arms above her head, giving her breasts to him as she closed her eyes.

"More?"

"Yes."

Such things he did to her breasts while she stretched against the tree. At his urging, she wrapped her hands around two branches, and then he gently unbuttoned the top of her gown. She hadn't bothered with stays on her midnight ramble. Just a shift beneath her gown, which was easily untied. Soon her breasts were bared to him, and she tilted her head to watch his large hands upon her flesh. His hands were tan, his fingers long. And in the moonlight, her skin appeared silver white.

"Yes?" he asked, and she had no idea if he meant the question specifically. Yes to the way he pinched her nipples making her gasp? Yes to the way his hands molded her breasts, making them feel a chaotic roll of sensation? Or just yes to more, more, more?

Whatever he meant, her answer was the same. "Yes."

Which is when he dropped to one knee before her. He put his mouth to her left nipple and sucked it in as he had sucked in her thumb earlier. She met his rhythm this time. Steady pulls that had her body rolling toward him. Her hands lost their grip and she dropped them to his shoulders. She gripped him hard there while he set his hands on her hips to steady her. And still his mouth did such things to her nipple.

She wanted to cry out but couldn't. She wanted him to pull harder, do more, do something, but she didn't know what. And before she could frame the demand, he broke away.

He tilted his head, pressing his face to her belly. She felt his breath saw in and out while his hands tightened on her hips.

She said nothing. How could she? She had no words, and to her shock, no real thought. Pure sensation as her heart continued to pound and her breath came in quick pants.

"Lady Gwen," he said, his voice sounding raw.

"Yes?"

His hands tightened in a quick spasm before he relaxed. His breath was evening out, though his broad shoulders seemed hard with tension.

"I will walk you back now." He pulled back. "You should cover up."

"What? Why?" She didn't want to stop. Not now, when she was feeling such things for the very first time.

"Because I swore I wouldn't hurt you."

"You haven't!"

"I said I would keep you safe."

"I am."

He pulled back from her, his hands leaving her hips at the very last moment. And then he slowly straightened to his full height. She watched him move while her breasts suddenly felt cold. Oh hell, she'd done it again. She'd done something odd, and he was pulling away. She raised her hands to cover up again, but he stopped her.

"Please," he rasped.

She froze. "What?"

"Wait a moment. Let me look."

She let her hands drop as she looked at his face and then down at herself. Her breasts were bared, her nipples tight. The moonlight made her skin bright and he extended his hands toward her, but stopped short of connecting.

"You're so beautiful," he murmured.

She looked down at herself then back up to him. There was no denying the hunger in his expression.

"You like looking at me?" she asked. She wasn't confused. She was interested. After all, he was helping her to learn what she liked. It was only fair that she learn what he enjoyed.

"Yes," he said.

She smiled, feeling a bit daring. "Is there a pose you prefer?"

His laugh came sharp then was quickly muffled. "Try a few out. Let me see."

So she did. She stretched her hands up high and arched her back. She left one up as the other dropped to her hip. She moved in a systematic way through different arm positions, different angles of her spine, even different tilts to her pelvis. She had once as a child done a study of flexibility. She had wanted to see the limits to the angles her body could move. She didn't go through all of them now. Indeed, she merely played with a few while he watched with flared nostrils and a steady regard.

Then she stopped and asked, "Well?"

"What?" His gaze rose to her face slowly.

"What was your favorite?"

"All of them. Absolutely every single one."

That wasn't logical, but it pleased her nonetheless. Then he tugged on one of the ribbons of her shift.

"Cover up now," he said. "I need to get you back inside."

She did as he bid, tying her ribbons and rebuttoning her dress. She waited until they were walking back to the inn to ask the question that had burned in her thoughts.

"What exactly did I do wrong? I want to learn."

She felt his jerk in reaction. "What? You did nothing wrong."

"Then why did you stop?"

"Because I swore to keep you safe and taking your virginity against a tree would be breaking my word."

She processed his words. "I would have told you to stop."

"Are you sure?"

She thought about it. She recalled how she had given herself over to the sensations, how her mind had stopped cataloging everything and had just grown silent as she experienced it all. And she knew that her breasts were still heavy, her gait languid, and every brush of her dress against her skin shot off sparks of feelings. If he had continued, would she have stopped him?

"Perhaps not."

He didn't respond. They were nearly at the inn, and as they neared, she lowered her voice.

"Was it hard?"

"What?"

"To stop."

"Very."

"Do you think we could try again? At some other time?"

He blew out a breath. "Lady Gwen, we are playing with fire. I am not always so honorable."

"I trust you."

"I know." It didn't sound like he thought that was a good thing.

"And I am on the shelf."

He groaned. "Don't dismiss yourself like that. You are much too vital to put yourself away."

"It is a fact," she countered. She was a spinster now and she had found an unexpected freedom in the appellation. Meanwhile, they reached the inn door which he opened slowly. Fortunately, the hinges were well oiled, and they made no noise. As they stepped inside the building, she whispered to him. "You will tell me if you wish to continue, won't you?"

He didn't answer as they climbed the stairs.

"Lord Sayres?"

"Jackson," he said. "My name is Jackson."

"I know," she said, but it wasn't proper for her to address him as such. Appropriate forms of address had been drilled into her from the moment she could speak.

"And yes," he said as he pressed a finger to her lips, presumably to silence her questions. "I will tell you."

Then he silently opened her bedroom door and pushed her inside. She went easily, and when she turned to see him one last time, he had stepped backward into the shadows.

"Good night Gwen," he whispered, as he gave her the most formal of bows.

Chapter Eighteen

Jackson's gut was tied into a knot by the time they arrived at his family's estate. Sitting so many hours in a state of lust while his thoughts bounced between his business idea and erotic fantasies made him irritable when he was trying to be calm, anxious when he was trying to be confident, and truly and completely mad.

It didn't help that Lady Gwen kept slanting him questioning looks. She would be bent over her sketching, then twist her head and give him a sideways look. It wasn't meant to be coy, and yet he saw the shape of her eyes and the curve of her cheeks. He also saw her mouth, looking wet and delectable since she often bit her lower lip in thought. It darkened the color of her mouth and swelled the tissues until he was thinking about all the things she could do with that mouth.

And now that they were arriving, she set down her charcoal and stretched. She arched her back in what tiny space there was in the carriage and extended her arms above her head. It was a normal thing. He'd done it himself. And yet, as he watched her, he remembered the way she'd looked breasts bared in the moonlight. Like a goddess of the night, tempting him with luscious breasts and an unabashed interest in how she was affecting him.

It had nearly killed him to step back from her last night. Never had he been closer to throwing away everything that made him a man. She was an innocent just waking to her desires. To take advantage of her would be like crushing a baby bird. He couldn't do it, and yet it had been so hard to stop.

"Are we here already?" she asked as she looked out the window.

Already? He had spent eons here, steeped in desire while every bump and jolt of the carriage had set her breasts jiggling while her arm or her thigh moved against him.

"We've made it through the village. If it were daylight, you'd see the manor right through those trees." He leaned forward and pointed, directing her gaze into the darkness ahead. There was nothing to see, but he could feel her back against his chest, inhale her sweet scent, and dream of burying his face in her hair while—

"Do they know we are coming?" she asked.

"I sent a message, but I don't know if it arrived before us." He took a breath and forced himself to move back from her. "I don't want you to be overwhelmed by my family. They're boisterous." It was a kinder word than raucous, uncivilized, or even vulgar. "They have good hearts."

She turned to look back at him, her eyes wide and uncertain. "I hope they will like me."

"My fear is that you will hate them." His sisters knew no restraint with their emotions. Now that he understood how carefully Lady Gwen held herself back, how fearful she was about appearing odd, he worried that she wouldn't know what to do when they dragged her into musical duets or hat-making afternoons or, God forbid, scandalous readings of some obscure poet.

"My lord," she said softly, "I am hardly one to judge another soul's oddities."

And right there was the problem. She thought so little of herself that she constantly tripped herself up trying to be what she thought was needed. If only he could find a way to tell her how amazing she was, how absolutely unique and enchanting he found her just as she was.

But in this he failed. He didn't have the right words and they were pulling up to the manor house. She leaned forward to open the door, but he touched her arm and spoke quickly.

"My sisters are Abigail, Beatrix, and Camile. Just think of them as A, B, and C. And my father—"

"Is the Earl of Allbury with a new wife, Jennifer." She smiled at him. "Don't worry. Mama tested me on their names and heritage. I'll get it right."

He gaped at her. "You studied my family history?"

"Mama insisted I learn it before the masquerade. She believes it rude to be ignorant of your host."

"I agree," he said.

"She was quite thorough. I believe she has a mind for pedigrees like I do for plants."

On that he had no doubt. Then there was no more time for talk as his sisters all came tumbling out of the house. Abigail bounced down the steps because she had so much energy, she had never been able to sit still. Beatrix had covered herself in paper flowers for some odd reason. She had them stuck every which way about her person and hair. Camile came last, her hands around their father's arm as he wobbled his way forward on his cane. Gout was destroying his health, and the man's expression appeared pained. Jennifer stood on his father's other side, a sturdy woman with a good smile, who was poised to catch the man if he stumbled.

His family. He grinned despite his worry. He adored them to the ends of the earth. Leaning across Lady Gwen, he threw open the carriage door and jumped out. Then he turned to assist her. He felt the tension in her body and winked to reassure her, but that was all the time he had as Abigail threw herself into his arms.

"We just got your letter today, but it didn't say anything about you coming. Have you gotten soft?" she asked as she poked his back. "Not enough work in London?"

"Soft?" he challenged, then he squeezed her until she squealed.

Even though she was the eldest of his sisters, she was the smallest. A great deal of energy in a small package. She laughed and kicked him until he set her down.

He turned his attention to Lady Gwen to make the introduction only to see her drop into a deep curtsey before his father.

"Oh goodness," his father blustered. "I'm not the king. Don't do that." Then he reached down and pulled her up, though he had to put weight on his bad foot to do it. "Jackson, tell us who this lovely woman is."

"Father, this is Lady Gwen. She's come for a short visit to help me prepare the daffodils for sale."

His stepmother frowned. "They're pretty now, but how will you get them to London?"

"We'll find a way," he said, praying it was true. "And we'll sell the bulbs too." He introduced everyone to everyone, including Lady Gwen's maid, who had finally roused herself from her sleep to step out of the carriage.

Five minutes later, the ladies were ushering Lady Gwen inside while his father joined him to care for the horses. He worried about leaving Gwen alone with his sisters—they were bound to pester her about something—but his father shot him a significant look. He wanted to talk privately, and so together they escorted the horses to the barn.

Their stable boy bounded forward. He was the child of one of their tenants who loved horses beyond anything else in the world, and he took the lead of one horse while Jackson began to rub down the other. His father leaned against a support beam, extended his bad leg in front, and then spoke casually.

"Lovely gel there," his father began, "though she didn't say much."

Jackson laughed. "No one can get a word in edgewise with our lot." He cast a worried look back at the house. "I probably should have stayed with her."

"Now, now, don't be over-protective. The girls are harmless."

"The girls are a lot."

His father chuckled. "Can't argue that."

Then the man grew silent a moment, and when Jackson looked up, his father appeared troubled.

"What has happened?" Jackson asked.

"What? Oh nothing. Camile fancies herself in love, is all."

"Camile?" he asked. He'd expected such from Abigail who was always falling in love with someone or something, be it a puppy, a novel, or a man. But Camile? "She's always kept to herself."

"Yes, but now she's writing letters. A lot of letters."

"To whom?"

"Her friend from school, but…" He shook his head.

"You think it's being passed on to a gentleman."

His father shrugged. "Maybe. Maybe not. I just wish they all could have more company than what's in our little village."

Meaning, he wanted them to have a Season in London. "I'm working on it," he said, doing his best not to give in to desperation. He lifted his gaze. If the stable wall weren't there, he'd be gazing straight onto the daffodil garden. The daffodils would sell. They had to.

"Strange thing to be selling flowers," his father said. "They're not a real crop. Just posies for ladies."

"There are a lot of ladies who like posies."

"Ladies like roses," he said firmly. "Not daffodils that are brown by the time they get to London."

Jackson straightened up as he studied his father. "What are you trying to say?"

The man whistled to their stable hand, calling the boy over. "Finish this up, will you Tommy?" Then he leaned heavily on his cane as they left the barn. Jackson joined him, shortening his steps to match his father's as they headed not to the house but around the side toward the daffodil garden.

"Father—"

"I got a letter from Lady Meunier."

Jackson stifled a groan. What trouble was Isabelle stirring up now?

"She's worried about you. Said you've fallen into a wild crowd, enchanted by a crazy woman, and taking insane risks with your money."

"She wants me to invest in her canals. I want something different."

His father arched a brow at him. "Flowers?" In that one word, the man conveyed all his contempt for anything so insubstantial as a daffodil. But in case Jackson didn't understand, he continued on. "Wheat and pigs, that's real commerce. Flowers are a woman's plaything. Something that doesn't last and isn't purchased when times are hard." His father gestured at the small patch. It was a riot of yellow right now, nearly the peak of blooms. Jackson didn't know what he'd do in two weeks if all the flowers were gone.

"It's a risk," he admitted. "But so are the canals."

"Not the same thing, and you know it." His father turned to him, his cheeks ruddy in the cold. "Just what has this gel got you into?"

"This gel," Jackson returned, "is Isabelle's niece. She's not crazy, and she didn't get me into anything."

"But it was her idea, yes?" His father shook his head. "She's pretty enough, but what does she know of commerce? If ladies liked daffodils, they'd have been buying them before now. It's all roses in London. Always been, always will."

Jackson drew breath, forcing himself to remain calm. His father wasn't being unreasonable. He was merely saying the same things Jackson had considered before. But he didn't like the way his father dismissed Lady Gwen. "I know what I'm doing. I've done well by us so far, haven't I?"

"No question about that," his father agreed. "It's been because of you that we've kept the house and the tenants going. You paid for the repairs, you kept many of 'em fed when the crop was bad, but you said it was because of Lady Meunier. Said it for years that if it weren't for her, you wouldn't have the foggiest idea what to do."

"She has taught me a lot."

"Took me aback, I can tell you. Never thought a woman could do what she has. You've been singing her praises for years."

He had. "But I learned. And now I want something of my own."

His father nodded, his expression softening. "I understand that, son. A man needs to make his own way sometimes. It takes maturity to see that a good thing doesn't come around often. And once you find it, you don't let go. It's the folly of youth to dismiss what works in search of something new." He snorted. "Especially something as frivolous as posies."

His father wasn't wrong. In his twenties and thirties, the man had pursued several bad investments in the hopes of restoring the family fortunes. None of them had profited, and so he'd become the epitome of conservative. Small profits that came steadily over years. The tried and true, because what he'd tried in his younger years hadn't paid off.

"I know what I'm doing," Jackson repeated. It was the truth, but it was also a lie. He had never done anything like this before. He had never tried to create a market for something rarely seen in London. There were several very real dangers, and it was folly to stake all the money he'd carefully saved on this one idea.

He was doing it anyway. And his family needed to help him or get out of his way.

Fortunately, his father knew him well enough to see his determination. The man pursed his lips and grunted in the way of an old dog sitting down for a nap. "You'll not be turned aside, will you?"

"No."

"And you want me to burn any more letters from Lady Meunier."

"I want you to give them to me." He was curious to see what lies she was spreading.

"I can do that. And I can be nice to Lady Gwen, even if her own aunt says she's peculiar."

"Well," he said with a smile. "She is unique. And I value her all the more for it."

His father turned toward the house. It was cold out here, and Jackson was grateful to head inside as well. It wasn't until they were at the door that his father stopped him with a heavy hand on his shoulder.

"I can be nice to the girl, and I can hold my tongue about what you're choosing, but I won't be putting any of the family money into your scheme. It'd be folly to throw away everything we've got. Can't risk it. I'm sorry."

Then he went inside leaving Jackson to stare in fury after the man's back. His family wouldn't have a penny if it hadn't been for his improvements to the farms. His father had turned over the management of the estate to him years ago, and so their coffers were full because Jackson had made sure of it. He'd left the bank accounts in his father's name because it had been convenient. And because he didn't want to embarrass his father. The man was horrendous when it came to management.

And now Jackson wasn't to touch any of it? It was his money! He'd merely allowed it to exist in his father's name out of kindness.

Damnation! Now he had to wrest control away from his father, and that would be an ugly fight that might tear his whole family apart.

Chapter Nineteen

THIS WASN'T THE first time Gwen had been surrounded by women who had an avid interest in everything about her. She'd gone through a dozen Seasons, after all, and there was always at least one event where she was the oddity on display. She'd learned to focus on something she could manage and ignore the rest. In this case, she intended to see her bedroom and perhaps air some of her clothing so it wouldn't wrinkle. It's what Lilah had suggested she do.

That was her plan, but it didn't work. Her mind latched onto something entirely inappropriate, as it was wont to do, and she was hard pressed to keep her mouth shut especially as Abigail kept asking her questions with barely a breath in between each sentence.

"It's so exciting to meet someone new. Tell us everything about yourself. Where are you from? How long are you staying? What made you come all the way from London with Jackson? He didn't say anything about you in his letter. I read it so many times, I've practically memorized it. And we just got it a few hours ago."

"Enough Abigail," Camile said, physically stepping between her sister and Gwen. "Let the lady breathe." Then she turned and smiled. "This will be your room. We'll have it set to rights in a moment."

Meanwhile, Lady Allbury cast her a sad look, as if she too were overpowered by the three sisters. "You must be hungry. I'll see that something is put together in the kitchen. Pray come down when you're ready. I was just about to make some tea." Then she turned and left, nearly bowling into Webster who was just then coming up the stairs. Gwen's maid tried to maneuver inside the bedroom, but there wasn't room with all the people, and so the woman stood in the threshold with her hands on her hips and a sour expression on her face.

Meanwhile, Abigail began speaking. "This is normally her room," she said, pointing at Camile. "She's the neatest of us all. You couldn't find room to breathe in Bea's room, and mine is—"

"A disaster?" teased Camile.

"Well-organized chaos."

"Ha!" The two bickered as they worked together to change the sheets and reset the room. Gwen tried to focus on them. She wanted to make a good impression, but her gaze kept going back to Beatrix and the lady's paper flowers as they adorned her body. The lady in question noted her regard, even as she dropped Gwen's valise with a thud.

"Do you like them?" she asked as she turned to show off all the flowers she had set about her body.

Gwen peered closer. They were not paper cuts, as she had first guessed, but painted flowers on canvas that had then been cut and pinned to the underlying dress or attached to an item of jewelry. The sheer multitude of the flowers was daunting enough, but no more so than in a garden. Gwen could manage the number of flowers. What she could not release was that many of those flowers were drawn incorrectly.

"Don't answer her," Abigail cried from the corner. "She'll want specifics, and nothing good ever comes from that."

Gwen turned to the woman. "The specifics are always important."

"No, they're not," Abigail countered with the ease of a long-standing argument. "Sometimes it's about the general system. The details obscure that."

Camile waved her sister back as she pushed the bed back into the corner. "Lady Gwen has had a long trip. I doubt she wants to talk philosophy right now," she said.

"Well, what would you like to talk about?" Abigail pressed. "Fashion? On-dits? How about pets? Do you have one? Are they hard to manage in the city?"

"Maybe she wouldn't like to talk at all. Maybe she needs to rest." Camile tried to shoo her family out, and they did back away. Unfortunately, they continued to talk during the entire process.

"But she's been in the carriage all day. Maybe she needs to walk a bit? I always feel sore after a ride and need to move about just to find some ease."

Words had been hovering on Gwen's tongue ever since she'd looked closely at Bea's painted flowers. She'd managed to hold them back for a bit, but even when she looked away, the mistakes in them continued to push at her until she couldn't contain it anymore. If only they'd leave, then she could say it into her pillow, but the women were still here, and finally the words burst free.

"They're not accurate," she blurted. Her words weren't exactly loud, but they did fill the room and all three ladies fell silent. Abigail was the first to recover.

"What's not?"

She looked at Abigail to answer, trying not to see the badly drawn flowers. But Beatrix stood right beside Abigail, and there was no way to *not* see them.

"I study plants, you see. The petals and stamen…well, the anatomy of the flowers isn't correct."

Beatrix looked down at the painted blooms on her bodice. "I was trying to evoke an emotion. The feeling of the flowers—"

"But how can something inaccurate evoke anything but wrongness?" It was the truth of her understanding, but she could see by the ladies' faces that she'd mis-stepped. "I'm so sorry," she said as she looked at the floor. "It has been a long day and—"

"Tell me more," Beatrix interrupted.

Abigail groaned. "Don't encourage her. She'll pester you with questions until you don't know what you're talking about."

Gwen frowned. "But I do know what I'm talking about. I have *studied* flowers."

Beatrix stepped forward. "Ignore her. Talk to me." She grabbed a painted daffodil off her bodice and thrust it forward. "Is this inaccurate? I was thinking of the sun when I painted it. I tried to make it like a burst of sunshine."

"The trumpet is too wide. The stamen too short." She looked up. "If you want to paint the sun, you should paint the sun, not a flower."

"But the point of art is not accuracy, it is to evoke emotions. I was trying to suggest that the flower reminded me of the sun."

Gwen thought about that, but she found the statement to be as illogical as it was inaccurate. "The sun is not an emotion. It is the sun."

"Ha!" cried Abigail. "She has you there!"

"Stop, stop," Camile said as she pushed her older sister out the door. "I apologize, Lady Gwen. We get so little company out here that we often forget that some people don't like to argue about every little thing." She shot Beatrix a hard look.

And here again, Gwen was at a loss. She hadn't been arguing. She'd been trying to answer the question of what she thought about Camile's flowers. But obviously Camile seemed to think it wrong, as she shot Beatrix a hard glare.

"Do you know," Beatrix said in a kind of sing-songy voice, "that Camile is the youngest of us all, but she is certainly the bossiest."

"Because I was the only one who listened to mother and Nanny about appropriate behavior."

"That's not true!" Abigail cried. "I listened. I just didn't obey."

Meanwhile, Camile touched Gwen's arm. "I am terribly sorry. Do you think us terribly countrified?"

How was Gwen supposed to answer that? She hadn't seen the

woman's movement, so had been startled by the touch on her arm. And while she was steeling herself to not recoil from the unexpected familiarity, the woman kept looking at her as if she wanted Lady Gwen to answer.

But Gwen couldn't think of what to say. She hadn't formed an opinion except that she had no idea what she was supposed to do. Unfortunately, she knew from experience that the longer she stayed silent, the more upset they would become. That's what always happened when she didn't know how to answer. But in this she was saved.

Lord Sayres came up the stairs with welcome news. "Tea's served. Come along, sisters. I can see that you've been alone with Lady Gwen long enough."

Abigail snorted. "It's not alone if everybody's here."

"Nevertheless. Go see if there are any tarts. I'm famished."

"I had planned to make them tomorrow," Abigail continued. "I didn't realize you were coming today."

"Well, then I shall look for them tomorrow," he said as he pressed a kiss to her cheek and then pushed her firmly toward the stairs. Beatrix and Camile followed as well. They huffed at him good naturedly. Both said something which Gwen immediately dismissed out of her thoughts. Instead, she focused on him. His broad shoulders, his easy smile, and the way his lips pursed when he looked at her.

What did his expression mean? Did he know she'd upset them already?

"Gwen?" he asked gently as the women were finally all heading down the stairs.

"My lord?" she returned. With the women gone, she could focus on him and not incorrectly drawn flowers. With the chatter down the stairs, she could forget the surprise of having a stranger grip her arm. With him looking at her without speaking, she could match her breath to his and settle herself down.

"Would you like some tea?"

She was thirsty. "Yes."

"Would you prefer I send it up here to you?"

Was that possible? Could she hide up here instead of facing his family? But Lilah had warned her that that was not polite. And while she tried to figure out what was the option that was the least disastrous, his expression tightened to the point that his mouth flattened into a hard, dark line.

"What did they say to you?"

"What?"

"What did they do to upset you?"

"Me?"

He blew out a breath. "I'll tell them you're exhausted from the trip. You don't have to see them anymore tonight, but you have to tell me specifically what they did. You're our guest here and I can't have them upsetting you."

She tilted her head. "I'm not upset," she said. "I'm confused."

"Well that's a polite way of saying it. Believe me, I know how noisy they can be. Always asking things, always doing things. I swear London is never so busy as my family at home. They don't realize it's not polite."

She tried to follow his words, but they made little sense to her. "I think I upset Camile. And she upset Beatrix."

"I assure you, you didn't upset anyone."

She shook her head. "Camile didn't like it when I answered Beatrix's question." She took a breath. She knew how to do this. After all, she'd been repairing her gaffs all her life. "I will go apologize, drink tea, and then maybe things will go better."

He lifted his hand, but he didn't touch her. Strangely enough, she found she wanted his touch, so she grabbed his hand and intertwined their fingers together. She liked that her smaller hand fit so well in his larger one, though the very notion seemed illogical to her.

And with their hands together, she found she could straighten her spine and smile. "I will apologize and tell Beatrix that I think her flowers are lovely."

She started to head down the stairs, but he held her back. "You mean you'd lie to Beatrix?"

She shrugged. "I do not judge beauty in the same way other people do. I prefer beauty to come from accuracy, and her flowers are inaccurate."

"Then why not say that to her?"

"I did. That's what upset Camile."

He smiled as he drew her hand up to his mouth. He pressed a long kiss there to her knuckles and spoke gently. "You do not need to go down there if you do not want to."

The temptation to hide was strong, but that was unworthy of her. She wanted to make a favorable impression on his family and disappearing into her bedroom was not how to do it. "I will go downstairs."

"Then I suggest you speak plainly to my family with no apology. I believe they will like you all the more for it."

She wasn't sure she believed him. In her experience—

"Trust me," he said before her thoughts could spin back to the many times she had spoken the truth only to upset the listener. "You have done nothing wrong."

She nodded because it was logical. He knew his family best and therefore would know how to best approach them. At least, that's what she told herself. In truth, she could not refuse him when he spoke so earnestly before pressing another kiss to her hand.

"As you say," she murmured.

He grinned then adjusted their position such that her hand rested upon his forearm as they headed back down the stairs. Everyone was gathered in the parlor, waiting while the tea sat untouched. Almost as a unit, they smiled at her, while Lady Allbury picked up the teapot as if offering it to her.

"It's my favorite blend of tea," she said. "Jackson makes sure to bring it from London every time he visits. Would you care for a cup?"

"I would, thank you," she said. She even remembered to smile.

"Excellent," the earl boomed. "And then while we drink, you can tell us how you have bewitched my son."

Chapter Twenty

Jackson bristled as his father began a not-so-subtle inquisition of Gwen. They'd barely arrived and already his father had made decisions about his money, Gwen, and her so-called influence on Jackson, all without the benefit of a single fact. Jackson was already angry, but to hear his father demand to know how she'd "bewitched" him, set his blood to boiling.

If his father said one thing to upset Gwen, Jackson was prepared to remove them both to Albury Castle several miles away. There were still a few habitable rooms in the crumbling edifice. She wouldn't mind the quiet, and he used to love spending nights there as a boy. It was great fun there in the summer when it wasn't quite so bloody cold at night.

He winced. It might not be the best place for Gwen.

Fortunately, she didn't seem upset at his father's initial question so much as confused. "I don't believe I have bewitched anyone ever," she said. Her head was tilted slightly to the side in the way she had when she was thinking hard about something. As if his father merited study for some reason. The man was being obnoxious.

"How did the two of you meet?" Lady Albury asked.

"I was a guest at his masquerade party," she answered.

"Oh yes! The masquerade!" said Abigail with a clap of her hands. "Tell me everything about it! What was the best costume?"

Jackson was all too happy to change the conversation, but before he could speak, Beatrix cut in. "I think you have a point, Gwen. Art should strive to be both correct and evocative. An anatomically correct daffodil can still suggest the sun."

No one responded to that. Beatrix was often in her own world when it came to art. In fact, Abigail drew breath to say something else, but she was forestalled by Gwen.

"I can help with the anatomy. I cannot help with the sun."

Beatrix smiled. "I would like that."

It was a simple exchange. A shared interest, an offer of help, and an acceptance for a later time. Except Gwen, apparently, didn't realize that most people would allow the conversation to wander to other topics. She immediately scooted her chair closer to Bea's and began discussing one flower after another. His sister, naturally, was beyond thrilled that someone took an interest in her art. Very soon, Bea was pulling flowers off her clothing. She grabbed a pair of scissors in one hand and a charcoal in another while making changes right there.

Camile tried to distract them. Abigail too, and Gwen would obediently lift her head, answer whatever question was posed to her before once again returning to Bea's flowers.

"It would seem that Beatrix has found a kindred spirit," his step-mother commented. And though he had never thought of Gwen as being obsessively artistic like his sister, he did see similarities in temperament. They both tended to focus on details to the exclusion of all else. And Bea could certainly seem very awkward at times. And yet he smiled when he looked at them both, his heart filling with tenderness.

The conversation moved on. Abigail wanted to know all the on-dits from London and his step-mother inquired about several of her school friends. Camile brought more substantial fare from the kitchen, and everyone had a delightful evening. Especially Jackson. Because he could see that Bea and Gwen had become fast friends, and even better, his father could not fail to see that Gwen hadn't the deceit to lead anyone astray, much less Jackson. She was forthright, brilliant, and supremely honest, a quality so rare he valued it beyond the others. He couldn't love her more if she were his wife.

He was in the middle of sending his father a pointed look when he processed his own thoughts. *He couldn't love her more if she were his wife.* Good God, he couldn't possibly have developed a tendre for her. Well, certainly he had affection toward her. And yet, the word "affection" was so pale compared to what he felt. "Lust" wasn't even strong enough, nor "passion." He delighted to hear her speak, not just her words, but her voice. He loved the way she thought, so straightforward without the normal byways and distractions that constantly plagued his mind. She often made him laugh, and for a man who rarely even chuckled, outright belly laughs were a miracle. She filled him with lust even when she was distracted and messy. Especially when charcoal smudged her cheek and her hair slipped free from its restraints. He had fantasized about that as much as he had relived how she'd seemed to dance bare-breasted in the moonlight.

Was that love? Was he *in love*? He rejected the very idea. He'd had absolutely no thoughts to court or marry her. In fact, he'd told her brother exactly that. Even Aaron had said it. And yet after all of that, the only word that fit his feelings was *love*. True, pure love like the feelings he had for his family, only so much stronger and more intimate.

Love. It boggled his mind.

"Jackson? Are you listening to me?" Abigail demanded.

"Of course not," he returned immediately. "You have found my limit to discussions of this year's fashions." He hoped she'd been talking about that. He wasn't at all sure.

"Idiot," she groused, though she smiled as she spoke. "I'd moved on to handsome gentlemen."

"Well, they bore me even more."

"Perhaps," inserted his stepmother, "we should talk of how long you intend to stay. Your letter indicated it would be a very short time."

He nodded. "Just long enough to fit out the daffodils for shipment and..." He turned to Gwen, but he couldn't manage to speak to her just yet. Not until he understood his feelings toward her. So his gaze landed on his sister. "Bea, why exactly are you wearing all those painted flowers?"

"Because of your letter," she said as she looked up from her sketchbook which was always by her side and was now spread out half on her lap, half on Gwen's.

Jackson frowned. "I'm sure I never asked you to wear flowers in my letter."

"You said, quote 'I should like to see how the daffodils would best interest ladies of the *ton*.' Close quote."

"And I said," inserted Abigail, "then they ought to be worn by handsome gentlemen." His sister threw up her hands. "And somehow that translated to Beatrix thinking her painted flowers would look best on lady's clothing."

"As I didn't have time to paint my gown—"

"Surely you don't intend to do that!" gasped his stepmother.

Beatrix frowned. "I didn't have time," she repeated.

Then Camile finished for him. "So she cut up her paintings and tried them all over her gowns with pins. We couldn't agree on the best position—"

"Bodice!" said Abigail firmly.

"Skirt," returned Camile.

"Hairpin," said his stepmother.

"I thought I'd put them all on and let you decide," Bea finished. Then she flashed a smile at Gwen. "And you, of course, but we didn't know you were coming."

"Very sensible," Gwen said with a nod.

His father grunted. "And that's what comes of letting ladies think." He gestured at Bea. "My daughter covered head to toe in canvas."

"Actually," Jackson said as he really looked at his sister's art. "I think that's a very clever idea. Though I can't believe you cut up your paintings."

She shrugged. "They weren't very good."

He doubted that. She was an excellent artist, though he didn't recall her working in oils before. That must be new. Meanwhile, he bent down and picked up one of the daffodils she'd dropped on the floor. Spinning it in his hands, he realized it was relatively stiff and yet still flexible enough to pin onto a dress. Lifting it up, he held it next to Gwen's hair, then shifted it to somewhere near her bodice, before finally positioning it near her knees on her skirt. The effect was odd, but distinctive. Here was a way he could highlight the Lincolnshire daffodils without worrying about keeping them freshly watered in a pin vase.

"How many of these could you make?" he asked his sister.

"As many as you like," she answered. "How long do I have?"

"They would have to be correctly drawn," he said. He looked at Gwen. "Can you teach her that?"

"Yes."

He grinned, then he turned to the room at large. "Never fear, family, we shall make a fortune from this for sure!"

Everyone gasped at that. Well, everyone but Gwen, who looked as if she never doubted a word he said, which he knew to be untrue. But it was his father who snorted out his disdain loud enough to silence everyone.

"Paint on canvas? Posies from daffodils? You're mad," the man said.

"No, father, I'm not." His voice was hard. He didn't want to have a confrontation with his father, not in front of everyone, but if the situation warranted it, then he would—

"Of course, you're mad," Gwen interrupted, her tone almost conversational.

He spun to her in shock. "What?"

She tilted her head as if surprised by his outrage. "Most experiments fail. More than 90%. Probably much more than that, but I haven't any way to measure it beyond my own work. Given that truth, it is madness to believe anything would succeed."

"See!" his father inserted. "Even she says your plan will fail."

"I didn't say that," Gwen returned. She spoke without heat—as if she were speaking about the way to grow a tree—and because of that, her voice carried weight. "Given the rate of failure, only a madman would attempt anything new. And yet without madmen, nothing new would ever get done. I don't know that we'd have invented the wheel, much less carriages and mills. Who thought it would be a good idea to try to sit on a wild horse? Or tame a wolf until generations later we have dogs? Only madmen, I assure you. And we are all the better for it."

His father folded his arms and glowered. "It's still a fool's choice to spend good money on such a thing. Canals," he said with a thump on the armrest of his chair. "Now there's a proven idea."

No one could argue that. It was a well-established business. "I don't own a canal," Jackson said into the silence. "I own daffodils."

"I own them," his father stressed.

"No dear," his stepmother said. She wasn't one to put herself forward. The woman hated arguments and Jackson wasn't sure he'd ever seen the woman openly disagree with her husband. But in this, she entwined her fingers in his. "The family owns the daffodils. Haven't you told me that often enough? You're a caretaker for the land. A steward for the Albury title."

"You're mincing my words."

"I'm repeating them exactly," she countered.

To the side, he saw Abigail open her mouth to speak, but Jackson cut her off with a quick shake of his head. He needed his father to soften. He needed the family money to make his idea work. And at the moment, his stepmother was the only one making headway. Or maybe not, because his father shook his head.

"I'll not risk everything we have now on foolishness. I know how it ends."

"No," he said to his father. "You know how it ended before. Not how it will end now."

"You're dreaming."

"Dreaming?" he retorted. "You haven't asked about my plans. You haven't seen the details." He didn't mean for his voice to rise, but it was a sore point for him. He hated it when he was lumped in with all the feckless youths who thought a good idea was all that was needed to make a profit. The idea was the beginning. The rest was hard work and a meticulous attention to detail. "You have dismissed me out of hand."

His father pursed his lips. Not exactly a reversal, but certainly a softening. So Jackson pressed it. "Would you like to see?"

"I could take a look at your plans."

"Good. Thank you." He started to say more, but his father cut him off.

"But all the details won't work if the idea isn't sound."

True enough. "You'll have one week to convince me, Father, because after that, I'm spending every penny I have on this."

His father shook his head as he glared at Gwen. "She's turned your head."

Far from being insulted, Gwen shrugged. "Your son's head is completely under his control. Mine, on the other hand, seems to have a fondness for madmen."

If he weren't in love with her before, that statement would have pushed him firmly off the cliff into devotion.

Chapter Twenty-One

What started out as a difficult week rapidly became tense. Gwen was so grateful to have found companionship with Beatrix. They spent a great deal of time together discussing the anatomy of flowers and that steadied her enough to face the rest of the family. She didn't blame anyone else for her awkwardness. Everyone was on edge, what with the earl and his son arguing night and day. Whenever possible they all escaped outside. Camile showed her their small store of daffodil bulbs. Lady Albury introduced her to the man who tended the daffodil garden, and together they built crates to transport both bulbs and flowers. Abigail helped with that, too. She even taught Gwen how to hammer in nails with the fewest number of whacks, which was incredibly satisfying.

In short, if it weren't for the men, Lady Gwen would likely have enjoyed this visit. But it was impossible to escape the constant bickering between father and son. At least it was until Lord Sayres found her one morning in the middle of the daffodil garden as she inspected the soil. She was on her knees in the far corner where the soil was wetter because of the slope of the land. She had a theory regarding water and how quickly the bloom grew. But when she heard her name called out in his deep voice, she popped up with a surprised gasp.

"Lord Sayres?"

"There you are." Relief echoed in his voice.

"Is there a problem?"

"No. Well, yes, but…" He blew out a breath. "I fancy a visit to my ancestral home," he said as quickly walked down the path toward her. "Care to see a moldering old castle with me?"

"I would be happy to," she said as she brushed the soil off her hands. Unfortunately, it was thick and moist as all good soil should be and so she smeared it all over her gardening dress. "I will need to change," she said.

"You are perfectly fine for the disaster that is my inheritance. But if you wish to clean up, then I shall grab a picnic for us. Meet me by the gig in fifteen minutes."

She agreed, but before she could depart, he held up his hand.

"And please, for my sanity, please do not tell anyone in my family about it."

She smiled. A few hours alone with him would be lovely. "I shall remain silent on the topic."

He grinned and held out his arm. "Then let me escort you back to the house."

His arm was solid, and the sun was warm. She settled her hand on his forearm and together they walked in perfect accord. Lincolnshire was beautiful, especially in spring, and she felt contentment settle into her heart now that she could not hear anyone arguing about anything at all.

That changed the moment they neared the house. Camile was clearly exasperated with Abigail. She said something tart that Gwen didn't hear well, but the tone was clear enough. As was Abigail's loud retort. Then Beatrix said something, and soon there were female voices speaking one over the other in such rapid words that no one could be heard clearly.

Gwen did hear Lord Sayres's groan as well as his muttered words. "I need to get them married. They all need separate households, preferably across the country from one another."

"That is the plan, isn't it?" Gwen asked. "Seasons for all three."

"Yes, but as you can plainly hear, it will not be soon enough. They need distance from one another now. For everyone's sanity."

She thought it might be his arguments with his father that were the real problem, but she didn't say it. She tended to hide away from raised voices, not delve into the reasons behind them.

"I'll be quick," she said when they made it fully inside the house. She rushed upstairs to wash her hands and change, and then found the gig in record time. He was there before her, finishing up as he hitched up the horse. They were tooling down the drive while his sisters were still arguing.

And as the quiet finally wrapped around them, he exhaled a tremendous sigh of relief. "Silence at last."

She said nothing. He didn't seem to require a response as he guided the horse onto the road. But apparently there was more of a conversation going than she thought because a moment later, he asked her a question.

"Has it been horribly difficult for you?"

She hated unspecific questions like that. She never knew how to answer and so usually ended up staring at people in confusion. Had what been difficult? Changing her clothes? Working in the garden?

He turned to look at her, and then abruptly flushed. "I'm sorry. I'm afraid I'm not making much sense."

"Perhaps you are finding things difficult. With your father perhaps?" She phrased it as a question because she wasn't sure of the answer. From what she'd seen of the three sisters, they enjoyed their arguments as much as they hated them. None of them seemed to hold a grudge, and an hour after the explosion, all three were in better spirits.

Meanwhile, Lord Sayres was staring out over the horse's ears as he spoke. "He will not listen to reason, and I am exhausted with trying to get him to hear. I thought if he could see everything I've done, all the details I've worked out, that he would see it can work. I've made allowances for bad crops, for disasters in transportation. There are risks, to be sure, but he simply doesn't believe in your idea."

"My idea?" she asked.

"That I can make the flower popular." He looked at her. "That I can make you popular."

She arched her brows at him. "If you recall, I don't think you can do it either. Not with me, at least."

"Yes, with you!" he huffed. "Only you!" Then when she didn't respond, he blew out a breath. "At least you are willing to let me try."

"I don't have that much at risk, though. If we fail, the worst I shall experience is some humiliation." She shrugged. "It will not be the first time, nor the last."

"You have invested your pin money."

In truth, she'd invested all her pin money plus some of her dowry, thanks to a long conversation with her brother. But Elliott would not give over her entire marriage portion, merely a small percentage, no matter how many times she repeated that the was on the shelf now and old enough to manage on her own.

Aunt Isabelle was still pressuring her—via a daily letter—to invest in her canals, but now that Gwen was in Lincolnshire, the missives were likely piling up at home. It was easy to ignore something she never saw. Meanwhile, Lord Sayres's hands tightened into fists on the reins.

"We are all taking a risk," he grumbled.

"But this is your entire family's money until next quarter day."

He fell silent, and she could tell he was brooding. She allowed him to do so as she used the time to look at the scenery. So much to see. So many plants. The air was clean, and the land uncrowded. She saw several sheep and only one other person far off in the distance. Compared to the crowd in London, this was heaven.

"You don't think it will work either," he said, his tone hard. "You have been humoring me."

"I don't think I know how to humor people."

"You do it all the time," he said. "You cannot tell me you wanted to play charades with Abigail last night. Or that you enjoyed corralling those children with Camile yesterday."

She hadn't *not* enjoyed it. "I was helping out," she said. "And I liked watching all of you play charades."

"And will you enjoy it when I cover you in flowers and take you to a several balls in one evening? Or will you be helping out?"

She thought spending the evening on his arm would be wonderful, but she didn't say that. She couldn't because the thought was so new in her mind. She didn't enjoy anyone's company as much as she did his. Not even Lilah's.

"Can't I do both?" she asked.

He nodded, but the gesture didn't hold any enthusiasm. "It doesn't matter," he finally said. "Without my father's money—money I earned for him, I might add—we cannot accomplish what I planned." He blew out a breath. "Worse, I believe he will invest it with Isabelle, but she cannot make that successful without me. I'm the one who would do the work to make the locks profitable again."

"And so you are once more under her thumb."

He nodded, then he abruptly frowned and straightened to look at her. "I never told you I wished to be out from under Isabelle's control."

"It was a logical conclusion. No man risks everything on a gambit like this unless he finds his current situation intolerable."

"Many men risk fortunes on the turn of a card or a roll of the dice."

"Yes, but you are not a gambler. Not in the normal way. And yet you are putting everything you can into making your flower popular." She arched a brow. "If you are not normally a gambler, then you must find Aunt Isabelle intolerable."

"I do," he said softly.

"Why?"

"Because what she wants is control. Not just of the business, but of the people who work for her, myself included. It is not healthy for anyone."

No one wanted to be controlled, least of all a man as strong-willed as he. But she could see no way around his difficulties. He had gone over the financials with her in detail in the carriage. She knew how much money he needed just to transport the bulbs to London, store them adequately, and then sell them. And that was after dressing her stylishly in the flowers and making her popular.

It seemed too daunting a task, but it was clear he believed he could do it. And she believed him. Which made her next statement logical.

"There is enough money in my full dowry to cover what you need."

She felt his entire body recoil from her. "I will not marry you for your money!" he said, every word sounding strangled out of him.

That wasn't what she meant. Even so, it was lowering to feel how very much he hated the idea of marrying her. He'd practically leaped out of the gig rather than sit beside her.

"Besides," he growled, "we are doing this so that you don't have to get married."

"I thought we were doing this so you could launch your sisters."

"That, too."

They were silent for a long moment while the air seemed laden with his anger. She had to make it clear to him that she hadn't meant marriage.

"I'm of age, aren't I?" she said in a low voice. "I'm on the shelf with no intention of marrying."

He turned to look at her, his expression tight. "Yes?"

He phrased the word as a question, but she didn't know what he was asking, so she ignored it. "When do I get my dowry for myself? Don't ladies who never marry live off their property?"

"It depends," he said slowly, "on the terms of the will."

She nodded. "I will press Elliott again. We can still go on as you intended, but with my money and not your family's."

"I will not take your dowry. Not without marrying you."

"Why not?" She twisted to look at him more closely. "As I said before, I have not risked so very much. If you believe in the plan enough to risk your entire family's fortune, then why can't I risk my dowry?"

"For one thing," he growled, "your brother will have me drawn and quartered."

"My brother cannot control what I do with my money."

"A nice thought in the abstract, but Elliott will not let you have it."

"But that is just the point. It is my money. He cannot—"

"He will. He will find a way. If nothing else, he will delay long enough that it is the same as saying no."

"He will give it to me. He loves me." After all, he'd already given her a little of her portion. How much harder would it be to get the rest?

"That is exactly why he will not. Damnit, Gwen, think! I wouldn't let you have your money if I were him. You cannot spend your fortune on a risky gambit with a known fortune hunter."

"But you're not a fortune hunter. And you want to take the risk with your sisters' money. Why not with mine?"

He had no answer to that. She could see it in his frustrated glower. She returned it with equal measure. And in such a state, they arrived at his titular castle. And a more ramshackle, disaster she'd never seen.

She loved it.

CHAPTER TWENTY-TWO

WAS THERE EVER a more maddening woman? He'd taken her on this trip specifically to propose to her. He wanted to marry her! But before he could even get to the romantic setting he'd planned, the woman brought up the idea that they wed for her money. It didn't matter that that wasn't her intention. She'd brought up the specter of fortune hunting, and he couldn't propose now without her thinking that he wanted her for her dowry.

It was his fault for doing this when he was ill-tempered. His father was immovable and, truth be told, Jackson couldn't fault the man for his caution. All she'd had to do was suggest in her gentle way that perhaps his father had a point, and it all came tumbling out. His frustration, his fears that he was taking too huge a risk, and his absolute determination to see it through to the end.

Then, just as they were crossing the moat into the castle grounds, she'd had the audacity to say she never intended to get married right before jumping out of the gig and running pell-mell into the castle ruins. He'd never seen her this gloriously uninhibited before. Most people would inspect the crumbling walls of the keep, the still-sturdy front archway, or the debris-clogged moat. Not Lady Gwen. She ran to a clutch of weeds and was already kneeling in the dirt to look closer.

She'd never looked more charming, especially when she turned to him with an excited grin. "Look what I've found!"

He sighed, but the sound soon turned into a chuckle. He loved it when she was happy. "Tell me what it is while I take care of the gig."

She began speaking, her voice rushed and barely heard, especially when she faced the plant and not him. He caught perhaps every third word, but it didn't matter. He gathered the plant was rare and she wanted cuttings.

Once he'd set the horse free to graze, he grabbed the picnic basket and headed toward her. "If I'd realized how delighted you'd be with this place, I would have brought you sooner."

"If I'd known it was here, I would have found a way to get here on my own."

So independent. "I promise to take you whenever you want."

She waved away his chivalrous comment. "You've plenty to do and no interest in watching me grub around in the dirt."

Now there was a turn of phrase. He'd wager anything those weren't her words. "Did your mother say that to you? When you were growing up?"

"Hmm? Oh yes. Nanny, too." She straightened up. "I don't have to take a cutting now. I can come back later, if you prefer."

"Heavens no. I delight in watching you be delighted."

She snorted as she inspected the moss on the wall. "I doubt that."

"And yet it's true."

She looked back at him. Her head tilted a bit to the side, and the sunlight made her honey colored hair appear shot with gold. It was beautiful, but what he liked most was the way her nose wrinkled at him.

"You're flirting with me," she stated, and there was curiosity more than accusation in her tone.

"Not really." He took a deep breath, and as he exhaled, he pushed aside all thoughts of risk and reward, money and management. He was with her now and nothing was more important than that. "Take all the time you want. Look at whatever you want. I'm going to take our picnic basket back to the chapel. It's through there and to the right."

She followed the line of his gesture and nodded. "Is the roof stable?"

"Collapsed years ago. Has all sorts of interesting things growing inside. You'll love it."

She grinned and hurried to his side. "I can't wait."

He laughed and held out his hand to her, feeling very pleased when she took it. His excuse was that the ground was uneven, and he was helping her past the crumbled ruins of some small structure. He had no idea what. But once she'd stepped over the patch of stones, he refused to let her go. He liked entwining their fingers together and she seemed content to remain with him.

As they walked, he gave her a brief history of the place. It had been built in the twelfth century on the ruins of an old Roman fortress. His family had lived here through the generations until his mother was pregnant with him and the chapel roof collapsed. That was enough to convince his father to pack up the whole lot of them—his grandfather was still alive then—and move to the dower property, which was where they lived now.

"You must have played here as a boy," she said as she paused to look at some early wildflowers.

"As much as I could." He grinned. "Too many girls at the house."

"I'll bet," she said with a laugh.

He took the long path, letting her exclaim over a patch of mushrooms and speculate over some young shoots. And as she delighted in every corner of his inheritance, he remembered the magic he'd once felt running through this place as a boy. He'd fought dragons here and even developed a ritual for knighting his friends. Some days he defeated pirates, and others he was the pirate. And every crack, every shadow held a surprise.

"You know, my father views this as nothing more than an enormous financial drain. We don't pay much for upkeep, but he resents even that little bit."

She straightened up from another set of interesting shoots and looked about her with a narrowed gaze. "I suppose even minimal work would be expensive."

"Very." But thanks to her joy, he was feeling that same magic from when he'd been young. "I want to restore it," he said. "Someday. After my sisters are launched. At a minimum, it should be safe for boys to run around in as they defeat dragons and rescue damsels in distress."

"Or you should teach the damsels to defeat the dragons on their own."

He nodded. "They can learn about the rare and exciting plants that grow here, too."

She looked about, perhaps seeing children at play here. He certainly did. He saw her pregnant with his child as she taught their other children the workings of the natural world. He, of course, was pretend fencing with their oldest, but when everyone had finished learning, they would run inside for a proper medieval feast. Or a good English picnic. Whatever his wife desired.

"Do you want to wander some more?" he asked, his voice thick from the need to create that future for himself and her. "Or would you prefer to eat?"

"I'm a contrary creature. I want to do both." She turned to him. "But that basket must be heavy. Let's set it down in the chapel, then you can show me all the things growing in there."

"Your wish is my command," he returned. And together they entered the chapel.

The roof was half-gone along with one wall, so the result was a kind of covered porch. Several years before, a child had broken his leg while exploring through the fallen timbers. Jackson had insisted that they clean up as much as they could and shore up the remaining structure. The stone altar remained, as well as a small archway the led to the main castle. But what had once been pews were now dirt. If there had been any stained glass, it was long gone. Instead, they enjoyed the shade of a pair of large oaks while the remaining structure blocked the wind.

As for the growing things, she'd already found what he called weeds. He pointed to where there'd once been a rabbit's den. She saw the squirrel nests, as well as a bird's nest. She climbed on some tall rocks to inspect them both. She knew the species of bird by the color and size of the eggs. Of course, she did. And he enjoyed the sound of her voice as she talked about driving her nanny to distraction one summer because she was always climbing trees to watch the baby birds grow.

Meanwhile, he spread the blanket and set out the food. He'd brought everything he could think of to tempt her, including the best wine bottle in their cellar, but he'd forgotten that she was tempted by their environment much more than any food. So he enjoyed the wine while she continued to poke at things and talk. And the whole time, he imagined many days spent doing just this: listening to her talk about her passions. And many nights exploring passion together. By the time she declared that hunger was overcoming her botanical interests, he was desperate for her love. Not just her physical passion, for which he was painfully hard just from his imagination. But he wanted her heart, too, and the life they could have together.

"Have I talked too much?" she asked as she knelt on the edge of the blanket.

"Not possible. I like listening to you talk."

She looked at him in that odd way of hers with her head tilted and her nose slightly wrinkled. "I cannot tell if you are teasing me."

"Why would you think that? It is the God's honest truth. I swear!"

"But you haven't the least interest in botany, except for the daffodils, of course. No one cares about what I say except other scientifically minded people."

"I care." And when she would have argued, he passed her a glass of wine instead. "I love hearing about what you love. I don't listen as much to the words as the joy in them. It is the most beautiful sound in the world."

"Now you are definitely flirting."

"Perhaps. But you are worthy of a little flirting. And maybe a lot more." He reached out his hand but didn't connect. Not until she shifted to sit closer to him. He let his hand settled on her forearm before stroking up to her elbow. "Would you like some chicken?"

She did. And some winter apples which he sliced up for her. And while she ate, he talked about his plans for restoring the castle. It was all pie in the sky right then, but it was glorious to talk to her about it. And then when she was leaning forward for the wine bottle, she overbalanced. Or perhaps he helped her overbalance such that she tumbled into his arms.

She laughed as she landed on his chest, and he was pleased to feel her body stay relaxed in his arms. She didn't flinch from him. Didn't even tighten. Instead, she stretched forward until their mouths were close enough to kiss.

"Lord Sayres?"

He rolled his eyes. "For God's sake, Gwen, call me Jackson." He cupped her cheek and brushed his thumb across her lower lip. He meant to say something more, but he lost it in the texture of her mouth and the nearness of her.

"I've been thinking," she said, as her eyelids fluttered down.

"You're always thinking," he teased.

"Yes, but I've been thinking about something specific. Something having to do with you."

He leaned forward, needing to touch their lips together. He didn't deepen it into a kiss but brushed his lips across hers. Back and forth while he heard her breath catch and his own lips tingled.

"With me?" he whispered as he darted his tongue out to wet her lips.

"Yes," she said, and the breathy quality of the word shot hunger straight to his groin.

"My favorite word."

He deepened the kiss. How could he not? She was in his arms, her body pliant, and with every shift of her mouth against his, she seemed to be asking for more. He hugged her to him, he plundered her mouth. And when she shifted her weight to the side, he rolled them both over until he could press her into the blanket. He kissed her as he had never kissed anyone in his life. He kissed her as if he had already asked for her hand and she had already said yes. He caressed her breasts as if they were already filling with milk for his children. And he gloried in her gasps as he would give pleasure to the woman he loved. Because he did.

His hands were full of her breasts when she spoke. He was trailing kisses along her neck, heading for her nipples when she put her hands to his shoulder. She didn't press him back so much as hold him steady. And when he lifted up to look at her in dazed confusion, she spoke words that he had to repeat three times in his head before he heard them over the roaring in his ears.

"I should like you to make love to me."

"What?"

"I'm on the shelf, you know."

"What?"

"Well, that means I shall never marry. I have already told you that."

"What?"

She pursed her lips, and not to kiss him. "Try to listen, Jackson."

His cock surged at the sound of his name on her lips.

"I don't think it's fair that I should never enjoy carnal pleasure just because I'm not going to marry anyone. So long as we ensure there will be no children, I see no harm in experiencing it." She looked uncertain for a moment. "And I should like to experience it with you, please. If you would."

If he would?

"Will you marry me?" he rasped.

"Oh, don't do that. You don't have to do that. I'm on the—"

"I am blasted tired of hearing you say that. You are young, beautiful, and incredibly attractive. Men want you."'

She simply blinked at him in obvious confusion. Frustrated, he grabbed her hand and set it to his cock. He meant to show her without words that he desired her. And perhaps he meant to frighten her a bit. The reality of a man hard and throbbing set many virgins to the vapors. Not her. Of course not her, because she immediately began to explore the length and breadth of him. And while his wits fled and his body thrust against her, she gasped in delight.

"I had not thought it would be so warm. Are you not hot? Do you wish to—"

"Don't say it."

"Open up and allow it free?"

He groaned and set his forehead to her shoulder. His blood was pounding and the scent of her filled him with a steady thrum of need. He wanted her, wanted her, wanted her.

"What can I say," he rasped, "that will convince you I wish to marry you? Not for your dowry, not for this act, but for life. With you."

She pursed her lips as she thought. How she could look so sexy and so academic at the same time was beyond him, but the sight nearly undid him.

"I think you should have to ask me when there is no need for me at all. When you do not need my dowry nor my body. When we are simply two friends sharing tea. Then you should ask, and I shall believe you."

He raised his head to stare down at her. "And what will you say then? Will you accept?"

Her expression softened and she touched his face. It was a slow caress of a wistful kind of happiness. "If that should happen, Jackson, then I would probably say yes." She smiled. "But I will not be sitting at home waiting for that wonderful day, because I doubt it will ever come. I am a woman, here for the moment. You are a man under enormous pressure to succeed in a way no one else ever has before." She coiled her fingers around his ear before stroking into his hair. "I should like to experience this now and I will not hold you to any promise for the future."

He looked into her eyes and saw how deeply she believed in her utter lack. She couldn't see her own beauty or that he could desire to have her as his own. Her own imagination couldn't make that bridge, but he could. For them both. And so he vowed in that moment to please her in every way, to show her exactly how wonderful she was. So that on that future date, she would have no doubt in her mind. She would know that he wanted her and only her.

"So will you do it?" she whispered. "Will you make love with me?"

"Will you marry me?"

"If you ask, then I will say yes."

"Then, yes," he said. Because in his mind, they were already wed. He had asked, and she had accepted. They were even in a church before an altar. To his way of thinking, it was as good as a ceremony. Better because the wedding night could begin right away.

Chapter Twenty-Three

Two weeks ago, Gwen hadn't realized what a gift it was to be on the shelf. Her mother had always spoken as if it was a pitiful state to be avoided at all costs. And yet, Gwen had discovered such freedom in being too old to care about acting like a girl straight out of the schoolroom. She was an adult woman who wanted to experience life. And finally she'd found a man who allowed her to do just that. He never laughed at her oddities, never chastised her for acting strange, and best of all, he let her explore when she wished to explore.

Which was now.

He was kissing her, deep and thorough. But she had experienced this before. She wanted something different. She wanted more. While he pleasured her mouth, she unbuttoned her gown. She'd chosen it specifically for this possibility, and so she managed it quickly. And then she began tugging at his shirtsleeves, since he'd already discarded his coat. Of course she was clumsy, and eventually he stopped what he was doing to look at her.

"You're very impatient," he drawled.

She blew out a breath. "You don't understand."

He rocked back from her. "Explain it to me then."

Fine. She would tell him it all. "I have studied anatomy. I have studied this act. I have looked at textbooks and read things that Mama would have locked me in the root cellar for even touching."

He nodded, clearly not understanding where she was going. "Yes?"

"I've read and studied, but I haven't actually *seen*."

"A man?"

"Yes!" She propped herself up on her elbow. "You saw me in the moonlight."

His smile widened. "I did. I have dreamed of it every night since."

"Well, so have I, but of seeing you. Men get to go to brothels, they discuss these things with barmaids and their older brothers. Women aren't told anything! All I know is what Diana has shared and it was not very helpful. I don't think she enjoyed it very much." At his concerned look, she quickly explained. "Not her current husband. He must be very good at it because whenever I ask, she blushes very red and giggles. And I can't get one word out of her beyond that she is blissfully happy."

"Then I am happy for her."

She rolled her eyes. "Well, that's all well and good, but I was talking about me. Seeing you. Naked." There. She'd said it though she felt her cheeks heat with embarrassment.

But far from laughing at her, he nodded solemnly to her. He began unbuttoning his shirtsleeves while she watched with increasing excitement. Finally, she'd been able to see and touch a man. And not just any man, but him, the most handsome specimen of manhood she knew.

Finally, he divested himself of his shirt. His torso was bared to her. And even better, he was in the sunlight. She could see every ripple and curve of his chest, tease her fingers through his wiry chest hair, and watch in delight as his male nipple tightened when she scraped at it with her nail. She heard his breath catch, watched his nostrils flare, but he didn't move while she explored. And it was wonderful!

But it wasn't exactly what she'd been hoping for. "Will you remove the rest?"

He nodded slowly, but he didn't move. "You must know that if we do this, there will be no going back. I will have you as mine."

"Well, of course you will have me. That's the whole point." And to prove it, she pulled a French letter out of her pocket. She had folded the envelope to hide it in the pocket of her gown, but she believed that would make no difference. "I brought this for you to use."

He sat up with a slight jerk as he took the envelope from her hand. "Where did you get this?"

She flushed a bright red. "I got it from Amber, my brother's wife. Diana wasn't helpful at all, but Amber was willing to show me preventatives."

"I see," he said slowly, as he opened the envelope and inspected the condom. "Have you handled this much?"

"No, no! Amber was very clear about that. I only touched it once and then very delicately."

He nodded. "Then it will serve."

She grinned. "Will you let me put it on you? When the time comes?"

"I will," his expression very grave. "You have put a lot of thought into this, haven't you?"

"I never do anything without thought. And this took a great deal more consideration than usual."

He frowned. "How long ago did you get this?"

She flushed. "A month ago."

"A month! And who did you think would…" His voice trailed away in a question.

"I didn't have anyone in mind. Not until recently, that is." She smiled. "I brought it on this trip just in case."

"Just in case," he said slowly.

"I like to be prepared."

He smiled, though he looked a little dazed. "My father is right," he said quietly. "I am bewitched by you."

"What?" she gasped.

He smiled. "In all the best ways, Gwen. It turns out I find a woman who takes control of her desires to be completely fascinating." He stroked his finger along her jaw. "Tell me what you want."

Finally! He asked the right question. "I should like to see you naked in the sunlight. Every part of you. And I should like to put this on you. And then…" She struggled for the right words. "Um…"

"Yes?"

"I should like to have fun then. I should like to blush afterwards and giggle into my fan like Diana does. I should like to smile like Amber does when she looks at my brother. I should like to know what it is like." She tilted her head. "Do you understand?"

"I do." Then he pressed a kiss to her lips. He was slow and tender with it, allowing her to luxuriate in the textures of his mouth. And then he pulled away. Standing up, he methodically removed his clothing as she watched. Every button undone, every ripple of his muscles watched, and every inch of his body revealed to her hungry gaze.

"I wish I was better at art," she murmured. "I would draw you so that I could remember this."

"I hope you will remember without benefit of your charcoals."

He was standing before her, his penis thrust long and thick in front of her eyes. Well, not exactly in front of her eyes, so she adjusted her position so she could look at it directly. Then she extended her hand to him but stopped short. Mindful of how she preferred to be asked before being handled, she glanced up at him. "I should like to touch it now, if that is acceptable?"

"I am at your command. You may do with me as you will." There was humor in his tone, but also a deeper note. One that throbbed in his voice and she heard only when they were kissing. "If you are bored, I could undress as well," she offered. "I am known to go a very long time when I study something."

He stroked her face with a tender caress. "I am not bored." He leaned down until they were nearly nose to nose. "But I should require a kiss every now and then."

"Agreed," she said. And to punctuate it, she stretched up to kiss him. He supported her back as she did and angled their bodies such that she was pressed flush against his leg. Her nipples tightened with the feel of his body and she wanted to be naked to experience the brush of his skin against her breasts.

Soon, she thought. Very soon. But at the moment, she had a penis to inspect. So when he released her mouth, she went back onto her knees to look at him. She noted the thick veins, she measured his girth, and touched the drop of liquid that had escaped his tip. She examined the cut of his circumcision, and with his permission, she ran her finger along the edge. And that was just what she did with his cock.

She also explored the cut of his hipbones, the curve of his buttocks. She felt the weight of his sac and heard his breath catch as she did. And then, who knew how much later, he rasped out her name.

"Gwendolyn, I should like another kiss now," he said.

"Of course." She straightened up with a grin as she pressed her mouth to his. And as his tongue toyed with hers, she felt the weight of her breasts and the wetness between her thighs. Her heart was beating fast, and she wanted to feel his body against hers.

When they separated again, he looked into her eyes. "Would you mind undressing for me now?"

"Not at all," she said. She'd just been thinking the exact same thing. Still, it was awkward taking off all her clothes in front of him. But it was hardly fair for her to be missish now when he had been standing in his full glory this whole time.

He must have noticed her hesitation because he whispered her name.

"Gwen? If you have changed your mind—"

"Oh no! Not at all," she said. "I want to. I just…" She flushed, words failing her.

"It's new."

"That never bothers me," she said as she tugged awkwardly at the ties of her stays.

"It's intimate."

She looked up at him. "Yes." But she was being silly. They had already kissed and touched one another. She had asked him to make love to her. That required a certain level of nudity. And she very much wanted to experience this.

"Let me help you," he offered as he reached toward the now tangled ties of her stays.

"Thank you."

His touch was gentle, but even the most casual brush of his fingers set her skin on fire. And he was touching her a great deal. He could have pulled off the stays within a moment, but he caressed her through her shift as he unknotted the ribbons. And once it was pulled away, he tugged at the shift.

"Shall we take this off as well?"

She nodded, her throat too tight for her to speak. The way he looked at her made her heart beat fast. The way he touched her made her skin tingle. And he so clearly was enjoying himself that she didn't think to question their actions. Especially since she had never felt like this before.

She was bare before now except for her stockings and shoes. "Shall I take them off?" she asked. It felt silly standing there in just those.

He nodded, his gaze hot as he watched her. She bent over and he exhaled in a long breath as she removed both shoes and stockings.

"I want to touch you," he rasped as she was still bent over.

"Yes," she responded. It was the only word she could manage. Then she felt his large hand, rough from callouses, as he pressed his palm to her lower back. Then he slid it down over her buttocks, and she felt her belly ripple in reaction.

"I have always preferred face to face," he murmured as he touched her. "But you are beautiful this way, too." Then he paused, his hand poised on the lowest curve of her bottom. "Do you understand what I mean?"

"Not entirely."

"Would you like me to explain?"

"Always."

So he did. He moved his hand lower until he slipped between her thighs. He went slowly and she straightened in reaction, but not all the way.

"Do you feel how wet you are? How ready for me?" he asked.

His fingers gently pressed between her legs and he moved them back and forth such that she felt the moisture there. She felt him press her intimately and her legs trembled from the sensation.

"Imagine my organ here," he said.

Then she didn't have to imagine because he stepped behind her and pressed it between her cheeks. He didn't invade. He simply pressed and she arched in reaction. She could feel him right there. She could imagine him penetrating her.

His hands coiled about her hips, steadying her. "From this angle, I can kiss your back." He pressed his mouth to her shoulder blades and lathed across her spine. "I can hold your breasts." He fitted word to action, and she gasped as he pinched her nipples. Her legs trembled and she thought she might fall, but his right hand flattened across her belly, pressing her backward into him.

"Lean back against me," he murmured.

She did. She felt his chest against her back, his heat against her body, and his breath next to her ear.

"Do you know what a quickening is?"

"Not exactly. I've read about it."

"Never experienced?"

"No." Then before he could ask permission, she rushed to reassure him. "Will you show me?"

"With pleasure. But perhaps we should sit down."

He showed her how to sit and she was grateful because her legs felt too weak to keep her standing. He braced his own back against a stone then settled her between the V of his legs. At his encouragement, she leaned back, trapping his cock against her back.

"Will this hurt?" she asked as she relaxed against him.

"It is pleasure for me," he answered.

Then as she relaxed back against him, he began to stroke her breasts. She was already sensitive and before long she was breathless from his touch.

"When you are ready, set your ankles atop mine."

It took her a moment to understand what he meant. His legs were spread in a V. To put hers on top of his…

He caressed her thighs, encouraging her to spread herself open.

"I wish we had a mirror so you could see."

So did she, but this was enough. To feel the cool air on her most private parts. And then to feel his fingers stroking down her belly. Further. Deeper. And then…

She gasped.

He rolled his long, thick finger across her clitoris. She knew the word, had learned it in a scientific text. But never had she felt it this way. Electric and alive. Every rub across it had her arching in reaction.

"Too much?" he asked.

She hadn't the breath to answer. So he shifted what he was doing. He bent his knees such that her knees lifted. And then he pushed a single finger inside her.

She cried out in shock and he froze.

"Should I stop?"

"No!" She took a breath. "I want to know!"

"Tell me if it hurts."

"It doesn't hurt. Not a bit!"

She felt him smile against her ear, but her attention was focused on what his fingers were doing. One deep inside her. In and out while she gasped in need. Then he pushed in two and her body accommodated the larger girth.

Her legs were gripping him, but his remained exactly where they were. So all she did was lift herself higher against him as he pushed in and out. In and out.

He was simulating the sex act, she knew. And it was wonderful!

In and out.

In and out.

In and out and up. A long roll against her clitoris and suddenly her body clenched and burst. Like a spring released, the muscles in her abdomen contracted and released in rhythmic pulse. Such pleasure she felt from it. Such glorious, beautiful, amazing pleasure.

He let her ride it while she gasped. And when she quieted against him, her body feeling languid and so sweet, he gently helped her stretch out on the blanket.

"Gwen," he said against her lips. "Gwen, do we stop? Do you want more?"

"More," she whispered. She definitely wanted more of that.

And then she understood what he meant because he reached for the French letter. He watched her face the whole time. He was slow in his movements and she wanted to put it on him, but she was feeling a little too lazy to move just then.

"Next time," he rasped. "Next time I shall let you put it on me."

It wasn't a question, but she nodded anyway.

He rolled the condom on while she watched. And then he leaned forward to kiss her. His movements were powerful, but not forceful. And she opened beneath him, happy to experience whatever he chose to show her.

He left her mouth to kiss down her neck and suck her right nipple into his mouth. She let the sensations roll through her. Pleasure. Excitement. Now she understood these words.

"Remember," he said as he moved to her other breast. "You have said it. You have told me when to ask and that you will say yes."

She had no idea what he was talking about. She was too absorbed in the feel of his masculine legs as they settled between her thighs. She liked the feel of him there, especially as she felt his penis slide between her folds.

"Gwen?"

"What?"

"You promised, remember?"

"What?"

"To marry me. When I ask, you have promised to say yes."

Oh that. "Yes." She couldn't imagine denying him anything at this point. "Yes, I promised. If you ask."

He thrust inside.

Her mind had been on the unlikely possibility that he would propose to her. She hadn't been prepared for his penetration. It startled her, but not in a bad way. In fact, it felt wonderfully expansive except for the sharp bite of pain.

He stilled, his body flush against hers, his penis as deep inside her as it could go. And it, apparently, could go a very far way.

"Gwen?"

"Yes. Marriage. I said I would."

"No. I mean, yes, but…how do you feel?"

How did she feel? "Like you are very big." She lifted her legs higher such that he settled more firmly against her. "But that we fit very well."

"Yes, we do." His voice was deep, and in the sunlight, she saw the muscles of his jaw and throat work. He was holding himself very still.

"Is that all?" she asked, somewhat confused. She thought there was supposed to be movement. In and out. In and… "Oh yes," she sighed. "That's better."

It was better as he withdrew and pushed back in. Out and then harder in. Out and deeply in.

His tempo started slow, but quickly increased. She found if she arched her back and tightened her legs at the right moment, she felt him impact her clitoris. It was a lovely feeling. It was a needful feeling, and it quickly became a demand.

He matched her desires. Harder. Faster.

Her belly coiled. Her breath caught.

Yes!

She burst into that place of pure sensation, pure bliss. And he shuddered against her, groaning in a way she'd never heard before. It was a masculine growl. If she weren't riding her own wave, she would have paid more attention to it. It sounded very distinctly like him, and she loved it.

And she loved…him?

CHAPTER TWENTY-FOUR

GWEN WAS QUIET afterwards, which was to be expected, but Jackson couldn't guess what she was thinking and that made him uneasy. It was hard to predict how any woman would react to her first sexual experience. He'd heard horror stories and he didn't want that for her. But she rested lazily in his arms and gave him absolutely no clue as to what to do next.

And the afternoon was wearing on. If they didn't get home soon, his father would likely send a search party.

Gwen turned and smiled at him, her eyes languid, her smile curved into a sweet knowing expression that melted his heart. "That was fun," she said.

"I'm very pleased to hear that." And relieved.

"Now I know why Amber and Diana are always giggling about it."

He raised his brows. "Always?"

She shrugged and her breasts moved enticingly against him. "It seems so sometimes, but they could just as easily be talking about china cabinets."

"Because they giggle about china cabinets?"

"Because they giggle, and I never know why."

"Maybe because they are happy." He pressed a kiss to his temple. "I look forward to the day I can hear your giggle."

She laughed lightly in a way that was more of a low chuckle than a giggle. "You may wait a long time for that, my lord. I am not the giggling type."

That was something he already knew. "We should get home soon. They will be wondering where we are."

"And what we are doing?"

He nodded. "Most likely. Tell them that you lost yourself in the plants around the castle."

"I definitely did that," she said. Then she touched his cheek. It was a tentative caress, but he cherished it all the more since she chose the connection. "Thank you," she said. "I understand so much more now."

"I am happy to expand your education as much you want." He blew out a breath. "But there may not be many opportunities before—"

"Yes, I know we will have to return to London. I much prefer it here."

He was going to say before they were married, but he didn't argue. "I have thoughts for the next few days as a way to help you prepare for returning to London. We can discuss them now, if you like."

She smiled and stretched against him. She wasn't being seductive. He doubted she knew how. But it was the single most erotic thing he'd ever experienced. "I know how to pack, my lord."

"I wasn't talking about packing. You're to be the vision of our magical daffodil. You need to practice becoming enchanting."

She frowned at him and he felt the withdrawal in her body as she eased away. "I'm supposed to be enchanted, not enchanting."

"No one cares if you are bewitched. They care that they are."

She opened her mouth to argue, but then stilled. "You are serious about this?"

"Deadly." Because if she failed at this, it would be the death of his financial dreams.

"You want me to practice?"

"Yes."

"And you will teach me *what* to practice."

"Absolutely." Then he added, "My sisters will help."

She blew out a breath. "I suppose you believe this is vitally important. As important as making sure there is enough aeration in the transportation boxes, but not enough room for vermin."

"Yes."

She pushed him back before she sat up. "Then I suppose I must bow to your greater wisdom."

She didn't sound like she wanted to do it. Hell, the last thing he wanted to do was make her fascinating to the *ton*. Especially since the process would likely make her hate him, at least for a while. "I hope you will see that it is time worth spending."

She shrugged and he was distracted by the shift of her breasts in the sunlight. "I shall view it as an experiment. And no matter how it turns out, the experiment is always time well spent."

He could see that she was trying to convince herself of that more than him, but he straightened up and extended his hand to her. "Tell me of some of your unsuccessful experiments."

She arched her brows even as she set her hand in his. "I just said they were all worthwhile." She sounded definite in her words, but he was beginning to know her better. It was in the tilt of her head, he thought. And the way she watched him out of the corner of her eye.

"You know what I meant," he said slowly. "You're teasing me. Or maybe you're testing me. I can't tell."

Her eyes widened. "What do you mean?"

"Oh no. You can't play ignorant like that. I know how smart you are." He leaned forward. "You are trying to tie me up in words and never answer my question. Why?"

She bit her lip and looked away. "I… I don't know. No one ever seems to know when I'm joking or not. Sometimes I just play."

He thought about that. He even cupped her chin—slowly—before turning her face so he could study it. "I think you are annoyed at me for making you do something you don't want to do, and so you turned it around on me. You play a verbal game designed to irritate me as a way to get even."

He wasn't angry. In truth, he was pleased that he had figured it out. He saw it as a harmless kind of fun for a woman who was so much smarter than everyone she knew. Except he was a match for her intelligence—or at least he came close—because he had figured it out. And her next words confirmed it.

"How did you know?"

He smiled. "Do you think I could make love to you, propose to you, and not make an effort to understand you? What kind of man would I be if I took what I wanted and never bothered to see you?"

She arched her brows. "I don't know how to answer that question. I never imagined a man would ever ask me that."

He grinned. "It would seem that I am as unique as you are."

"Yes," she said, her voice low as she drew her brows together. "Yes, it would seem so."

Then she set her hands to his torso. They both stood naked and so close that he felt the heat from her body. His cock bobbed between them, erect again and more than willing to lay her back down on the blanket. But he didn't move to do so. First, they had no time. And second, he wasn't willing to break the spell she seemed to be in as she moved her hands across his chest and onto his shoulders.

Finally, she lifted her chin to face him eye to eye.

"You have my attention, my lord, and that is rare indeed for a person. More than that, you have my respect." Then she arched her brow. "I cannot fathom how you accomplished it."

Coming from her, that was high praise indeed. "I did it by listening to you, Gwen. By being interested in you because you are a fascinating woman."

"Don't give me Spanish coin—" she began, but he cut her off.

"I'm not flattering you," he said harshly. It irritated him that she didn't see her own worth. But rather than repeat—again—how impressed he was by her, he went another direction. "I'm teaching you. You become fascinating by being fascinated by the person you are with. You become magical by being magical with them."

"That doesn't make sense."

"It does to me." He touched her mouth. As always, he went slowly, but he wanted to stroke that part of her. Or any part, really. "Will you try it?"

"If you give me more specifics on how it is accomplished."

"I will."

"And if we can come up here again." Her eyes seemed to dance. "Soon."

His cock jumped at that, but he held himself back. There wasn't time, and he didn't want to make her sore. "It would be my absolute pleasure."

She nodded. "Oh, but I don't have any more French letters."

"I can get some."

"Excellent." Then she wrinkled her nose. "I am getting cold. We should either dress now or return to the blanket."

He groaned. Did she know how much she tempted him? Especially when she licked her lips and looked up at him like a botanical temptress?

"If we lay back down," he said, "we will tarry much too long."

She sighed and stepped away. He wanted to watch her dress, to see the sensuous way she moved her body even when she was doing nothing more than pulling on her stockings. But she glanced over her shoulder not at him but the location of the sun. He looked too and was startled to see it already heading toward the horizon. They had definitely tarried here too long.

With a groan, he dressed as well. It was hard tucking everything back away, especially when he knew she peeked at him. His cock was hungry for more, and she was making him regret promising to wait to propose to her. He wanted her now and not in a year's time when his finances were settled. Even total disaster would be easier with her by his side and in his bed. But in this—as in all things with her—he knew that patience was the key. She needed the slow approach, and so he forced himself to wait.

And in the meantime, he packed up the remains of their meal. She went to gather "a few cuttings" while he hitched up the gig. He worked as quickly as possible, but his mind kept replaying moments from this afternoon. He ought to think about his plans, but she filled his thoughts and—

"Jackson! Jackson! Come quick!"

Her cries startled him and the horse as she came tearing full tilt from around the side of the castle. He spun and broke into a dead run straight at her. As he moved, he scanned her face and body but could see no injury, no blood. Nothing but the excitement in her face and the wind through her hair.

He caught her with a rush, grabbing her around the torso rather than have her flatten them both. He spun her around merely to absorb their momentum so they could both remain upright. And when he finally set her onto her feet, she giggled—actually giggled—at him.

"You look so terrified."

He could already see that she was happy, so at least his terror had subsided. "You gave me a scare," he said. "What happened?"

"Come see!" she said as she grabbed his hand and headed back up the hill.

"Gwen, we must get back."

She rolled her eyes. "Come. See!"

So he did. And the time he took was worth a month's delay in all his plans. Fortunately, just like her, it was a miracle dropped into his lap at just the right time.

CHAPTER TWENTY-FIVE

GWEN LAUGHED AS she tugged Jackson around the corner. "I was going to the kitchen garden. There always is one and who knows what could have grown there since the place has been abandoned."

"Slow down, Gwen," he said as he intertwined their fingers.

"I have slowed down!" She wanted to run, run, run with her arms spread wide and the wind flowing through her hair.

"The kitchen was over there."

"I know! But I got turned around and stumbled upon the bath house."

"Good lord, that caved in decades ago."

"And a good thing too," she said. They cleared the last tree, and she made an expansive gesture. "Look!"

He did, and she saw his eyes widened. "Are those—"

"Daffodils. Not yet bloomed. Because of the remaining walls, this place must have kept the snow longer than the rest." Plus there was shade from the nearby trees as well. And now they had a small field of young daffodils.

"This is fantastic!" he exclaimed as he stepped closer to look. He stopped just short of the closest flower, clearly not wanting to crush any of the crop. "We can take these with us to London when we return." He grinned. "And now we have extra plants to sell." He looked around. "Maybe enough to cover this year's expense and invest in next year."

She nodded. That was her thought exactly.

He rubbed a hand down his face. "There isn't time to figure this out now. I need to think."

She stayed silent, respecting his need to think. Her mind was spinning with the possibility of timing their crop such that they weren't flooding the Season with daffodils for two weeks, then nothing for the rest of the year. She'd often wondered if the environment could be adjusted to speed up or delay blooming. This dilapidated bath house told her it could. Nature had already set it up for them. She just had to figure out how to maximize the late blooming yield—

"We need to go back to the house now. We're going to be very busy in the next couple days and I need you to start training now."

She grimaced. "Must I?"

He chuckled and pressed a kiss to the edge of her mouth. "I'm going to teach you how to be popular and pretend it was all because of a flower."

It sounded silly, but it was hard to doubt his air of total confidence. She found herself entering into his enthusiasm as they headed back toward the gig.

"It's very simple," he said, "and we're going to practice on the drive back, but it boils down to this: an honest compliment."

She frowned at him. "Are you joking? I cannot tell."

He handed her into the gig. "Not a joke. No matter who it is, you must say something honest to them about your feelings toward them. And it must be a compliment."

"But I don't have many feelings toward people. And those I do have are usually not complimentary."

"That is why you have to practice." He flicked the reins and they started moving. She had one last moment to look over the dilapidated and thoroughly magical castle. Such things she had done and seen here! But as soon as they passed the moat and were on the road, such as it was, her thoughts dimmed considerably.

"Gwen—"

"I don't think this will work," she said glumly.

He blew out a breath. "Gwen, I cannot be constantly fighting you on this. You have agreed to trust my judgment, so I would ask—"

"Yes, I know. I will." So far he had proven himself correct about so many things. "I will do what you ask."

Except it was very hard.

He began simply. When they returned home—filled with the tales of plans for their unexpected daffodil harvest—Jackson enlisted his sisters in teaching her the art of an honest compliment. She couldn't just say she liked someone's jacket or shoes. She had to listen to whatever they said and respond with a true admiration within five minutes. Five minutes! By that time, she was usually bored with whomever spoke with her.

"You're a smart woman," he chided while his sisters were preparing their first test for her. "You're well-read in a variety of subjects. Surely you can find something to admire in everyone you meet."

"The two do not go together," she returned. "Just because I find books fascinating, does not mean I find people the least bit educational."

"But there is so much more to admire in people," he said. "Take my father, for example." The man was reading a newspaper on the opposite side of the room. "Surely you find something worthwhile in him."

"Of course, I do. I find his determination to protect his family honorable. So many men ignore their responsibilities in favor of frivolities."

"So go tell him that."

"What?"

"Say that to him."

She wrinkled her nose. "Won't he find that odd? We have not

discussed anything together beyond the price of corn."

"If you speak from the heart, he will hear the honesty in your words."

"But—" She cut off her words at his expression. His brows were raised, his head cocked to the side, and most telling, his arms were folded across his chest. He was trying to be encouraging, but she knew he was exasperated with her constant questions. She bit back her arguments and vowed to please him in this. Or at least try. The sooner he saw that she was hopeless at it, the sooner they could make other plans.

She approached the earl. "My lord," she said tentatively. "I…I wish to say something to you."

He set down the newspaper and eyed her over his glasses. "Yes?" The word carried all the dismissal she'd heard from men all her life. He was tolerating her presence out of politeness, but he truly wished to return to reading rather than speak with her.

Normally she'd make an apology and leave. She had no interest in speaking with someone who would rather be reading, but she had promised and persevered.

"I, um, wished to say that I admire how fiercely you work to safeguard your family's welfare. I know you and your son have disagreed. I wish to say that I admire that determination."

He frowned at her, his lips pursed. And then the frown turned uglier, as did his tone. "It does him no credit to send you over with sweet words to change my mind. I don't care—"

"He didn't send me!" She frowned. Well, that wasn't exactly true. She wouldn't be here if Jackson hadn't forced her. "Oh, this is ridiculous," she said. She would have said it to Jackson, but he wasn't even in the room. He'd left for some reason.

"I quite agree," the earl said as she picked up the newspaper again.

"My lord," she huffed out. "Your son is teaching me to give compliments. I am to give one to every soul in this household."

"That shouldn't prove difficult. He's always been adept with a glib tongue."

"Maybe he has, but I have not. He tells me it must be an honest statement, and so I said it to you." She folded her arms across her chest. "I know you think his daffodil idea is a mad scheme, but it is a hard thing for anyone to stand against someone as persuasive as your son, myself included. But you have. You are not thwarting him out of hatred or petty jealousy. You are standing firm to protect your family's assets. Indeed, I believe you have set your life to the careful, conservative management of your finances. That is admirable indeed." She blew out a breath. That was the longest statement she'd ever made to someone who was not part of her family or interested in botany.

And it was clear that the earl had no idea how to respond to that. He pulled off his glasses and leaned back in his chair. He regarded her with a heavy stare. "And what do you think of his idea?"

She considered her words carefully. "I believe in him and the work he has done. Despite the risk, I have pledged my dowry to his use."

"What?" the man exploded. His foot—which had been crossed over one knee—dropped heavily against the floor and he leaned forward to bellow. "You are marrying him?"

She leaped back a foot. "No! No, I am giving him my dowry."

"The devil, you say."

She had never understood that expression, not knowing whether the speaker was arguing with her statement or with her. Fortunately, she was saved an answer, as Jackson came back into the room. His expression was locked down, but his jaw was clenched tight and so Gwen guessed he wasn't happy. But about what she wasn't exactly sure.

"Father, I believe you have startled our guest."

"No, no," Gwen rushed to say. "I think I startled him."

"I'd say she did," the earl barked. "You are marrying her?"

"No!" she rushed. "I am old enough to manage my own funds—"

she began, but no one appeared to be listening to her.

"Would you object?" Jackson said, his voice sounding more like a threat than a question.

"I won't have it!" his father said as he pushed to his feet. "Bad enough you are destroying your money, but to take a naïve girl's dowry is heinous."

Jackson didn't answer, but Gwen could see his jaw tick in fury. Fortunately, she had the right response now. And she said it before more angry words could flow between the two men.

"What I find heinous," she said into the silence, "is that you could dismiss my intelligence so completely. That you have no understanding of your son's integrity. And that you would feign outrage over my dowry when in truth you object to the idea that your son would stoop so low as to marry one such as me."

Jackson spun to her, his eyes wide. "That's not what he meant."

"Try to see this logically," she said. "If you had come here with a polished lady of the *ton* and presented her as your bride, he would have embraced me with open arms. He has not. Instead, you have fought night and day over your plans for the daffodils. And now he accuses you of marrying me for my dowry."

Jackson shook his head. "The fault is between me and my father. It has nothing—"

"Did you argue with him before I came?"

"No, but—"

"Then you can see how my conclusion is sound." She turned to his father. "You do not approve of me, correct?"

She wasn't sure he would answer honestly, but in this he was very much like his son. Despite the way his teeth ground together, he spoke the truth. "Jackson has always chosen the right path, seen the right way, but he's never been smart with women."

"What?" Jackson gasped.

"You turn their heads, and then they turn yours. It happened with

Lady Meunier."

"Isabelle has nothing to do with anything."

The earl shook his head. "All the heiresses you could have charmed. Every single one of them an excellent choice for your bride. Instead, you pick a widow who might as well be a man. She dines with bankers, speaks often on how useless men are, even pushes the vote for women."

"Isabelle is a woman of many opinions, and I learned a great deal from her."

The earl took a step forward as he glared at his son. "She turned you away from the normal way of things. Find a wealthy woman, marry her, and launch your sisters."

"That is not the only way to make money."

But his father wasn't to be deterred. Now that he was finally speaking his mind, he would not stop. "Always the odd women with you, strange ideas and ridiculous chances."

Jackson straightened up to his full height. "You don't know what you're talking about."

"Why can't you do things the normal way? You never listen. Always one wild hair after another, and all because of your women."

"And by my women, you mean Isabelle and Gwen?"

"You need to find a woman like your mother or my Jenny. A solid woman who settles you and doesn't encourage you on wild tears. Daffodils! What's wrong with corn?"

Jackson didn't answer his father's tirade. Instead, he turned to her and bowed deeply before her. "Lady Gwen, I apologize for my father. He is in his cups and has forgotten himself."

Was he? Gwen looked back at the earl. It was true, his eyes did shine bright and there was the unmistakable odor of port. But she doubted that was the real reason for the outburst. Then she turned to see Jackson's sisters at the base of the stairs, looking on with stricken eyes. They were dressed oddly, but Gwen dismissed it as yet something new she didn't understand.

But the outrage on the earl's face and the pain in Jackson's stiff bearing was something she did comprehend. So she touched Jackson's arm and tried to gently draw him from the room. He didn't move at first. Instead, he shot his father a furious glare.

"We will speak of this later," he said. Then he gave Gwen his arm and together they walked past his sisters and out of the house. They didn't stop when Camile touched his shoulder or Abigail pulled off a heavy gardening hat and threw it onto a bench. They didn't even stop when Lady Albury ducked her chin and headed back into the kitchen without saying a word.

They headed out the doors and ended up in his mother's daffodil garden. It wasn't until he was standing there among the blossoms that he turned back to her.

"I'm terribly sorry. That was inexcusable."

"You've never seen it before, have you?"

"What?"

"The things men say about odd women."

"Don't be silly."

"Didn't Aunt Isabelle mention it?"

"Well, of course there are always ignorant people who refuse to take orders from a woman. I was there at her side telling them to shut up or lose their job. I never thought my own father would…"

He shook his head.

"I was engaged for one night, did you know that?"

He jolted. "What?"

"A gentleman in my third season proposed and I accepted. He had a fondness for science, and we got along well. Then I chanced to overhear him speaking with his oldest friend." She smiled. "I've learned to be quiet in rooms and often overlooked. I've heard the most interesting things that way."

"It must have been idiotic, whatever you heard."

"The exact words don't matter. Suffice it to say that he said something very similar to what your father said. That I was an odd duck, but my dowry was worth it. His mama would just have to get used to it."

"Who was this blighter?"

She smiled. "He married someone else two years later and I'm told she's a terrible shrew."

"Good. I hope he's miserable. Saves me from calling him out."

She touched his face, gently encouraging him to look directly at her. "Jackson—"

"I cannot apologize enough for my father's abominable behavior—"

"I think he was right," she said.

"What?"

"You do like odd ducks, don't you? Your sisters, every one of them, is unusual in her own unique way. I gather it is only your stepmother and mother who were traditional society women."

He nodded slowly, though she could tell he didn't want to agree.

"Lilah told me once that parents have dreams for their children. They imagine all sorts of futures, but often become especially fond of the future they'd wanted for themselves. Mama had all sorts of requirements for the man I was to marry, and not a one of her requirements meant anything to me. Similarly, I'd guess that your father had dreams for your wife as well. A future countess to carry on the title and bear him grandchildren worthy of your name."

Jackson gave her a diffident nod that was half shrug. "Whenever he comes to London, he makes sure to introduce me to entirely suitable, very dull women."

"Not at all to your tastes."

He gave a mock shudder. "Average looks, average fortune, and average intelligence. There was nothing wrong with them—"

"Except they did not spark your interest."

He shook his head.

"Instead, you became involved with Aunt Isabelle."

"I worked for her," he stressed. "It was only in the beginning that there was anything more."

"And she is not the usual choice for a young, titled man about town."

"Definitely not."

"And in all that time, did someone not tell you how strange your preferences were?"

"Of course not. It would be damned impertinent if they did."

"And yet, they say that to odd women all the time."

"Stop saying that! I hate it when you do not see your own worth."

"But I do see my own worth in my own way. And thanks to you, I see much more of it than I ever did. But now, I think, you begin to see the cost of spending time with an odd woman. Even your own father thinks you are daft for it."

"My father can go to the devil, then. I find you everything that is appropriate." So saying he abruptly cupped her face and kissed her. A few days before, she might have stiffened at his touch. He had moved quickly without her seeing it coming. The press of his lips, the invasion of his tongue, were forceful and dominant. And yet, she softened, though it took a conscious decision on her part. And before long, he relaxed his fervor which in turn allowed her to melt into his arms.

All in all, it took three seconds to go from stiff to completely at home. And now, when he lifted his mouth from hers, she smiled at him.

"You are not odd," he said.

"Yes, I am. And so are you, so I think we match in that." She smiled. "It is only because you are a man that people have not been saying so to your face."

"Even so, my father had no right to say what he did."

She shrugged. What did she care about his father? It was the pain in his eyes that tore at her. "What will you do now?"

"Exactly what I was going to do before. I am going to show the world your beauty. And in so doing, I'm going to sell a lot of daffodils."

"Excellent—"

"And when that is done, I'm going to come to you with my fortune and ask for your hand in marriage."

"And when you have made your fortune, you will have your pick of women. The odd ones or the heiresses who are intelligent and acceptable. They do exist, you know."

He nodded gravely. "Remember that, will you?"

"What?"

"That when I have made my fortune, I will have my pick of women. Then you will believe that I freely choose you."

She smiled. "I will not hold you to your promise, my lord."

"I don't care," he returned tartly. "Because I am holding you to yours." Then he kissed her again, and she reveled in it. Except that she could feel the anger in him still. She didn't know what to do about it. She had no words to console him. She had long since learned to feel pride in her strengths even if her intelligence, for example, was considered unusual.

He would have to find his own peace with his oddity.

Then he surprised her. He pulled back from their kiss and pressed another one to the tip of her nose.

"No one," he rasped. "No one will ever disparage you like that again. Not in my presence. Not even my own father."

His words were illogical. Even as formidable as he was, he could not stop everyone, nor could he see what the future held. And yet, his words warmed her nonetheless. Warmed her until she kissed him as desperately as he seemed to need her.

It was many hours before they returned to the house.

Chapter Twenty-Six

Life progressed very quickly after that. Jackson spent the bulk of his time with Gwen, helping her learn the art of conversation, and he was proud of how earnestly she worked. Once she'd given her word, she did as he asked with little objection. He saw how difficult it was for her. Conversation was often awkward, but she got better with every dialogue.

Fortunately, his sisters threw themselves into the task as well, dressing up as one character after another as they pretended to be boorish or bad smelling or whatever their inventive minds could make up. Then Jackson took Gwen to meet every single soul in Lincolnshire. He found himself showing her off with pride and was inordinately pleased when she did well with them.

Oddly enough, she was much more at ease with the laborers than she was with anyone else. They spoke about crops or medicinal plants, and she listened closely to whatever their ideas were, even if their opinion was that it was stupid to change a good oat crop to flowers.

A total success—in Lincolnshire. But tomorrow dawn they headed for London and the real test.

"But don't you want to talk to your father before we go?" she asked Jackson as they strolled one last time through the daffodil garden.

"The man has been drinking since supper. No good can come of a conversation now."

"I hate being the cause of a rift between father and son."

"You were merely the catalyst. The reaction would have happened eventually." He felt proud of himself for using a chemical comparison, and she smiled in acknowledgement. Though her silence told him that he had not made a perfect analogy. He would have to study more if he wanted to keep up with her brilliant mind. Or maybe he would just have to make sure he satisfied her in other ways. In the short five days since their trip to the castle, he had found ways to expand her education in sexual pleasure. If it weren't for the prune-faced maid who was going to sit with them during the carriage ride, he would have looked forward to their travel. As it was now, he was simply anxious to get it over with.

"I have memorized the facts you gave me," she said. "Lord Blackstone revels in his military past, Lady Morgan enjoys a fondness for pugs." She blew out a breath. "I am able to memorize lengthy facts about various plant specimens, but this taxed even my skills."

He had given her notes on every member of the *ton*. It had taken him years to amass that information and she had memorized it in a few hours. "You amaze me."

"Just don't hate me if I fail to take in London."

"If you stumble, that will be from my mistakes, not yours. And since neither of us is prone to failure, I believe you shall be a complete success."

She shook her head. "I was less nervous at my first come out."

"Then allow me to distract you for a time."

She did. She always did, and it pleased him to feel how easily she allowed him to touch her now. She never flinched anymore. In truth, she tended to lean into his caresses and even initiated many of her own. How far they'd come from the very start.

"In three nights, you will be the belle of the ball."

"Then I suggest you make sure your distraction techniques last a very long time."

He grinned. "I will do my best."

And he did. But even the best seduction techniques faded after a day in a carriage. By the time they arrived in London at the end of the second day, they were both a bundle of nerves. Everything depended on the ball the next evening.

But the moment he stepped out of the carriage at her home, he knew there was a problem. It was early evening during the Season. Gwen's home should have been quiet as her mother went to parties. Instead, the house was ablaze with lights and at least two coaches were waiting on the street for their owners to return.

"Is your mother hosting an entertainment tonight? Perhaps an intimate supper?"

"I don't believe so," Gwen said as she pressed her fingers against her eyes as if to clear them. She'd been dozing against him in the carriage and he loved seeing her appear slightly tousled and very dreamy. Sadly, he could not do what he was thinking at the moment. Instead, he extended his arm and together they walked toward the house.

"Maybe someone else on the street is having an event." He said the words, but he didn't think it likely. Hers was the only home lit brightly this evening. And then as they were just about to raise the knocker, the door was pulled open to reveal a woman donning her hat. She took one look at the two of them, and her eyes widened as her mouth shaped into an O of horror. Or perhaps it was delight, because she immediately spun around.

"She's home! Patricia, she's alive!"

Gwen flinched at the words and he tightened his grip on her arm in support. But then she spoke, her voice level and seemingly unaffected though he knew from the tension in her body that she was covering her confusion.

"Yes, I'm alive," she said as they made it to the door and the butler stepped out as if to greet them. "Mr. Parry, was there some reason to believe I'd perished?"

The man sniffed as he all but tugged her off Jackson's arm. He did it under the guise of taking her coat, but his haughty expression was aimed directly at Jackson. "His lordship's character has been called into question," the butler said heavily. "We have been most worried about you, Lady Gwen."

Gwen surrendered her coat, but not her wits. "Lord Sayres has been a complete gentleman. You do no good to impugn him like that."

Jackson winced. Truthfully, he had not behaved gentlemanly at all with her, but her defense of his character warmed him nonetheless. "Perhaps we should step inside," he said, as he attempted to do just that. Unfortunately, the butler blocked his way and though he could have easily overpowered the older man, Jackson did not want to resort to fisticuffs before he knew what was going on.

Meanwhile, Gwen's mother came rushing forward from the front parlor.

"Thank God! We have been in such a state of worry." She embraced Gwen in a dramatic rush of skirts and perfume. Gwen tolerated it, but her gaze went over her mother's shoulder to the crowd of women standing in the hallway watching.

"My lady," Jackson said loudly. "Please tell us what has occurred. We are at a loss as to why you appear so worried."

One of the older ladies pushed forward through the press of women in the hallway. He recognized her as the Dowager Countess Highburn, and a more bitter shrew never existed. "How dare you!" the woman wheezed. "You dare enter the house of good people? Begone sirrah! We will have none of you here."

At that, the butler tried to push the door shut, but Jackson's foot firmly blocked the motion. Hell, his reputation had never been stellar—he'd need a full coffer for that—but he'd never sunk so low as to have women cursing him in the parlor.

"My lady, I cry foul. What have I done to earn such recrimination?"

Rather than answer, the woman hissed, "Degenerate libertine!"

And the others nodded their agreement, all repeating that phrase or several others. One of the women, however, made a different choice. She gestured Gwen forward with urgent motions. "Come away from him, Lady Gwen."

Gwen just stared at all the people in her front hallway as she disentangled herself from her mother's embrace. "Mr. Parry, step aside. Lord Sayres is attempting to enter."

"Lord Satyr, you mean," the Dowager Countess Highburn retorted.

"No," frowned Gwen as she raised her voice. "Lord Sayres." She spoke his name as if to a deaf woman, and Jackson would have laughed if the situation weren't so serious. If his reputation was in tatters, so too would his flowers and all their efforts would be for nothing. Then she turned and tried to pull him inside, but the damned butler prevented her and that he couldn't tolerate. He would not push inside of his own accord, but Lady Gwen would not be stopped in her own home.

So he gently elbowed the man aside. And when a gentle elbow didn't suffice, he reached around and tapped the man on his opposite shoulder. Mr. Parry twisted around because that's what butlers did when tapped, allowing Jackson to neatly step to Gwen's side.

Given that the other choice was to manhandle the butler, he thought his trickery was well done. Apparently, Gwen thought so too because she whispered, "You must teach me how to do that."

The dowager countess, on the other hand, voiced her objection loudly. "The nerve!" she shaped. "How dare you—"

"Why are you here, my lady?" Gwen interrupted. Her tone of voice was calm, but Jackson could feel the tension in her as she gripped his fingers. "Why is everyone here?"

"They believe he has ravished you," came a voice from the stairs.

It was Lilah, Gwen's half-sister. "And they are here to…console Mama." The pause before the word "console" indicated that they were here for gossip more than anything else.

"Ravish me?" Gwen said. "Why?"

He assumed she meant why would they think that as opposed to why would anyone want to ravish her, but with Gwen, one never fully knew. Fortunately, Lilah answered the relevant question as she descended the stairs.

"There are rumors—"

"Witnesses!" huffed one lady.

"They claim all manner of malicious intent."

"From me?" Jackson asked. "What have I done?"

Several ladies began speaking at once with others agreeing in rising volume, but it was Gwen's mother herself who finally put an end to it.

"Be silent everyone. I swear this whole mishap has given me the headache."

It took a moment, but the ladies did quiet enough for him to speak. "I gather that Lady Meunier has been at the rumor mill again," he said, making an effort to keep his voice light.

"It is not rumor, but fact!" the dowager countess cried.

"Truly?"

He stepped forward, alarmed to see many of the ladies shying backwards as if he were a leper. Gwen stepped up beside him, obviously wanting to defend him, but in this she would only damage herself. He needed to stem the tide of public opinion, and he needed to do it now. Fortunately, the right woman was in the crowd, though her presence here hurt. He'd once counted her a friend.

"Mrs. Bradley, I didn't see you in the back there. Well met."

She huffed and drew herself up to her full height. She opened her mouth to speak, but he didn't give her the opportunity.

"How is your dear little dog? Muffin is his name, isn't it?" A decidedly too benign name for the sharp-toothed terrier she adored. By way of explanation, he turned to the crowd in the hall. "Dear Muffin was ill, and Mrs. Bradley was beside herself, Mr. Bradley being, um, indisposed." The man had been in his cups and fully insensate as the dog had lay moaning at his feet. She sent a message to her son asking for his help, but the boy had been equally indisposed. So it was that Jackson had come to her aid, sitting with her all through the night as the dog slowly recovered on his own. He had held the lady's hand and talked with her gently throughout the night. "I believe I spent the night with you then, the two of us taking turns giving poor Muffin water through a dropper. You told me then I was an angel among men."

Mrs. Bradley looked down at her hands and mumbled, "You were most kind."

"Did I make any heinous attack on your person?" he asked. "If I am a reprobate, surely I would have made some sort of advance."

"Of course not!" she said, outrage in her tone. It was the only answer she could give, first and foremost because it was true, but also because to suggest otherwise would damage her own reputation. After all, they had spent the night together as they tended the dog. That could only happen if his reputation were unimpeachable.

"Just because you were kind once—" began the dowager countess. Fortunately, he had sited his next target and was able to interrupt her.

"Mrs. Saunderson," he said. "How is your housekeeper's health? And your cook? It was last Season, wasn't it, when both ladies and indeed half the staff took ill just days before your ball. You begged me to help as you were beside yourself with worry for the dear ladies." She'd actually been terrified that she was sick herself and was importuning all of her intimates to help her. He had been only one of three who had given her aid, but he had spent several hours closeted with her because no one else would risk infection. "We wracked our brains for a solution and finally—after several hours' discussion—managed to pull together a perfect menu. Everyone said your ball was the best that

Season, and your staff recovered quickly, thank Heaven."

"I did most of the work."

"You did," he pressed. "But I believe—"

"You told me he was a Godsend," said Gwen's mother, her tone sharp. "I remember that now. You told me you couldn't have done it without him." She straightened up. "And you said Violet developed a tendre for him, but he never laid a finger on her. You said he was the perfect gentleman!"

Oh yes, he remembered Violet now. Mrs. Saunderson's daughter, not yet out of the nursery. She had big eyes and the most adorable laugh. He'd teased her to make her smile, nothing more. He had no idea she'd turned him into a romantic hero.

"I don't remember that," Mrs. Saunderson said stiffly.

"But I do," retorted Gwen's mother with heavy tones. "As does Mrs. Lawrence, Lady Wattingham, and Mrs. Burke. We talked about it over tea for three afternoons straight."

Jackson had no idea if the ladies had indeed discussed it, but it didn't matter. The three women nodded rather than argue with their hostess.

"Why, I believe Lord Sayres had helped any number of us over the years. When our husbands and sons fail us, he has stepped in to help. Esther, didn't he find you a new coachman when your other one left? Agnes, didn't you tell me he found a jeweler to repair your necklace when it was broken?"

Finding decent servants was easy if they were well treated. Esther had needed a new coachman who didn't mind being screeched at whenever her ladyship was late. As for Agnes, he'd found her a fence to replace the stones with paste.

It was how he existed so easily on the edge of society. He was around when ladies sent frantic messages to their husbands or sons. When family had no interest in helping, he often lent a hand. It endeared him to the ladies and their men, which made it easy for him to find investors for Isabelle. It was also an easy way to keep up on society gossip, which always came in handy.

"Well that just proves the point," the Dowager Countess Highburn cried. "He's always around, always sniffing around ladies. Whyever for if not—"

"To enlist you in an orgy?" Gwen cried. "Do you hear how ridiculous that sounds?"

Absolute silence filled the hallway as everyone turned horrified looks on Gwen. She didn't understand that ladies were not supposed to even know the word, much less utter it aloud. Meanwhile, Gwen continued as she pulled off her gloves as if she were about to throw them down like gauntlets.

"That is what he's accused of, isn't it? Orgies? Relations with every woman about town, often several at once. My goodness, can any of you imagine a man with such stamina as he is accused? Truly? He's a fine man, to be sure, but when would he have the time, much less the strength?"

Countess Highburn was not to be deterred. She curled her lip. "You are too young, Lady Gwen, to understand these things."

"On the contrary," she began, and Jackson tightened his grip on her hand. She could not mean to reveal what they'd done together. Thankfully, she was smarter than that. "I have a married sister and a sister-in-law. They tell me things." She stepped forward. "Ladies, you are all married. Are your men able to…act over and over, several times a night? Don't they just fall asleep?"

The embarrassed shuffling of feet gave answer enough.

"So is it logical to assume that Lord Sayres has done…" She gestured vaguely with her hands. "Whatever it is that's been said? All while tending to sick dogs, helping arrange balls, and hiring coachmen?" She turned to him. "I believe, my lord, that you have an enemy with a vicious tongue. One who is illogical, thankfully, so it is easy to see the truth of it."

He nodded. He knew exactly who had done it. Indeed, he had said so, but the women hadn't been interested in targeting her. So he left it open to their speculation.

"I believe you are right," he said. "But who could want to tarnish me so badly that she would tarnish every one of your reputations as well as mine? Who hates you, Mrs. Saunderson? Mrs. Bradley? I cannot imagine such perfidy. Thank God it was so easily exposed. Otherwise, how would your daughters fare if your reputation was impugned? Or your nieces? Not to mention sweet Violet who is so innocent, I believe a false word would hurt her deeply."

That was enough to turn the tide. The women had a mystery that included a subtle threat to every lady here. Gwen's mother called for more tea, and the women returned to the parlor, apparently eager to discuss the problem.

Well done, he thought, but this was just one group of ladies. There were likely several others comparing him to Satan right now in parlors and in ballrooms throughout London. That made everything more difficult. And in case he didn't realize it, Gwen's mother turned her hard gaze onto him.

"There, Lord Sayres," she said with a hard glare. "I have stopped the worst of it here, but this must end or you may not ever come near my daughter again."

He nodded as he looked to Gwen. "I must double check all of our plans for tomorrow night. We cannot debut the daffodil in the midst of a scandal."

Gwen's eyes were dark with worry. "We cannot delay either. The flowers for tomorrow night have already been cut. They will not be fresh beyond tomorrow."

He was well aware. "I must talk with Mrs. Ross immediately." It was at her ball that Gwen was going to make her debut.

"No, no," her mother said impatiently. "She has denounced you. It was either that or lose her reputation completely."

"What?" he gasped. He and Mrs. Ross had been friends since he first arrived in London a decade ago. He'd introduced her to her husband and stood at her wedding.

"She had no choice. They've been saying the two of you were lovers. Her husband is furious."

Her husband wasn't the only one. Damnation, just how far had Isabelle gone to destroy him? The answer was obvious. She'd done exactly what she excelled at. She destroyed his reputation among the financial set, and now among the *ton*.

"You must appear somewhere at the height of respectability," Gwen's mother said. "Somewhere no one would question as part of your network of evil."

He had a network of evil?

"Almack's, then," Gwen said.

Both he and her mother frowned at her. "What?"

"We must debut our flower at Almack's. There is no place more respectable than that."

He groaned. She was right. No place was more respectable, but could he get in? Could he convince the patronesses to display his flowers? He had a smooth tongue, but no one was that clever. Not with those biddies.

"Promise them popularity," Gwen said. "That's what you promised me."

Her mother huffed. "Is that what he offered you? My goodness, Gwen, you could have asked me."

Gwen didn't respond to her mother's gibe. Instead, she looked him in the eye. "Can you do it?"

It was a simple question, and yet he responded to it like a clarion call. "I will," he said firmly. He had to or they were both done, and he'd never be able to ask for her hand in marriage.

"Excellent," she said, as if that settled everything. Then she turned to her mother as she headed toward the stairs. "I am going to change out of these wretched clothes. And then I have to find Elliott. I am done waiting for my dowry. I should like the money now." She glanced at Jackson. "In case you need to bribe your way into Almack's."

Chapter Twenty-Seven

"I WANT YOU to come." Five words that Gwen had been repeating over and over. "If it can't be him, I want you."

Lilah smiled as she finished admiring Gwen's earbobs. They were tiny daffodils painted with the correct anatomy and then cut and glued onto ear dangles, all made by Beatrix. "These are beautiful," she said as she handed them to Gwen. "And he'll be there."

Gwen stared down at her hands and did her best not to fiddle with the pin vase at her bodice. It had water in it, but no flower. Not yet. Not until the very last moment. "Aunt Isabelle has made him out to be a… a…" She couldn't find the right word to describe all the things that had been attributed to him.

"A satyr?"

"Yes! And it's just not true!"

"Of course, it's not true."

Except it was, at least where she was concerned. They'd made love several times while in Lincolnshire. She'd been the one begging for it every time, but that didn't change the truth. He was an excellent lover. Almost mythical in his abilities, she thought. And every time she claimed that he was the purest, most moral gentleman she'd ever met, she was lying. He was the best, most amazing man she'd ever met, and that was enough for her.

"Gwen? What are you thinking?"

That she was in love and that was uncomfortable. He made her laugh, and she never felt awkward or odd in his presence. He challenged her mind and let her say whatever she believed as forcefully as she wanted. And when he touched her, everything else disappeared. She always felt safe in his arms, and often she felt so much more.

She was in love with Jackson, and she didn't know what to do about it. Did she tell him? Wouldn't he feel forced to marry her then? Did she want a husband who came to her out of guilt and obligation?

"Gwen?"

She jerked her attention back to her half-sister. "Mama says Lord Sayres has been banned from Almack's. So I want you—"

"I am a bastard, Gwen. I've never been allowed there before, and I won't be allowed inside now."

"That's not fair! You deserve to dance and find a husband just like everyone else."

Lilah didn't respond. She didn't need to because they both knew the world wasn't fair. But if ever a woman deserved happiness, it was Lilah.

"When this is over," Gwen declared loudly, "I will set my mind to getting you a good husband."

Her sister squeezed Gwen's hand. "When this is over, I have plans of my own."

"What plans? They must be very smart because..." her voice trailed away as Lilah shook her head.

"No more talk. Tonight is about you."

The panic that had disappeared when she focused on Lilah returned now with renewed power. "I can't be clever on my own! Not without him, not without you. I'll resort to talking botany and that's not what we need right now."

Lilah pressed a kiss to Gwen's cheek, then stepped back. "You look beautiful. Mama will be there to help."

"She never helps—"

"And if you get self-conscious, remember that he thinks you're perfect just as you are."

Gwen frowned at Lilah. "How do you know that? He's never said—"

"It's in the way he looks at you. And besides, I know it too. You're perfect." And with that, she pulled the first of several daffodils from the vase on the dressing table and began slipping them carefully into the holders tucked into Gwen's hair. She saved the last for the largest pin at her bodice. "Ready?" Lilah asked.

"Not in the least. I hate Almack's."

"After tonight, you're going to love it."

"LADY JERSEY, YOU cannot deny me entrance tonight." Jackson struggled to keep his voice even. He stood outside the entrance to the Marriage Mart. It was society's most holy place where virginal girls went to find husbands while five patronesses watched over the proceedings like queens. Lady Jersey was only one of the five, but she was his last hope. If she denied him entrance, then he would be forced to cool his heels in worry while Gwen struggled on her own to make their dreams come true.

"You don't understand how important I am to Lady Gwen. She needs me there. Everything depends upon her shining tonight, and I help her relax."

"Poppycock. Lady Gwen doesn't need to relax. She needs to learn how to smile prettily and pretend that she needs a man."

Lord, how was he to make Gwen popular without being in there himself? "Surely there is something I can do to convince you."

"My lord, Almack's is a place where proper young ladies and gentlemen can meet. Your reputation—"

"Is completely fabricated. I did not do any of the things of which I am accused!"

"Nonetheless, appearance is as good as a fact."

"That's not true!"

"It is tonight. I do not know what you have and have not done, and until I do, you will not be allowed inside."

"Lady Jersey, I implore you. Perhaps I could—"

"Good evening, Lord Satyr."

"Sayres!"

"What? Oh yes. My apologies. And good evening." And with that she swept inside, past the large footmen left standing there to prevent anyone without a voucher from entering Almack's hallowed halls.

Jackson wracked his brains. There had to be some way he could get inside. Certainly, he could sneak in, but once there, any of the five patronesses would see him tossed outside within minutes. He couldn't possibly make Gwen the center of attention if he was constantly being removed from the ballroom.

He descended the stairs down to the street where he paced back and forth. He watched as young potential brides descended from carriages, all giggling behind their hands while their mothers corralled them with clucking sounds. Many of them noticed him, and it was clear his notoriety had reached their ears. Mothers glared him away, though he never approached any of them. The girls went from giggles to outright gasps, and in what had to be the most humiliating slap of the evening, two young gentlemen passed him their cards in the hope of being invited to his next night of debauchery. They even had a name for his revels—Satyr's Seder—in the most revolting mix of mythology and religion he'd ever heard.

He tried to set them straight, but the young men didn't want to listen to a lecture, nor did they believe his denials. No one did. So he was forced to wait for Gwen while trying to hide his face away from every glaring mama and overeager son, not to mention the girls, the papas, and even the servant staff who cut such a wide berth around him that he might as well have been a leper.

"Lord Sayres? Is that you?"

He spun around at the sound of Gwen's voice, but then was stopped short at the sight of her beauty. She was dressed to perfection, a vision in blue with those beautiful Lincolnshire daffodils making her look like the goddess of spring. Which was wonderful, except her face looked pinched and anxious.

"Gwen, you look wonderful."

"They won't last," she said as he looked down at the flowers in her bodice. "I need to give them more water, but it spills on the dress. You'll have to help me. My hands are shaking." She held them out to him. "I have never done well at Almack's. Always end up standing next to the wall and drinking their horrible lemonade until I'm sick. I swear I hate the very sight of the building."

He gripped her hands and pressed his lips to them. He didn't want to tell her of his failure. The one thing he'd promised her from the beginning was that he'd be by her side as he made her into the most famous woman this Season. And now he had to abandon her, and it cut him to the quick.

"I was able to get a maid inside the dressing room. She has a large vase of daffodils for you and will help you replace any that have wilted."

"That's a good idea," she said.

"And I've told everyone I can think of that you'll be here. That they'll not want to miss seeing you."

"Oh my. You're adding to the anticipation. I'll have to do something amazing."

"You are amazing. All you have to do is be exactly who you are, exactly how we practiced."

She nodded. "I remember."

"And when they compliment me, tell them it's all because of the magic of your daffodil."

"Yes."

"And they'll buy because they're that stupid?"

"Because they won't be able to resist trying to copy your success."

She shook her head. "I'll have to be successful for that."

"You will. I believe in it with my whole heart."

She nodded and he watched her chin firm with determination. Then she turned for the front door. "Come on. Let's get this over with."

He held back, gently disentangling their hands though it gave him a physical pain to release her. She waited by his side, her hand raised to set it his forearm so he could escort her in. And when he didn't offer her his arm, she realized the truth.

"They won't let you in."

"I tried everything I could think of. I even tried to bribe Lady Castlereigh." With the last of his funds, no less.

"It didn't work?"

"It did. She allowed me to set daffodils for your use in the retiring room."

"But not…?"

"Me? No."

She shook her head. "I'm going to have stern words with Aunt Isabelle very soon."

He smiled. "Aunt Isabelle is powerless if you remember who you are."

"I'm an odd bluestocking with an affinity for your daffodils."

"You're a brilliant woman who sees the best in everyone."

"That's Lilah."

"It's you too." He chucked her under her chin. Sometime between Lady Jersey's refusal and this moment, he'd come to a decision. He needed to say it now before Gwen went inside. She needed to know that no matter what happened—even if he had to work at Isabelle's locks until he near drowned—that she was the one woman he wanted.

"Gwendolyn!" her mother called from halfway up the steps. "We need to go in now."

"Yes, Mama," Gwen said. Then she squeezed his arm. "I'll do my best."

He couldn't let her go. Not with anxiety still haunting her eyes, and not with his words unspoken. "Gwen," he said as he tugged her back to her side. "I don't care what happens tonight. I don't care what the future brings. I care that you marry me. I love you. And if you will have me, I want to marry you as soon as possible. No matter what happens tonight."

Her eyes widened. "I'm getting the rest of my dowry for you. You don't need—"

"No!" he rasped. "No, Gwen. I want you." He pressed his mouth to her gloved fingers. "Just you. I can do anything if you are by my side."

When he straightened, her mouth had parted in a word he couldn't hear. He didn't even know if she said anything because her mother chose that moment to descend the steps and physically pull her away.

"This does not help your cause," her mother hissed.

"But—" Gwen said.

"It's all right," he said. "We'll speak together tomorrow."

"Tonight," Gwen countered. "After this ends."

He nodded. "After this ends." Then he watched her go inside carrying all of his hopes and dreams with her.

Chapter Twenty-Eight

Trust Jackson to completely overturn her life right before the most important party of her life.

He loved her?

That's what he'd said and butterflies of giddiness inside her told her that she loved him, too. Except she knew enough about feelings to know they didn't last. Even her most exciting scientific moments had faded when the next curiosity grabbed her attention. But this didn't seem like it was going to fade. It was too intense, too real, and too special.

"Gwendolyn! Mind your step!" Her mother hissed at her. "I don't understand this flower thing you're doing, but I can tell you that tripping over your own feet will not help your cause."

"Yes, Mama," Gwen murmured, taking the admonishment to heart. She needed to focus on what she was doing here and now because both their futures depended on her making a good showing. So she tried to set her mind to making a good impression. She tried to push her actions to appropriate ladylike behavior. She tried any number of things to make herself behave just as she ought.

It all faded under the rainbow excitement of Jackson's words. *I love you. And if you will have me, I want to marry you as soon as possible.*

Lord, the flush of feeling that came over her whenever she thought of those words! Hot then cold, tingly then giggly. All the things she never associated with…well, anything but science and him.

"Gwen!"

Brought back—again—to the present, Gwen stepped forward and handed her voucher to the doorman. She and her mother were announced, and she stepped into the one place where she always felt like a desperate, old leftover woman. The room was relatively small, but it was designed for dancing. Tepid lemonade in one corner, the orchestra in another, and seats for the patronesses in the third where they reigned like queens. And all around the edges stood the young girls with their mothers. Her mother called them *dewy fresh*. Gwen called them pastel cut-outs of people. If any one of them had a passion, it had been thoroughly stamped out of them. Certainly one might sing well, another play the violin with skill, but not one dared speak out or carve their own path. They were too young to realize they could, and their mothers had been too determined to teach them "proper manners."

It reminded her forcefully of the little girl in the park so long ago. The one who had been watching an insect only to have her nanny swat it away. Every single one of these girls was a result of that kind of education, and Gwen thought it a crime. Because if they never fought back, if they never thought for themselves, then they'd never find the kind of joy she found in science or a man like Jackson who valued her passions as much as his own.

She stepped into the room and she heard the whispers begin. She was notorious in Almack's because she was the cautionary tale. Every girl here was being admonished to be nice to the gentlemen or they'd end up like Lady Gwen—on the shelf and damned as a bluestocking.

Normally Gwen would deflate within ten seconds of hearing the first whispers. She would mentally retreat into her plants, thinking of science rather than whomever was in the room. And she would pray for the evening to end.

I love you. And if you will have me, I want to marry you as soon as possible.

But today was going to be different.

A gentleman approached and bowed to her and her mother.

"Mr. MacDonald," her mother said. "What a pleasure to see you here tonight."

Thanks to Jackson's coaching, she knew he was the second son of a Scottish earl on the hunt for a wife. He enjoyed dogs, horses, and boxing, and he was a year her junior. Within two minutes' conversation, she also found him rather silly. Usually she'd just turn away from him or accidentally spill lemonade on him just to get away. Instead, she heard Jackson's voice reminding her to find something honest she could say to compliment him.

"I really admire how you are keeping yourself fit," she said in absolute truth. "So many men forget that they will age into heaviness which is not at all attractive."

He brightened at that, preening as young men often do. He was only one year her junior, and yet she couldn't escape the feeling that he was still a thirteen-year-old boy trying to prove himself manly.

"You are most kind and…" he added with a wink, "most perceptive. Might I have the honor of a dance?"

She agreed and offered him her dance card. Very soon others were coming to speak to her. It wasn't much different from any other time she went to Almack's. She was never completely without partners, and the fact that she was wearing daffodils certainly sparked a bit of conversation. But after the first set it was clear that she wasn't making anything like the impact they needed to sell the flowers.

She needed to be special very soon or this would all be for nothing. But how? Without Jackson here she couldn't do anything new, couldn't *be* anything new. Her only choice was to get a message to him, and the only way to do that—short of leaving—was to use the maid in the dressing room. Besides, the flowers she wore were indeed drooping. It was time to replace them with new.

She headed into the ladies withdrawing room. Since it was between sets, there were several girls there refreshing themselves, getting the hems of their skirts resewn, or just clustered in a corner talking to one another away from their mothers. Personally, she had never found the room to be a respite from anything. As bad as her mother could be, the girls in the dressing room could be ten times crueler, but there was no other choice.

So she went in, saw the maid right away as she tried to keep a couple girls back from the vase of daffodils, and quickly maneuvered through the crowd. One thing about being long in the tooth, she'd had more time to learn how to use her hips to good effect.

"Please, step back. Ladies, if you want these exclusive Lincolnshire daffodils, then you'll have to buy them tomorrow. I've already paid tonight for these."

"I'm going to wear roses," one woman huffed. "I don't want your silly yellow trumpets."

She almost said something cutting back, but once again she heard Jackson's voice in her head. Only nice words, no matter what they say. An honest compliment.

Except she knew the speaker. A spoiled, mean brat if ever there was one. But she would do what Jackson wanted even if it was a million times harder to think of an honest compliment to the shrew.

"You used the correct terminology!" Gwen managed to cry with false enthusiasm. "This part of the daffodil is called the trumpet. Your education really was excellent." Well, that part was a lie. Only boys got a good education. Girls got the leftovers.

Miss Esme Atkinson frowned, completely thrown by Gwen's words. Unfortunately, that only lasted a few seconds. Moments later, she lifted her chin, sniffed in disdain, and said, "Of course I do," before walking away with her group of followers trailing behind.

Gwen watched the women walk away, waiting for the familiar bite of loneliness to cut through her chest. Here was yet another example of how she didn't fit in. But instead of pain, she felt a curious detachment from the situation, similar to what she felt for Mr. MacDonald and his need to appear manly. Miss Atkinson seemed just as young and silly to her as Mr. MacDonald did, and that was a surprise. Beyond politeness, she had no more need to be friendly with her than the child in the park with her nanny.

What a surprise.

And on the heels of that shock came another. She was busy pulling out the daffodil from her bodice when a voice interrupted her.

"Don't worry about Esme. She was born awful."

Gwen turned around, startled to hear anyone speak to her in a kind fashion. That wasn't usual in the ladies retiring room. "She doesn't bother me," she returned honestly. "Miss Atkinson was born young and apparently has remained that way."

The woman's eyes widened. She was a mousy girl with nut brown hair and sweet brown eyes set beneath thick eyebrows. She also had a beautiful smile as she looked longingly at the daffodils. "Are they really magical? I heard they come from a fairy mound."

Obviously, Jackson's efforts had succeeded. He'd begun the rumor that they were magical for just this kind of reaction. Here was a young woman desperate to believe that anything would make her special even if it was the false belief in magic. And Gwen was supposed to agree with that, reinforce that, even promote that because it was the only way to make the flower popular.

But she couldn't do it.

Well, not exactly. Jackson had challenged her to answer honestly but in a positive way. She lowered her voice and drew the woman forward.

"What's your name?" she asked.

"Nora Moss," she said as she dipped in a quick curtsey.

"Pleased to meet you, Miss Moss. I'm–"

"We know who you are Lady Gwen. We *all* know your name."

That was disconcerting, but she didn't want to focus on something that might upset her. She had to sell the flowers. "Come look at these blooms," she urged as she pulled one from the vase. "See how there are two sets of petals? These outside ones are a little pale, I think, but that's because they open first. It's the inside–the trumpet—that looks like the sun to me. Like a bright light bursting forth. But then if you look very close at the center—"

"The stamen and the stigma."

Miss Moss knew her flower parts. "Yes. That's where the fascinating things begin."

They discussed the plant for a while longer, but Gwen got the feeling that the woman didn't have a true love of botany. She seemed to want something else, and it wasn't hard to discover what.

"You were hoping for magic, weren't you?"

Miss Moss looked away. "I like the idea of magic. I like imagining fairies and leprechauns. Something that takes the ordinary and makes it special."

Gwen nodded. "A month ago, I wouldn't have understood that," she confessed. "But then I met someone who saw that I was special in my own strange way. These are his flowers, and every time I look at them, I remember…" *That he loves me.* "That I am special just as I am."

"That's what men tell women when they want…" Miss Moss cut off her words but the blush that stained her cheeks told Gwen everything she needed to know about how that sentence ended. And it was worse because Gwen's cheeks heated in memory. Yes, she had explored that as well, but it had been her choice.

"The difference is I feel special now as I am. It doesn't matter what did or didn't happen. I am perfect as I am." She never would have realized that without him, but now that it was part of her, it would always be part of her.

"That is magic," Miss Moss said softly.

"It definitely is." Then she looked at the girl wondering what had brought her to this desperate need. "Do you know," she said, "I find you quite interesting and intelligent. I would like to further our acquaintance, if you'd like to as well."

Miss Moss's eyes widened. "I would, too." Then her gaze dropped to her hands. "But my mother thinks you've been debauched."

"What?"

"By Lord Satyr."

Ah. So that was why everyone knew her name. "I can tell you it's absolutely not true." If anyone did the debauching, it was her. But she knew better than to say that. "Shall I prove it to you?"

"How?"

"A debauched woman is ashamed, afraid, and..." She shrugged. "I don't know. Less than everyone else somehow. Do I seem like less to you? Like someone who—"

"No," Miss Moss said quickly. "You seem confident. And happy?"

"So happy it's magical." Her gaze went back to the flowers. "Do you understand now where the magic of these blooms come from?"

"From you," she stated firmly.

"No, silly. From you."

Miss Moss shook her head. "No, it's you. And I—"

"I think you should wear them yourself and find out. Can these blooms make you feel magical? Or can they just remind you that you have magic inside?"

So saying, she pulled the vase pin off her bodice, set the bloom inside, and clipped it onto Miss Moss's dress.

"Now," she said firmly. "Do you feel special?"

"I...?" Suddenly she lifted her chin. "I feel special because of you. I want to be as confident as you are."

Well that was a first. No one had ever said anything like that to her before. "Then shall we go dance? I think I should like to see how a confident Miss Moss smiles."

She looked at Gwen. "Exactly like you do."

Well, not *exactly* because they were different people, but Gwen didn't quibble. In truth, she appreciated the support of Miss Moss especially as they stepped out of the retiring room to a seemingly hostile room. She didn't know if Miss Atkinson had been whispering things or if it was just the way she always felt at Almack's, but it seemed as if everyone was staring at her. Or rather at the two of them because they were together.

"We are special," Miss Moss whispered to herself, but Gwen took the words to heart.

"And we're smart too!"

Miss Moss grinned and then their mothers converged on them, both speaking in low whispers that were completely unintelligible to Gwen.

"Stop, stop. Please," she said to her mother, but it managed to silence both of the older women. Then she looked at Miss Moss who gave her an apologetic look. "Miss Moss, would you care to walk with me? I should love some lemonade before the dancing begins again."

"Definitely not—" began the woman's mother, but Miss Moss was made of sterner stuff. She lifted her chin and held out her arm.

"I would love to."

They walked together to the lemonade stand which would have been unremarkable alone. But apparently Miss Moss knew quite a few of the more awkward women. By ones or twos, they came and used their friendship with Miss Moss to meet Gwen. Mindful of Jackson's advice, she found herself giving genuine compliments to every single one of the ladies, which in turn seemed to brighten them to a noticeable degree.

Soon the lemonade area was filled with girls' laughter and Gwen was rather bemused to be at the center of it. She was, however, quite pleased to notice their extraordinary interest in the Lincolnshire daffodil. Mostly on the discussion of whether it was truly magical, but there was some scientific talk as well comparing it to other flowers. And naturally, where there were girls, there were soon men.

The gentlemen all asked her for a dance, and she accepted when she could, but she was more interested in talking to the women who were Miss Moss's friends. Every one of them was shy or odd in some way. Before she'd met Jackson, she wouldn't have even noticed that. But the moment she focused on trying to learn something about them that she could compliment, the more she realized every single one of them felt awkward in some way. It was a revelation to her. And since she had no interest in dancing to find a husband, she took great pleasure in matching up gentlemen with the ladies around her.

In truth, she was a terrible matchmaker, but it didn't matter. So long as everyone got a partner, everyone was happy. And none more so than the blossoming Miss Moss.

"It is magic!" Miss Moss said just before she left with her newest partner.

"No—" she began, but there was no time to deny it as a girl asked if she could have Lincolnshire daffodils for her official come-out ball in three days' time. And once she was heard asking, all the other girls clamored for flowers as well.

And there it was. Somehow, some way, Jackson had made her and his daffodil popular. She couldn't believe it. And she couldn't wait to tell him.

"Magic," she whispered to herself only to have the other ladies echo it.

"Magic," they all concurred.

Until a strident tone cut through her happiness. She knew the voice as well as the tone. It was Aunt Isabelle, and with one word, she effectively destroyed everything Gwen had accomplished this evening.

"Rubbish!"

Chapter Twenty-Nine

JACKSON COULDN'T FORCE himself to leave, even if he couldn't go inside. He wanted to be near Gwen just in case. So he lurked in the shadows, paced the street, and generally wondered what she was doing, what she was feeling, and—preeminent in his thoughts—would she say yes? Did she feel for him the aching need he had for her?

And then he saw Isabelle.

What was she doing here? Causing trouble, obviously, and he couldn't leave Gwen vulnerable to her aunt's venom no matter what damage it caused to their daffodil business.

As usual, Isabelle was flanked by gentlemen companions. There were three tonight, pretty boys who were trained in gossip—the getting and making of it. Two would follow her in, flanking her on either side in a show of power. The third would slink in behind, his entire job being to hear everyone's reaction to whatever commotion Isabelle began. And in that moment, Jackson saw his opportunity.

He took it.

Isabelle chose her men for looks, not pugilistic skill. He waited until Isabelle and two of her men began climbing the steps. She would pass through the building door before climbing the steps to Almack's which was on the second floor. The moment she was far enough away to not hear any noise, Jackson slipped behind the carriage and grabbed the third man by the collar. He'd knocked the blighter flat, then dragged the man into the shadows before he climbed the steps two at a time. He made it inside the building door in time to hear Isabelle instruct the Almack's doorman above.

"Another gentleman follows directly behind me. You will allow him in."

He grinned. That's what she always said, and like always, the servant was quick to obey.

"Yes, my lady."

Then she swept in. Jackson waited long enough for her to have moved into the ballroom, then followed. The doorman recognized him, of course, but he couldn't go against Isabelle. Excellent. He flashed the man a jaunty grin, then slipped in as unobtrusively as possible and tried to locate Gwen.

He didn't see her at first, and when he did, he felt ashamed that it had taken him so long to find her. He'd expected her to be at the edge of the ballroom, watching the proceedings from the sidelines. It wasn't that he doubted her ability to shine, just that he knew she preferred to stay in the shadows. And yet there she was, in the center of a crowd near the lemonade stand, beaming with happiness as she looked at the crowd around her. He didn't know what she'd done, but it was clear that she'd truly stepped into the beauty that was all her.

His heart swelled with pride.

Then one word rang out from Isabelle, so loud it silenced everything else.

"Rubbish!"

He jolted, along with everyone else. Then he pressed forward, intent on getting to Gwen's side. He needed to support her. But before he could do more than take three steps, he heard Gwen's clear tones, sounding melodic against Isabelle's gong-like voice.

"Aunt Isabelle, I didn't know you were coming to Almack's tonight."

"Neither did I," the woman snapped. "I came to save you from yourself." She tsked. "You were the smart one, Gwen. I cannot understand why you allowed yourself to be duped by that terrible man. Not only has he poisoned your mind, but he has brought you into his evil schemes. Imagine suggesting that a flower is magical. He's a liar and a reprobate. You need to denounce him immediately."

"He was your friend and employee for a decade, Aunt. And I have deceived no one." She shook her head. "You were never one to make cruel assumptions about anyone. What has happened to your logic that you do so now?"

"GWEN," ISABELLE SAID in the heaviest of accents. "You have been deceived! And I am at my wits end as to how to protect you."

The words had their intended effect. Not on Gwen, of course, who seemed completely unruffled by the drama, but on the mothers in the room. As one, they gestured their children away from Gwen. Gentlemen frowned, unsure how they should react. And the ladies shifted uncomfortably, using the motions to step back.

"But Aunt," Gwen said with a laugh. "You were the one who told me that a woman of maturity didn't need anyone's protection." She stepped forward. "I am a woman on the shelf. Even my mother has said so. My mind is clear, and my soul is happy. I have no need of your protection, least of all from the man who gave me such beautiful daffodils."

"Don't be ridiculous—" Isabelle began, but apparently Gwen had had enough. She threw up her hands in frustration.

"Why are you so afraid of a yellow flower?"

"It's not the flower, you idiot girl. It's Lord Sayres! He has led you down a garden path."

"Yes. To buy his flowers!"

"My God," Isabelle cried. "Patricia, can't you manage your own child? What has happened to her mind?"

Gwen's mother looked confused as her gaze hopped between her daughter and her nearest relation. "Isabelle, I don't think this is seemly."

"It most certainly isn't," Isabelle gasped. "Lord Sayres—"

"Has just this night proposed to me," interrupted Gwen. Then she glanced at the gentlemen around her. "It's why I was encouraging you to look at all these other lovely ladies." She looked back at her mother, her eyes shining. "He professed his love just this evening, and…" Her gaze found his. "I have discovered to my shock that I am head over heels in love with him. I should like to accept your proposal, my lord. If that is agreeable?"

That was his cue. He stepped around the crowd and walked forward, dropping to one knee as soon as he was close enough to clasp her hands and kiss them. "It would be my greatest honor," he said. And he meant it.

All around them the ladies sighed in delight. All except Isabelle, who cried out.

"He is doing it for your dowry! Can't you see?"

"My dowry? But he already has it."

"Not without marrying you, you idiot."

She blew out her breath, speaking in the tones of a woman patiently explaining something to a simpleton. "But don't you remember, Aunt? You told me yourself that I am of age to control my own fortune. You told me that less than two weeks ago. And you were right."

"But—"

"I have already invested my dowry. It's all gone," Gwen said with a grin. "All Lord Sayres is getting is myself and my love."

He looked up at her. "That is more than enough for me."

"You see, Aunt. There is nothing to worry about from Lord Sayres. Except to ask if I could perhaps wear his flowers at our wedding."

"You outshine them," he said, as he straightened to his full height. "And you may have anything you want from me." Then he touched her face, silently asking her if he could do what he had wanted to for so long. Could he kiss her now? In front of everyone?

She smiled as he leaned forward, and she rose up onto her toes. Around there were other sounds. Sighs of delight. Isabelle's ranting. Gwen's mother telling her to keep quiet because Gwen was going to marry a future earl. All of it swirled about him, but none of it mattered.

"I am so proud of you, Gwen," he said. "I don't know how you did it, but you have made it all perfect."

"We did it," she said. "I would never have learned to value myself without you." Then she stretched up on her toes just as he clasped her around the waist. Their mouths met, their arms entwined, and she said, "Yes," one more time. A whisper against his lips and a promise shining in her eyes.

Nothing else in the entire world mattered.

EPILOGUE

One year later

VAUXHALL WAS COVERED in Lincolnshire daffodils, much to the awe of the assembled guests. But of all the beauty surrounding him this morning, Jackson had eyes for only his bride. Gwen was everything he'd ever wanted, and when she said, "I do," his heart pounded out a steady rhythm of joy.

"I love you," he said right before he kissed her in such a way that every man, woman, and child here would know she was his forever.

And when he was done, she held on for a moment longer, letting him know that he was hers as well.

Then she turned to the guests and threw her bouquet into the crowd. But since she still held the ribbon, the flowers scattered apart to rain down upon the congregation, much to everyone's delight.

"Clever girl," he said.

"It was your idea."

It had been, but the design and execution had been all hers. And then they both watched in pleasure as the women and a few men scrambled to gather up the "magical" blooms in the hopes of grabbing luck for themselves.

"Are you sure we haven't emptied your flower gardens?" Gwen asked. The flowers were here not just for the ceremony and bridal breakfast this morning, but also for his annual masquerade tonight.

Though tonight, Lord Satyr intended to remain tamely by his wife's side through the revels. And then, of course, there would be their own private celebration afterwards.

"We planted well in advance." And even if they hadn't, the orders for daffodil bulbs from last year had made enough profit for Abigail's come out. Even better, orders for the blossoms this Season were coming in as fast as his secretary could record them.

The Lincolnshire daffodil was a sensation. As much in demand as Prussian blue ever was, and Jackson no longer feared for his family's wellbeing. They would soon be extraordinarily wealthy. But the real prize was holding his hand and smiling at the on-rush of well-wishers.

Always protective, he watched Gwen for signs that she was becoming overwhelmed by the attention, but something had changed in her that night at Vauxhall. She was poised now where she was uncertain before, and she never once referred to herself as odd anymore. Unless it was as a good thing. She even had the wherewithal to invite Isabelle to the wedding and laugh when the lady refused to attend.

"More breakfast for everyone else," she'd chortled.

And now she was laughing again as her sisters, his sisters, and the two mothers pulled her away from him. He had no idea where they were going, but everyone was laughing as they ushered her away. He managed to grab Lilah before he lost sight of his bride altogether.

"They're going to bring her back, aren't they?"

Lilah smiled. "I believe your sisters have a surprise for you both, but they need her to accomplish it."

"Oh dear," Jackson moaned. No telling what his sisters had done.

Lilah chuckled at his mock horror, but the humor didn't last. Her eyes appeared misty as she looked back at the altar. "It was beautiful," she said. "I'm so happy for you both."

"Thank you," he returned, his mind shifting uncomfortably back to his promise to his Aaron regarding Lilah. He'd sworn to keep the lady distracted until his friend could get his affairs in order and propose, thereby ruining his political career and possibly his entire life.

Instead, Jackson had encouraged Gwen to take her sister along with her to every ball and rout after that night in Vauxhall. He'd hoped that Lilah would set her matrimonial gaze elsewhere. It hadn't worked. And now Jackson was in the difficult position of watching as she scanned the guests for the one man she couldn't have.

"I'm sorry. Aaron couldn't make it today. His father—"

"Yes, I know. He had to go home. I understand his father is gravely ill." Then her gaze sharpened on him. "How did you know I was looking for Lord Chambers?"

"Aaron mentioned to me that you two enjoyed a lovely walk at the masquerade last year." He watched her face closely as he referred to their romantic wanderings down the Dark Path. What he saw wasn't reassuring. Her gaze grew dreamy, and her smile was private as she nodded.

"He was a gentleman with me in every way."

Given her parentage, that was probably rare for her. And it was directly at odds with Aaron's claim that he'd ruined her.

"No matter," she quipped airily. "That was last year. This year—"

"You intend to take London by storm? Gwen has already plans for your gowns and the daffodils. She wants to make you this year's sensation."

Lilah's smile turned indulgent as she shook her head. "I know she has plans, and I've told her they won't work."

"Of course, they can. We made her a sensation last Season. There is no reason we cannot do the same for you this year."

"That is very kind of you, my lord, but I have other plans. Exciting ones that have nothing to do with the Season or even London."

"Really? I'm intrigued."

"Oh yes, I shall—"

Whatever she said next was lost beneath a great clashing of cymbals. He was sure his sisters were the cause, so he turned toward the sound with a feeling of indulgent dread.

Then he saw it. Gwen dressed in a gown painted like the sun carrying a basket of what looked to be painted flowers. So that's what Bea had been working on. Gwen was at the far side of the lawn from him, and as she walked through their guests, she gave every woman a painted blossom.

He had no desire to wait for her to make it to him, so he joined her before she was even halfway through. And then he held the flower basket as she spoke to every guest. By the time they made it to the top table—the one set for bride and groom—he lost every thought in his head except that she was the most exquisite creature he'd ever known. "You are everything to me," he said to her, as he set a painted daffodil into her hair.

"You are my love," she returned. Then they kissed in front of everyone, and such joy filled his heart that he couldn't imagine ever being happier. Unless it was the next morning when he woke with her in his arms. Or the next, and the next, through their entire life together.

About the Author

A *USA Today* Bestseller, JADE LEE has been scripting love stories since she first picked up a set of paper dolls. Ball gowns and rakish lords caught her attention early (thank you Georgette Heyer), and her fascination with historical romance began. Author of more than 30 regency romances, Jade has a gift for creating a lively world, witty dialogue, and hot, sexy humor. Jade also writes contemporary and paranormal romance as Kathy Lyons. Together, they've won several industry awards, including the *Prism—Best of the Best, Romantic Times Reviewer's Choice,* and *Fresh Fiction's* Steamiest Read. Even though Kathy (and Jade) have written over 60 romance novels, she's just getting started. Check out her latest news at www.KathyLyons.com, Facebook: JadeLeeAuthor, and Twitter: JadeLeeAuthor. Instagram: KathyLyonsAuthor.